PRAISE FOR
THE EVERLASTING LIFE
OF CHARLIE WALL

The Life of Charlie Wall is a distinguished addition to the State Literature of Florida. Paul Wilborn brings Tampa's Ybor City vividly to life both in its present and its past incarnations. Ybor's past is a story of Italian, Cuban and Spanish immigration, replete with gangsters and their molls, with ladies of the night and Grande Dames of the best houses, and with Pols both of rectitude and dubious ethic. The Life of Charlie Wall abounds with action, violent and erotic, local color strikingly rendered, and the pungent steam of tropical nights and roasting coffee. It's all told in a style as muscular and beautiful as the wrought iron on the balconies of Ybor's Septima Avenida.

Sterling Watson, Author of The Committee and Night Letter

"Paul Wilborn's The Everlasting Life of Charlie Wall melds richly drawn characters with an engaging premise - what if infamous Tampa mobster Charlie Wall survived his 1955 hit and lived into the gritty Tampa of the 1980s? Drawing on the City's unique underworld history and blending it with his own experiences, Paul crafts a story that is as much about relationships and the passage of time as it is about gangsters. A wonderful read."

Published by St. Petersburg Press
St. Petersburg, FL
www.stpetersburgpress.com

Design and composition by St. Petersburg Press and Isa Crosta
Cover design by St. Petersburg Press and Karen Saint-John

Paperback ISBN: 978-1-964239-44-6
Ebook ISBN: 978-1-964239-45-3

First Edition

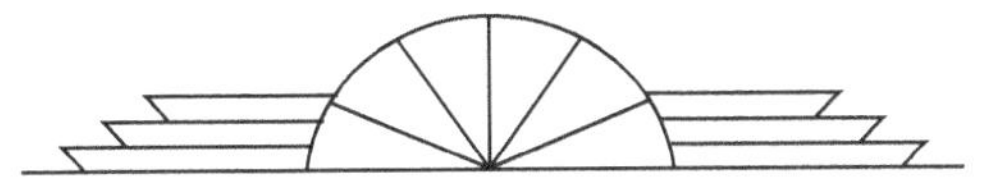

THE EVERLASTING LIFE OF CHARLIE WALL

A Novel
By Paul Wilborn

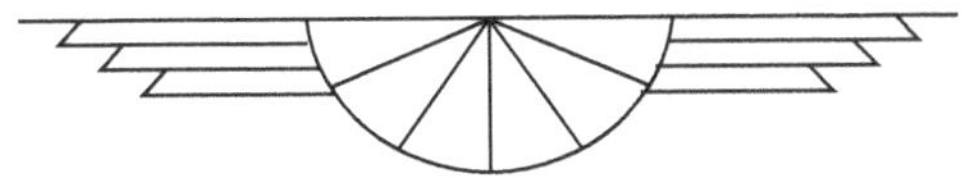

Why is it that the only time he was happy before was in the Argonne Forest in 1918 when he was shooting at Germans and stood a good chance of being shot by Germans?

—

Walker Percy

For Ferdie Pacheco and Jack Espinosa,
two of my favorite Tampa bananas.

CHAPTER I

An arrow—its tip shiny silver, its sleek red shaft trimmed at the base with a tuft of lime-colored feathers—swooshed by Charlie's head, slamming with a "thock" into the frame above the front door. In the snapshot silence afterward, Trip Armstrong thought he could hear the arrow quivering, like someone had plucked a taut string in the guts of a grand piano.

"Holy undershirts!" Charlie gasped, as Trip turned the key and pushed the old man through the open door, slamming it behind them.

"Whoa Betty!" Charlie shouted. "What in Hades was that?"

Trip suppressed a grin. It tickled him when his boss made up his own curse words. They stood for a long beat in the dark, listening to the ticking of the grandfather clock before Trip flipped the light switch.

Charlie's mouth twisted up into a tight smile. "They keep trying. They keep failing."

Stepping to the closed door, he shouted to his would-be assassin: "You should know by now you can't whack Charlie Wall!"

But, at least for a moment, they could scare him. When Charlie turned back, Trip noticed a growing stain around the zipper of his seersucker trousers. Charlie dismissed the stain with a wave of his hand.

"I told you I had to pee. Dalmation! Now I gotta clean this suit." Charlie pulled a pocket watch from his jacket, scanned it, then looked up at Trip, as if it were any other night. "How'd it get so late?"

Trip knew exactly how it got so late. Waving a limp twenty at Betty, the longtime bartender at The Turf, Charlie had insisted on a fourth Old Fashioned.

"You sure, Charlie?" Betty's face was a mask of bones and wrinkles, her sparse curls yellowed by six decades of cigarette smoke. "I think your level is good."

On most subjects, Charlie had a philosophy he lived by, except when he didn't feel like it. His philosophy of drinking was like that. He believed a wise man should know how to hold his liquor. About once a night, usually in The Turf, his favorite among the dark, old-school joints around downtown Tampa, the drunken philosopher would rise slowly from the barstool and straighten his shoulders, his lanky, Abe Lincoln frame draped in his standard uniform—a seersucker suit that seemed to grow larger every day—Or, maybe after 85 tumultuous years on the planet, Charlie was shrinking. His pale blue dress shirt hung loose around a wattled neck, his paisley bowtie dangled, his straw boater rested upside down on the bar. "People drink the wrong way," Charlie would say to his barroom companions—often total strangers—his high lonesome voice a mix of southern aristocrat and cracker cowpoke.

"A wise man only drinks to here." He would draw a flat hand across the middle of his chest, where his shirt was rorschached with soup and gravy stains. He'd wiggle his fingers.

"A little higher. A little lower. It's okay. When a man gets in trouble is when he drinks to here." Charlie's index finger slid like a knife blade across his neck. "It's neck drinkers that give liquor a bad name."

Betty had heard it plenty of times. Usually after Charlie had let the booze rise to neck level. But she knew you didn't argue with Charlie Wall. People had died after disagreeing with Charlie. Sure, it was a long time ago, but they had died. In cars. On front porches. In trash-strewn alleys behind Ybor City dive bars. All rising to meet their maker courtesy of a double-barreled blast from a sawed-off wielded by one of Charlie's guys.

Betty set down a fresh Old Fashioned. Easing off the stool, Charlie took the drink down the bar where a couple of 30ish women were giggling at a private joke.

"I'm Charlie Wall," he announced. "Ever hear of me?"

The women wore the business-blue pant suits and pastel blouses that said they worked just down the street at the court-house. Likely court reporters, Trip thought. Their hair styles were identical, all scrambled-up curls, though one was dyed blond, the other chocolate brown.

"You a lawyer?" The brunette asked.

"I'm a crook." Charlie eased onto the stool next to them. "Used to be anyway. Long time ago. Call your Momma. I bet she's heard of me."

Trip shook his head and checked his watch. Dammit! We're gonna be late. He waved to Betty for another club soda and lime.

In Charlie's driveway an hour later, the motion sensor spotlight turned the inside of the car prison-yard bright. Trip switched off the key, but the Cadillac's massive V-8 shook and sputtered, refusing to die.

"She hates to quit." Charlie said from the passenger seat, the alcohol removing the spaces between his words. "It's like when I put my head on the pillow at night. Always afraid I won't crank up again in the morning."

When the car finally thudded to a stop, Charlie patted the metal dash. "There, there, Betty. Rest a bit. We'll be back to-morrow, I promise."

Stepping from the car, Trip turned in a slow circle to check out the decaying neighborhood for any signs of danger. Although Charlie had been out of the rackets for decades, he insisted that what he needed was not just a driver, but a body-guard.

"Come on Charlie." Trip yanked on Charlie's door; heard the familiar screech of metal raking metal. Charlie hooked his corn-stalk fingers over the doorframe and pulled himself slowly from the car. Trip put his hands on the old man's shoulders to steady him, but Charlie shook them off.

"I'm good. You check around?"

Trip nodded. "The coast, as they say, is clear."

Charlie swiveled his head slowly left then right, making sure Trip was correct. During his criminal days, trusting his bodyguards had almost gotten him killed. Satisfied that all was quiet, Charlie slapped the hood of the car twice. "Okay, let's go."

It was twenty paces from the driveway to the three steps leading up to Charlie's porch. The sidewalk, like the driveway, was now a few stray shards of concrete tucked into the thick green lawn.

Charlie shuffled up the steps onto the porch. At the door, he turned to Trip, who held the key. "Get it open, man. I'm about to race like a pee-horse."

That's when the arrow passed a few inches above Charlie's comb-over.

Inside, with the door locked, Charlie yelled at his would-be assasins, then sighed like a man who hadn't slept in weeks. He padded slowly toward his side of the house. At the hallway door, he turned back, his head and shoulders washed in buttery light.

"You going out to see, right?" An expanding stain darkened the front of his slacks.

Trip picked up the 8-iron he kept by the door for moments like this. Not that there had been other moments like this, but Charlie had insisted that his bodyguard carry some kind of weapon.

"I got a gun, you know?" Charlie said. "Do you much better than that country club swatter."

"I told you. I don't do guns. I grew up swinging one of these. I know how to use it. Anyway, whoever did this is long gone."

"You don't know that. But you're probably right. Those jaw-dragging Sicilians. They still got it in for Charlie Wall."

"I don't know about their ethnicity, but somebody obviously wants you dead." Trip cracked the door warily, the club shaft resting on his shoulder. "Lock this after I go. I got a key."

"Bring me that arrow, will ya?"

Outside, Trip leaned the club against the porch wall and wiggled the arrow from the door frame and leaned it next to his 8-iron. When he heard Charlie turn the bolt, he hurried down the steps. The sidewalk and the brick street in front of Charlie's house were empty. The archer stepped from behind an oak tree and stood in the pale glow of a streetlight. "How was that?"

Charlie's would-be assassin was a gangly teenager; his face blistered with pimples. Danny Hernandez was the star of Tampa Catholic's archery team. Trip pulled some folded bills from his pocket and pressed them into the kid's outstretched palm. "Maybe a little close for comfort, but yeah, it was good."

"Can I get my arrow back? They're expensive. And I had to wait an extra hour. You said nine, not ten. My mom's gonna be pissed."

Trip stuffed a few more crumpled bills into the kid's shirt pocket. "Buy another arrow. He wants this one. He collects souvenirs."

CHAPTER 2

SIX MONTHS EARLIER

Trip was speeding. It was something he didn't do when his leather saddlebags were filled with first-degree felonies. But the night was cool, the traffic thin, and his ebony Ducati 450 was happiest at 50 miles an hour or more.

A large black sedan lurked at the edge of a convenience store parking lot, the wide, chrome nose just inches from the street.

Unmarked, Trip thought. Shit!

He geared down. He wasn't speeding when he passed the sedan, but the car pulled out behind him and quickly closed in, the circling siren wailing. Red and blue lights pulsed off the trees and parking lots lining Hillsborough Avenue.

After countless bouts of 3 a.m. anxiety—imagining himself cuffed in the backseat of a patrol car, breathing in the skunk smell of body odor and vomit, hearing the clap of the judge's gavel, or cell doors slamming shut—this was the real thing. He chased away a panicked fantasy about gunning the bike down back streets and alleys. That's a fool's game. You can't shake a police cruiser.

A gas station sign appeared ahead. Trip rolled into the parking lot, wondering what he'd tell his father on the one call they'd allow him from jail. He eased off the bike, setting his helmet on the seat.

The sedan pulled in. The lights swirled, but the siren went silent. The man who emerged wore a dark suit, white shirt, and a narrow black tie that fell to his belt buckle. This is a plainclothes cop, Trip told himself, in a plainclothes cop suit. The man in the suit was tall and lean. No doughnut belly on this one. A holster bulged under the suit jacket.

Trip waited until he was a few feet away. "Officer, was I...."

The man lifted his arm, his palm open showing a gold badge. He had the tanned face of a golf pro, or a tennis instructor. What he didn't have was a smile.

"Just turn around and put your hands behind your back." It was not a voice you could argue with.

"But I-"

The man cut him off.

"Just do it."

Trip turned slowly. He was sure this was no random stop of a suspicious looking character. When Trip was making his deliveries, he worked hard not to look suspicious. He wore his South Tampa preppy outfit. His pants were khaki. His shirts madras, with button down collars. The logo on his zippered jacket was Members Only.

The cuffing was swift and unfriendly. The cop spun Trip around and pulled him to the dark sedan. He pushed him hard against the front fender. The car was warm on his back.

The cop leaned close to Trip's face. "Stay!" He spoke like a dog trainer.

Cars slowed to take in the handcuffed man in the swirling lights. Trip lowered his head, to hide his face. The cop walked to Trip's bike and flipped back the cover of one saddlebag. He lifted out a clear quart jar of dark liquid. He stared over at Trip, lifting the jar so Trip could see it. Then, he eased it back inside the saddlebag.

Trip fought back tears. It was finally happening.

At least once a week, he had told himself that he wasn't a drug dealer. His products were natural—gooey buds harvested in Jamaica and magic mushrooms he and his cocker spaniel gathered from cow pastures north of Tampa and boiled into a black tea. If someone asked about his profession, he described himself as "an entrepreneur of inner visions." But in 1985, under the laws of Florida, he was a hard-core felon who simply hadn't been caught. Until tonight.

As his business had grown during his senior year at Plant High, Trip had considered himself a connoisseur who liked sharing with friends and friends of friends. The connoisseur part was true; Trip was always his own best customer. From age fifteen to thirty Trip had smoked up vast pastures of Jamaican and Colombian buds, swallowed sheet after sheet of Orange Sunshine, and downed a tank car full of 'schroom tea. He loved how psilocybin set time adrift, his square, blank window on the world slowly polaroiding into a glowing jewel box of colors.

A tow truck pulled into the parking lot. The bearded driver wore blue jeans and a stained T-shirt that stretched over his belly. The cop showed him something written in a small note-book. The driver nodded.

The plainclothes cop returned. He stuffed Trip into the back-seat of the cruiser. Trip could feel the blood leaving his hands. The cop said nothing as he eased out onto the street. The sedan rolled onto the Interstate, headed toward downtown. The jail was there. So was the police station.

The sedan took a downtown exit but cruised south to a four-lane road lined with mansions and condo towers. Bayshore Boulevard was the scenic route to the upscale neighborhoods of South Tampa. Trip considered asking where they were going but thought better of it.

Moments later, the sedan turned off Bayshore and then up MacDill Avenue toward the Palma Ceia Country Club. Trip had grown up in a sprawling ranch house that backed up to the fifth green. The sedan stopped in the cuticle shaped driveway in front of Trip's family home.

The cop held the door open, so Trip could climb out. He spun Trip around and removed the handcuffs. When the cuffs were off, the cop wrapped his fingers tight on Trip's upper arm. Trip was rubbing his wrists when his father emerged from the red front door.

"Dad, what the hell?"

"Shut up, son. Don't talk right now."

Ronald Armstrong's hair was gray, but he still had the body of an athlete. In the 1950s, he'd been a starting linebacker for the University of Florida under Coach Bob Woodruff. At 55, he skied the black diamond slopes at Vail twice a year and played competitive tennis three nights a week. His golf handicap was six.

Trip's grandfather, Ronald Armstrong, had occupied a powerful seat on the Hillsborough County Commission for 40 years. Ronald Jr., Trip's father, was president of Tampa Electric, the city's utility company. Trip's birth certificate listed his name as Ronald Armstrong III.

His father led the plainclothes officer a few steps away from his son. He handed him an envelope. Without another look at Trip, the cop got into his car and drove away. Father and son stood in the yellow glow of the front porch light.

"Dad, I..." His father waved away Trip's words.

"Don't say anything. The next time, the cops won't bring you here. Do you understand what I'm saying?"

Trip nodded.

"If there is a next time, I won't help you. I won't bail you out or hire a lawyer. You'll be on your own. You understand?"

Trip nodded.

"How old are you son?"

"You know how old I am," Trip whispered.

"Yeah, I do. I'm wondering if you know."

The tow truck pulled into the driveway. The driver unhooked the chains and eased the motorcycle from the flat bed of the truck. Once the bike was leaning on its kickstand, Trip's father handed another envelope to the tow-truck driver.

Trip's stepmother watched from the living room window. Lynn Armstrong was slim in her pastel robe, her head covered by curlers and a scarf.

Trip stood rubbing his sore wrists. His father walked to the red front door and turned back.

"It's up to you son. Choose your path before it's chosen for you."

His father disappeared inside. His stepmother eased away from the window, the curtain falling back into place. This was a neighborhood Trip knew better than any other. The winding brick street. The mossy overhang of the water oaks. The pulsing thump of the golf course sprinkler.

He hated to admit that his father was right about anything. But he was 30. And some mornings, when his head was clear, he was bored with himself and his life. His childhood friends were out of college, starting families and careers. He had a loose cadre of friends and customers. He lived alone, in a fishing shack far from the city. He spent most days floating on an innertube atop a crystal blue lake, his belly and his brain full of magic.

The lights inside his parent's house dimmed. Trip walked slowly to the motorcycle. He lifted the flap on the saddle bags. The jars were still there!

It was time for a change. No question about it. But like his father and grandfather, Trip was a practical man. Before he quit the business, he would at least liquidate his stock.

The tow-truck driver had left his helmet on the seat. Taking a long, deep breath, Trip slipped his head inside and returned to his route.

CHAPTER 3

In Trip's business, it was better if your customers didn't know where you lived. He took orders by phone, and twice a week, he made deliveries. His last stop this night was in Ybor City, a district that had once been home to dozens of red brick cigar factories and thousands of immigrants from Cuba, Spain, and Sicily, part of a European exodus that had started in the 1880s and continued into the 1930s. By the 1980s, the immigrants had moved on and Ybor (*pronounced E-bore*) was empty except for a few dozen artists who had taken up residence in cigar worker houses and the large but squalid apartments above Seventh Avenue, the quarter's main drag. Trip had a lot of customers in this ad-libbed arts district.

Frankie and Josh shared a large, antique-filled bungalow on Fifth Avenue that had once been home to Frankie's grandparents. Trip handed Josh a jelly jar of sludge-colored mushroom tea.

"This is the last one. I gotta get out. I feel like it's all closing in on me." He didn't tell Josh about the roadside stop or his conversation with his father.

A slender, wisp of a man, Josh nodded solemnly. "Oh, I get it. Living on the bad side of the law is romantic for a while, but sooner or later, everybody's luck runs out."

Josh led Trip to a vintage, wood-trimmed couch, the wide arms draped with lace doilies crocheted by Frankie's Sicilian grandmother. Trip had spent a lot of stoned evenings in this living room, or back in the extra bedroom, where Frankie had dropped in a hot-tub, replacing the room's pine walls with glass that opened onto a lush jungle of up-lit palms and exotic shrubs.

"I had a dream about you," Josh whispered, his voice soft and almost girlish. "You were locked inside a wooden box. The key was in your pocket, but the lock was outside. You couldn't reach it. I woke up shaking. I was planning to tell you next time I saw you. You gotta be careful, Trip. Avoid the box!"

"I definitely want to avoid the box. But what am I going do? I can't go back to the parents, and I don't think I could handle a straight job."

"Oh, God no! Not that!" Josh moaned. "But listen, tonight, we're doing the 'schrooms and floating in Frankie's tub. Tomorrow, we'll get to work on finding you a new occupation."

Trip shook his head. After riding handcuffed in an unmarked car, and being confronted by his father, he wanted to head home for some serious, sober thinking on the front porch. He certainly wasn't going to get high.

Josh stopped him with a wave of his hand, then lifted the jar brimming with magic tea. "You're about to change your life. We need to discuss it. In depth. So, you're going nowhere, except our hot tub and the bed in the guest room."

Josh led Trip down the hallway to the kitchen in back and pulled glass tumblers from the kitchen cabinet. He poured two fingers of juice into each and added a fistful of ice cubes. "Let's toast to Trip Armstrong avoiding the box!"

Trip wanted to say no, but the glass was in his hand. The muddy, earthy smell was in his nostrils. Why the hell not, he thought. I'll take a farewell voyage.

He raised the glass. "Avoiding the box. I'll drink to that!"

* * *

In his dream, Trip was rising through pale pink clouds, like some psychedelic Superman, arms outstretched toward a bright blue stamp of sky in the distance. A ringing phone brought him back to earth.

"Wake up! Trip! Rise and whine, brother."

"Wha..." Trip muttered.

"Come on! Wake up. The early bird gets the sperm!"

Trip held the phone to his ear, his head sunk in the pillows of his own bed. He'd answered mostly to stop the infernal ringing. "The what?"

"It's 3 o'clock, pal. You're still young, but the day is about to get a gold watch and a house in Sun City."

Trip recognized Frankie's West Tampa accent. Frankie was a Jesuit High jock who'd realized in his '20s that he liked the jocks more than the cheerleaders. He and Josh had been lovers for years. Frankie had joined them in the hot tub at some point the night before. Just before dawn, Frankie and Josh, wrapped in blue-striped beach towels, had said goodnight and stumbled off to bed. Still enjoying the last mellow dregs of the high, Trip had decided to skip the guest room. In the pale wash of dawn, he had raced home on the Ducati, ignoring the speed limits, knowing his saddlebags held no trace of contraband.

"What?" He coughed into the phone.

"I'm saying, wake up, sleeping booty. I got news for you."

"Jesus, Frankie. Hold on." Trip eased himself up into a sitting position, pushing an extra pillow behind his back. There was a glass of water on the bedside table. He took a long drink.

"Okay," he whispered hoarsely, his voice not ready for actual talking yet. "What's up?"

"I've got something for you. I didn't remember last night, but today, I did. I checked the guest room and you'd split, so now I'm calling..."

"And now, I'm listening," Trip whispered. Frankie was clearly excited.

"I ran into Manny at Rough Riders the other night. You met him, right? He was telling me some old guy in Ybor was looking for a driver and bodyguard and did I know anybody? I didn't. But this morning, okay, early this afternoon when I woke up, I thought of you. I mean, you know, you're kinda built like a bodyguard."

"Who is this guy?"

"Wait, I got a note here," Frankie said, and after a brief pause: "Named Charlie Wall, apparently he was somebody once."

Trip didn't read newspapers or watch the local news, but he had heard of Charlie Wall. Charlie was Tampa's most famous gangster. A legend. "You mean THE Charlie Wall?"

Frankie, known for the thick black curls atop his chiseled head, and not the brains inside, had no clue. "Hell, I never heard of the guy. You know him?"

"I thought he was dead," Trip said.

"I guess not. Sounds like this could be pretty far from a straight job." This struck Trip as funny. He started to laugh but instead fell into a fit of coughing.

"You okay?" Frankie asked.

Trip managed to catch his breath. "You got a phone number?"

* * *

At sunset, Trip reclined in the wooden rocker on his front porch, Neil Young on the stereo, a half-smoked joint in his right hand, a phone number scrawled in blue ink on his forearm. The porch looked west across a small gravel street to a pine forest and a vast swatch of crimson sky. He'd spent hundreds of afternoons like this one blissfully enjoying Florida's sunset show, but today, instead of savoring the oranges and pinks cast by the sinking sun, Trip saw flashing blue and red lights, felt the cuffs on his wrists, heard the wailing siren.

Getting high had always untethered his brain, his thoughts drifting like butterflies from one fragrant flower to another. But lately THC and psilocybin triggered only dark thoughts. The high life didn't make sense anymore. He had rebelled against the idea of being something. But maybe being nothing wasn't such a good alternative. The scene with the cop and his father had only added fuel to the smoky peat fire that had clouded his head with doubt for months.

Closing his eyes to blot out those images, Trip tumbled into a well of familiar memories:

He was a boy growing up on the oak-shaded streets and manicured lawns around the Palma Ceia golf course. Ronnie

Armstrong had a natural swing and placed in some junior tournaments.

"Get your putter right and you could win some of these," his father told him.

But Ronnie didn't want to spend time on a putting green or a driving range. He had grown into a stocky, athletic teenager. The coaches at Plant saw him as a linebacker, but that didn't interest him either. The world outside of Palma Ceia was changing and being a jock wasn't part of it. He had watched the evening news with his father and stepmother. The story was about a San Francisco neighborhood called Haight-Ashbury. Hairy people, just a bit older than Ronnie, wore crazy outfits and danced, tribal style, in Golden Gate Park. His father had shaken his fist at the television.

"Bunch of goddamn freaks!" he shouted.

The wave from California took a while to reach Florida, but when it did, it swept Trip off his feet. He put away his golf clubs. He spent weekends at a riverfront park where teenagers gathered to make music on acoustic guitars, bongos, or overturned buckets. Joints were passed. Tabs were swallowed. Scraggly hair, patched jeans and tie-dye T-shirts were the required uniform. He moved from the Palma Ceia house to the family's weekend place on Lake Keystone, on an acre thick with ancient oaks.

The flatlands north of Tampa were filled with citrus groves, cow pastures, and watery stands of cypress. After a rainstorm, piles of cow dung sprouted off-white toadstools, their crowns brushed with bark-brown streaks. Pluck them and their cream-colored bases turned a deep purple, the telltale footprint of all the psychedelic goo festering inside. Trip learned where the fences were easiest to breach. He trained Satin, his floppy-eared cocker spaniel, to sniff out the magical buttons.

His father and stepmother only came out to the lake on Sundays, leaving Trip alone for most of the week. In the wide, marble-countered kitchen, he boiled the fruits of his labor into a tea, black as pitch and almost as thick. He sold the tea in jelly jars to friends, and eventually, to friends of friends. In 1973, when the Grateful Dead played a two-night stand at Tampa's Curtis Hixon Hall, his 'schroom juice was marinating in the brains of dozens of dancing Deadheads. After that legendary weekend, Ronald Armstrong III, then age 17, was known as "Trip."

Despite a spotty attendance record, he managed to graduate from high school with the class of '73. He missed some of the multiple-choice test questions, but he always aced the essays. Trip could write. At 12, he and his younger brother had produced a mimeographed newspaper called *The Palma Ceia Post*: "Errant golf balls—hazard, or opportunity?" The paper lasted three issues, but Trip kept writing, keeping his GPA afloat on the strength of short stories dashed off at the last minute, often as substitutes for the assigned topics.

"Ronald, this is lovely and sad," a stern-faced Edna Jackson told him as she handed back a story about a pregnant high school girl who leapt to her death from the Skyway Bridge. The title page was marked with a red "A+".

He hadn't read much poetry or fiction, but he liked telling stories and the thought of being a writer appealed to him. In the storefront coffee houses, or around a campfire in the woods, somebody was always reciting Allen Ginsburg, Bob Dylan or Rod McEwen.

His father pulled a few strings and got Trip accepted at the University of Florida, the alma mater of three generations of Armstrongs'. Trip tore up the letter. He refused to cut his hair or join the family for Sunday services at St. John's. He didn't consider himself a druggie. Coke, downers, speed, and opiates never appealed to him. And he was always polite and never stole from his family to buy drugs. He dealt pot, 'schroom juice, and acid at school and used the proceeds to keep himself happily stoned. He loved how pot made the world shimmer with possibilities and how mushrooms and acid showed him a hidden truth—he was just a cellular speck adrift in a vast pulsating universe.

Ron Armstrong Jr. wasn't pleased with the changes in his namesake. He'd seen his son's dazed expression and red-streaked eyes. One Sunday at the lake house, he found Trip's stash, hidden under an empty flowerpot in the shed. A week later, he delivered his son to a prison-like campus in St. Petersburg called Straight Inc. where ex-stoners and reformed addicts led him around by his belt-loops. Trip struggled at first but quickly figured out there was no escaping the compound. At the rap sessions he smiled and mouthed platitudes from the Straight handbooks. He cleaned bathrooms and peeled potatoes. He made his bed. Three months later, when he was released, Trip returned to the park and his tribe of happy stoners.

A few weeks after his release, his father yanked him out of bed. Trip was groggy after a 12-hour ride on a tab of orange sunshine. Like a Marine drill sergeant, his father stuck his face an inch from his son's. He told him he was taking away the keys to the Palma Ceia house, the Keystone house, and the silver BMW. Trip was no longer welcome around his family.

"Come back when you're ready to become an Armstrong. Until then, you're on your own."

Trip had no interest in becoming an Armstrong, whatever that meant. He didn't know why his mother had left, but he was convinced she had rejected the straight life of a South Tampa wife and mother. He was his mother's son. He didn't want to follow anybody's prescribed path. College. Career. Marriage. Kids. Trip was 18. The whole idea of becoming someone and doing something seemed foolish. He was just a speck in the vast cosmos. Being nothing made sense to him.

Trip expanded his pot and mushroom business and used the proceeds to buy the Ducati and pay the rent on his new residence—a rustic fishing shack on a pristine lake, with a wide front porch, and pecky cypress walls adorned with two large stuffed bass. It was thirty minutes north of the city, surrounded by pine forests and cow pastures.

When he wasn't hanging out with his pals, or on the motorcycle making deliveries, Trip spent lazy afternoons stretched out on an inner tube atop the cobalt-blue lake, like a frog atop a lily pad, watching eagles and ospreys circle slowly above. Closing his eyes, he envisioned a lined sheet of notepaper, and his own hand scrawling words in a crisp cursive. Riding the ripples from a distant bass boat, he moved the words around on his eyelids until they resembled something like poetry.

Years slipped by. His friends were all stoners or backsliding prepsters. Girls and women came and went. They were around when he wanted them, but he had never become attached. A relationship would have been something. Trip liked to tell friends he lived in a country called "Nadastan." He turned 20. Then 25. And now, here he was at 30, half-stoned, spending another sunset in the rocker on his front porch. The forgotten joint scorched his fingertips and Trip struggled back to the present. It was a gray and dreary dusk. A ghostly mist circled the branches of the pine trees. The cicadas scratched out their skittering harmony as Neil Young sang "Old man take a look at my life/I'm a lot like you."

He tossed the smoky roach to the porch and rubbed it out with his boot. Maybe it was time to flee Nadastan. He wasn't sure exactly where he would go, but he'd start with the seven numbers scrawled on his forearm.

CHAPTER 4

The next afternoon, wearing his cleanest jeans and a blue oxford cloth shirt with a button-down collar and no burn-holes, Trip parked the motorcycle in front of the address he'd been given. The house was one-story, but it covered most of the corner lot. It was built in the standard wood-frame, Ybor style, but this was no simple cigar shack. It was the house of someone with money. A wing in back extended deep into the lot, and the front porch was wide, its roof resting on carved columns that rose from red brick pedestals. It had once been the best house in a bustling neighborhood, but times had changed.

Trip had come to Ybor in the '80s for the parties and the poetry readings. He knew the history of the district. In the early 1960s Interstate Highway 4 had plowed through, dividing Ybor City in half. On the south side was the aging downtown—red brick buildings with shops downstairs and apartments upstairs, their ornate balconies hanging above the sidewalk. There were three-story yellow brick social clubs built by Italians, Cubans, and Spaniards. Dues-paying immigrants had come to the clubs for weddings, concerts, and visits to medical and dental clinics and a pharmacy. With the immigrants long gone, the clubs were empty and Ybor's downtown was just a shell. A loose cadre of artists, musicians and aging hippies, looking for cheap rent and some urban authenticity, had moved in.

North of the highway, Ybor had always been residential. But the economics had changed. Except for Charlie Wall and a few stooped widows too stubborn to leave, the current residents were mostly poor and mostly Black. Charlie's house was the only one on the block with a fresh coat of cream-colored paint.

Trip opened the gate. The lush St. Augustine lawn was

trimmed and edged. On the wide porch, he looked for a door-bell. Not finding one, he rapped on the door. A minute passed with no answer. Trip had reached into his back pocket for the paper with the address, when a man's voice barked an order from behind the door.

"Show me your hands!"

The voice was raspy, but resonant, the words clearly a command. Trip raised his arms like a man at gunpoint. He stared at the metal peephole.

"Now turn around. Slowly. And keep your hands where they are."

Trip followed instructions. A few seconds later, the door eased open.

"Get in. Now! An open door is just asking for trouble."

Inside, the house was dark, his host shrouded in shadow.

"Over there," the voice instructed. "That big chair."

The house stank of mold and cigar smoke, as though the windows hadn't been opened in a long time. A few shafts of light, penetrating the heavy maroon curtains, helped Trip find a leather chair. With a moan, the stork-like figure crumpled onto what appeared to be a couch, then stretched to switch on a floor lamp.

The room filled with light and Trip finally got a good look at Charlie Wall. Old, he thought. Seriously old. His face was long and flat like the backside of a shovel. His chin, his jiggly neck and cheeks were dotted with spikes of gray hair. His nose, swollen and lined with blue veins, had once been regal. For this noon-time job interview, Charlie wore a paisley bathrobe, his bone-thin calves exposed above a pair of leather slippers. Apparently, his potential employer had just pulled himself out of bed.

As the old man gave him a slow, foot-to-head look, Trip could see the couch was covered in gold brocade, the coffee table was buried beneath yellowing copies *The Tampa Tribune*. An Oriental rug, its colors as muted as one of Charlie's fifty-year-old tattoos, lay across the heart-pine floor.

"You're a big boy," he said finally. "Ever used a gun?" Trip shook his head. "Typical. Your generation believes all that love and peace crap. Ever hit anybody?"

"I was a wrestler in junior high. But I never punched anybody if that's what you're asking. Probably because people look at me and don't want to get into anything."

"Got a driver's license?"

Trip nodded.

"So, I'm not sure about the name, Trip," the old man continued. "Sounds like some hippie nickname to me. What name did your daddy give you?"

"Ronald. Ronald Armstrong." Trip hesitated, then finished, "the third. They called me Ronnie. And you, I'm guessing you're Charlie Wall?"

"The one and only. Still breathing, despite everything." Charlie was quiet a moment. Trip could sense gears moving inside the old man's head.

"You Ron Jr.'s son?"

Trip nodded. He hadn't heard anyone speak his father's name in a while.

"I thought so. Saw a family resemblance. He's the top Tampa Electric man now, am I right? I knew your grandfather well. He ran this county. We did some business back in the day. So why does a rich Palma Ceia boy like you want this job?"

"You knew my granddad?"

"I know everybody. Or I did. So, answer me. Why do you want this job?"

Trip thought about it. He had many reasons, but he gave just one. "I've been on my own a while. I like it that way. I've made my own money since I left home but my current business..." Trip stopped himself, not sure how much to tell a prospective employer, even one like Charlie Wall. "...I'll just say it has a lot of drawbacks."

"Like what?" Charlie asked.

Trip was silent.

"Son, nothing you can say will shock me. I've done it all and much worse. I suspect you know that much already. So, tell your

Uncle Charlie the truth. What's the drawback?"

"Jail, for starters."

A narrow smile settled on Charlie's lips. "The rebel son?"

Trip nodded.

"I spent some time on the dark side myself." Charlie said. "But as I said, I'm sure you already know that. Now, I'm just a simple retiree, enjoying my golden years. Or some baloney like that. There's nothing golden about getting old. But dying is worse. And over the years—how should I say this?—some people have gone out of their way to hurry my departure from this earthly plane. That's why I need something more than a driver. Someone with good eyesight. Someone who looks kind of scary. Someone like you. You understand?"

Trip nodded again. He felt comfortable enough to try a joke.

"So, you need a guard dog that drives?"

Charlie coughed out something close to a laugh. "I hadn't thought of it like that, but yes, that is exactly what I need."

"Can I ask one more question?"

Charlie nodded. "I thought you might have more than one."

"Just this one, I think. I wouldn't be doing anything illegal, would I? I'm trying to get away from that type of work."

Charlie's head rocked back, and he released a spit-slinging laugh that led to a round of choking and coughing. When he regained his breath, he grabbed a sheet of newsprint from the coffee table and loudly hawked into it. He carefully folded the sheet and set it on the table.

"My days on the wrong side of the law are in the rear-view mirror. In fact, I'm at an age where most of my days are in the rear-view mirror. You want to hear about the job?"

Trip nodded, thinking for the first time that he might have passed the audition.

"I go out at six. I'm generally home by nine. That's when I need you—between 6 and 9, six days a week. The other hours of the day, and Sunday, your time's your own. You get the apartment in back and all the groceries you can eat. I'll pay you twenty a day in cash. And I'll pay for seven days, and you only work six. That's 140 a week, though I'm sure a businessman like you already did the math. You can come and go as you like, but if you ever leave the frick-frackin' door unbolted, or a window unlatched, I'll sack you like that." The old man snapped two bony fingers.

Trip felt comfortable enough to tease.

"Did you say 'frick-frackin'?"

"Son," Charlie leaned closer. "My mother taught me that a gentleman never curses. It's a sign of a poor vocabulary and a shoddy upbringing."

"I'll remember that. So, when do I start this frick-frackin' job?"

The old man struggled to his feet. He winked at Trip and snapped his fingers. "How about tonight?"

CHAPTER 5

Normally, Katrina Carey skipped open-mic night. She worked hard at her poetry and had a well-received chapbook and a BFA from Michigan to prove it. Katrina had little patience for amateurs, but here she was, in a wooden folding chair in the third row of a makeshift performance space, watching a string of very bad poets strutting and fretting, and, in Katrina's mind, making much ado about nothing much.

She hadn't planned to come out, but this lonely Sunday had seemed never-ending. After she had finished a home-cooked dinner for one—a boliche roast with white rice and sautéed plantains that would have made any Cuban chef proud—she had felt the plaster walls of her second-story walk-up narrowing in on her, like the intergalactic garbage compacter in Star Wars. She had thought about writing, but had no fresh ideas, and the golden glow of the Seventh Avenue streetlights promised, if nothing else, a break from her own dark thoughts.

Open mic night at the Trolley Stop Bar, with a smattering of the local arts crowd and some high school kids fresh from the 'burbs, had not improved her mood. Amateur poetry made her think of Brian, who had sworn he was a poet, but turned out to be a poseur. Memories of her one-time fiancée—gone now for almost a year—always hit her like a rogue wave. She struggled against an undertow of grief.

She slapped her face with both hands, hoping to knock Brian's strong-jawed, asshole-next-door face from her mind. Since Brian's abrupt departure, pity and remorse had taken up residence in Katrina's brain and signed a long lease.

After scattered applause, Michael Poole, the host of the Thirsty Ear poetry series, stepped to the mic. He was too good a poet for this mid-sized southern city where amateur community theater and open mic nights passed for high culture. Built like a middleweight boxer, with tight curls and a stubbled face, Michael "could'a been a contendah" in New York City. Katrina loved his tough but tender poems, delivered during his curated poetry slams. He wouldn't read tonight. For his open-mics, Michael's talent was how, with a shake of his head or a crooked grin, he let the audience know what he thought of the evening's litter of wanna-be poets.

"Well, wasn't that something?" Michael quipped, as a slight, pimpled teenage boy stumbled off-stage. Katrina had zoned out when the boy rhymed "shooting stars...fast cars...jangling guitars."

Michael shook his head, his eyes wide, apparently trying to evict the last poet from his brain. "All I know about our next poet is that he rode up here on a very cool motorcycle, and like Cher and Prince, he goes by a one-word moniker. Please welcome, for his first time at Hungry Ear, it's..." Forgetting the name, Michael glared at his run sheet. "It's...shit, oh, here we go...it's Trip!"

An unshaven ruffian, his tangle of thick blond hair yanked into a mini ponytail, lumbered onstage like a tackle returning to the scrimmage line. He was handsome, even Katrina, who had sworn off men, noticed that. His grass-stained jeans and the untucked Grateful Dead concert tee, pocked with charred holes, told Katrina all she needed to know. A stoner, she was sure, the burn marks left by pot seeds sparking off hand-rolled joints. He projected the air of a scruffy romantic bard, but Katrina refused to fall for it. He's trying too hard to look like somebody who doesn't give a shit, she thought. Probably just some rich rebel from the 'burbs having his boho moment.

The poet's hands held no paper. He scanned the room, apparently savoring his moment at the microphone. Damn! She thought, he's doing it from memory, always a bad idea. The poet snatched up the mic stand, causing more than a little screeching feedback. Tilting it away from him, he leaned in, his eyes pressed shut, like some well-fed rock god. Expecting the worst, Katrina was relieved to hear a voice that was oaky and strong.

She dances
With galaxies
Clothed in the belt of
 the huntsman
tracking love's prey.

The poet took a slow breath and looked up, letting the words settle, a glimmer of a smile on his lips.

She somersaults into a
 milky sea of stars.
Backstroking through the glittering phosphorescence
Her incandescent
 mandala
Igniting
Alnitak
　　　Alnilam
　　　　Mintaka

He paused again, letting the names of the stars in Orion's Belt resonate, and then, staring directly at Katrina, he drew another slow breath and began:

Light years away
Immaculate on a ridge above a
 muddy river
I snatch the tail of the fiery comet
And carry it home
 in my pocket

That was it. With the final word he bowed his head, acknowledging the applause. The man-child threw a sly wink in Katrina's direction, his confident grin showing off the dimples in his cheeks and his cleft chin. When the applause faded, he stepped out of the single spot and into the audience, moving in Katrina's direction.

Oh God, don't sit here! She stared ahead as the bulk of him slumped into the chair beside her.

There was one more poet that night, a mouse of a girl, in

thick black glasses, her tiny feet—stuffed into pale blue ballet slippers—rose *en pointe* so she could reach the mic. "I'll be reading some of my original haikus," she said in a squeaky voice that belonged in a middle school, not a bar. She took a deep breath, then closed her eyes. Katrina sighed.

"June too soon
Spring flees forgotten
Harsh sun shakes, bakes"

Katrina shook her head. Thank God I don't own a gun because I would kill her!

Mercifully, the girl only had two more haikus, including one that rhymed koi with boy. Katrina wanted to scream: Haiku doesn't rhyme! The girl gave a slight head tilt—her version of a bow. Katrina saw her neighbor staring in her direction. She returned his stare but said nothing. She wanted to look away, but she was a sucker for a guy with dimples.

"So, what did you think?" His smile showed off a set of well-tended teeth.

"Her?" Katrina knew that wasn't what he was asking. "She sucked in so many ways, I don't know where to begin."

He grimaced. He ran his hand over his mouth, then raked it across his stubbled chin.

"I guess I was asking about mine." His eyes locked on hers. "It was just, you know, a work in progress. What did you think?"

I think you're sexy, is what she wanted to say. Brian was also a dimpled, sexy guy. They had met in a poetry workshop in Ann Arbor. After the Brian fiasco, Katrina had sworn off men for good.

Dimmed for the performance, the lights in the bar brightened and Katrina noticed that her next-door neighbor's eyes were drizzled with tiny red lines. His engorged pupils were black and round. Katrina didn't do drugs, but she knew buzzed when she saw it.

"I'm sorry?" Katrina asked. "What did you say?"

"Uh…I'd be happy for a little feedback. Like I say, it's just a work in progress. You know…"

The T-shirt and blue-jeaned crowd ambled toward the door. Michael and his girlfriend folded the metal chairs. When Katrina stood, the poet rose with her. He brushed back a cascade of yellow hair and smiled. Katrina knew he didn't want criticism. He was angling for a compliment, but he had dropped his hook in front of the wrong fish. When it came to poetry, she refused to offer faint praise. This handsome wastrel, a cocky interloper in the world of serious writing, needed a wake-up call.

"Don't take this the wrong way," she said, holding his gaze. "You can put words together, but come on, that spacy, drugged-out shit was bad enough in the '60s. Wake up! It's 1985."

She watched his smile contract into a frown of shock and confusion. Katrina felt bad. Clearly, he was trying, but somebody had to let him know where he was going wrong.

Taking his hand, she led him over to a table where lidless cigar boxes held the accessories for the Trolley Stop's coffee bar. She picked up a pink packet of saccharine. "This tastes like the real thing but it's not. How about you show me something you've written when you brain isn't artificially sweetened."

The big guy looked stunned. He seemed to struggle for words. Katrina patted his shoulder twice, her way of saying "There, there," and turned toward the front door, hoping he might try to stop her.

"Wait!"

Suppressing a smile, she turned back.

"If I had something to show you. Something better. Where could I find you?"

Katrina lived just a few steps from the bar, but she didn't want this guy knowing that. If he followed her home tonight, she might be tempted to invite him in.

"I work some night shifts at Rough Riders. You can find me there."

* * *

The Trolley Stop was tucked into a narrow Ybor storefront;

the name stenciled in red letters on the wide front windows. Inside, the walls were unpainted bead-board, the shabby-chic bar made of pine from a dismantled barn, set with wicker baskets of fresh peanuts. The discarded shells littered the floor.

The bar ran the length of the storefront, and Trip sat near the front window. The dark-haired woman's scolding and the lingering lethargy of that afternoon's dose of 'schroom juice, left him feeling lost. There was a half-empty glass of beer in front of him. He stared out at the sidewalk where he'd last seen her walking away. Most of the Monday night poetry crowd had fled. Jonathan Richman, an Ybor favorite, sang from the jukebox: 'I was dancin' in a lesbian bar..."

Three weeks into his job with Charlie, Trip had given up his drug business and stayed sober for his driver/bodyguard duties, but he still spent his free time getting high. Quitting was not as easy as the thought. And here he was again, all jagged on a Monday night.

He felt a hand on his shoulder. He turned, hoping the dark-haired woman had returned but it was Terry Krasner, an old stoner pal. Trip and Terry had spent their teen years and part of their '20s, smoking joints and hanging with the tribe. They were both tall, but where Trip was brawny, Terry was lean, needing a belt to keep his faded dungarees around his waist. The guy standing in front of Trip was still thin, but he had traded his druggie uniform for club clothes—cream-colored bell bottoms and a polyester Nik-Nik that opened halfway down his hairless chest.

Like Trip, Terry was a refugee from Straight Inc. He'd been at Curtis Hixon Hall with Trip for the legendary Dead concert, and they had shared a sheet of blotter acid the night Patti Smith fell off the stage during her show. In those crazy days, Terry kept his mop of khaki-colored hair pulled into a ponytail, but tonight his hair was trimmed and parted along the side. It was a grown-up haircut.

"Saw you through the front window!" Terry patted Trip's shoulder. "Long time..."

Trip and Terry had avoided college at 18, but while Trip was earning an advanced degree in psychedelic studies, Terry gave in. The last time they got high, Terry was finishing an economics degree at the University of Florida, where his roommates grew their own hydroponic weed and harvested bags of mushrooms from the cow pastures just outside of town.

"How's school?" Trip wasn't sure how long it had been since he'd seen Terry.

"Man, that was six years ago. "I milked it as long as I could, but at some point, you gotta graduate and go do something."

Terry waved at the bartender for two more drafts, and Trip caught the glimmer of a wedding ring.

"Is that a real ring or a cigar band?"

"I did the deed, my brother. The whole ride. I tried to invite you, but your parents didn't have an address or a phone number."

"I took some time off from all that," Trip said. "Please tell me you didn't do it at the church in Hyde Park with the tuxedo and the white dress, and the drunken reception at Palma Ceia with a top 40 band?"

"Cecilia kind of wanted the whole South Tampa wedding thing. I would have been happy to elope."

The beers arrived and Terry downed his in two long gulps. He made Trip do the same.

"Come on." Terry dropped a twenty on the bar and pulled Trip toward the door. "I got something you'll like."

Five minutes later, Trip was in an Ybor alley, halfway through a potent joint of Columbian, that Terry had rolled up in yellow paper. All that THC, on top of the beers and the lingering effects of the 'schroom juice, had Trip feeling like a boat that had run aground. He closed his eyes and leaned back, using the red-brick wall for support. The alley smelled like rotting fruit, but when Trip opened his eyes, the overturned trash bins, empty beer bottles and tumbleweeds of plastic grocery bags disappeared behind a cascade of floating hieroglyphics.

"You okay, brother?" It was Terry. "I gotta get over to El Goya.

The place is crawling with gay guys and straight women. The women love it when a hetero asks 'em to dance."

Trip shook his head, trying to get his bearings.

"Didn't you say you were married?"

"Trip, my wife is six months pregnant. She goes to bed at 7. Sometimes I gotta open a window and slip out, you know? You sure you're okay?"

Trip managed a smile and patted Terry on his cheek.

"Never better. But I gotta go home."

"And I gotta Goya."

Terry pulled Trip's head down and kissed him on the hair.

"Good running into you. Same old Trip. I like that."

Trip dragged Terry into a drunken bear hug. Terry broke free and stepped back to brush off his shirt and trousers. "Call me sometime. I'm at dad's office. You know, the one downtown?"

Looking like a loose-limbed blend of Fred Astaire and John Travolta, Terry soft-shoed to the mouth of the alley, then turned and yelled back at Trip.

"Track me down, brother! We'll do the crazy thing, for old times' sake."

Trip lingered in the shadowed alley, hoping the spinning world would slow down. When he tried to walk, the hieroglyphics skyrocketed around him. He tripped over something and went down hard.

CHAPTER 6

—

B uster Maniscalco wasn't a breakfast guy. His morning ritual was a cup or two of strong espresso ladled with steamed milk, the Ybor brew known as *café con leche*. The kitchen crew at Our Lady of Perpetual Help Senior Community knew what the old Italian, Spanish, and Cuban residents liked, and they kept a big pot of espresso and a tankard of steamed milk on a heating table just inside the wide, high-ceilinged dining room.

At 7:30 a.m., Buster stood at the counter, stirring his milk and coffee together in a white ceramic mug. He wasn't the first one up. The residents at Our Lady, in bed by 8 or 9 each night, rose with the sun. Most had finished breakfast by the time Buster stumbled in. He looked around at the human relics filling most of the scarred wooden tables—heads bent, some muttering to themselves, canes dangling from chair backs, walkers lined up just inside the front doors. This place is full of old people, he told himself. What am I doing here?

A resident for less than a month, Buster was still adjusting to the realities at Our Lady. For most of his life he had lived in squalid, rent-by-the week rooms, often above beer-and-a-bump bars. He wasn't used to a place with cream-colored walls, Danish modern tables and chairs, fresh flowers in ceramic pots, and a battalion of smiling servers and attendants. Buster and the other functioning residents had their own rooms on the upper floors. The failing ones withered away in tiny hospital rooms on a first-floor wing. Buster had been passing the hospital wing when the double doors opened with automated whoosh. He had seen wheelchairs, metal carts and stretchers, and a single nurse walking down a wide, fluorescent-lit corridor.

Not that the folks on the upper floors were in such great shape. Buster's next-door neighbor was a tall, mustachioed man, always stately in his tan suit, dress shirt and tie, who sat alone at dinner, arguing with some invisible crony. And there was the wild-haired woman, who walked the halls in her floral Moo-Moo, her face coated in cold cream, her lips fire-engine red.

From the coffee station, Buster watched an emaciated woman, wearing what looked like a prom dress, aim her metal walker toward the front doors. Her pace was glacial. At least I'm moving under my own power, Buster thought. And I know where I am.

He turned back to the dining room and noticed that the tall woman was waving at him again. She had been smiling and offering Buster a seat at her table for the past two weeks. Never a sociable guy, Buster had pretended not to see her. But here she was, alone at a four-top, aiming her perfect smile in his direction. When their eyes met, her smile amped up a few thousand watts. She leaned forward and patted the chair beside her. Buster almost turned away but changed his mind. Why not? He decided. She looks nice and I got nothing else going on. He ambled over, but instead of sitting beside her, he took the seat across the table.

"I'm Angie" Her voice was breathy. Her eyes were clear and wide. Buster felt a twinge of something that might have been desire. "You're Buster, right?"

He grunted, his way of saying, "Yes."

"I always see you with just a coffee in the morning. Don't you want some breakfast. A turnover? Some Cuban toast?"

"I'm not really…"

She didn't wait for him to finish.

"At our age, we need to eat. Ferdie always said our bodies were like coal-fired locomotives. They only kept going if you stoked 'em regularly. Food is fuel."

She slid a white plate, holding a single apple turnover, across the table, stopping when the plate reached his coffee cup.

"Who's Ferdie?" Buster asked.

"He's my husband."

Buster struggled to corral a thought—a question really—why did he feel a hot spike in his belly when this woman mentioned a husband? Buster was no good at romance. Never had been. In his younger days, whenever that annoying stiffness pushed against his boxer shorts, he got himself to Eighth Avenue and handed a twenty to Vivica, one of the "working women" who lived above the barber shops and dry goods stores. She knew how to relieve the pressure quickly and professionally.

In his 84 years on the planet, Buster had never had an actual girlfriend, let alone a wife. He had been comfortable with his monthly visit with Vivica. He liked her jowly, clownish face, powdered white, eyebrows drawn with what looked like charcoal. Her lips were the color of strawberry jam, her black hive of hair teased and then tamed, somewhat, by a single blue porcelain clip. He never actually saw her naked, but he loved how her tremulous breasts rose from her lace-trimmed decolletage like loaves of freshly baked bread. Whenever he showed up at her door Vivica teased him—"Well, the big man has peddled back in my direction!"—and, in the middle of the business, she always pretended to be impressed by the size of his kickstand.

Whores he understood. Civilian women were confusing and unpredictable. Buster avoided them. So why this hot poker feeling now? He kept his voice calm. "You got a husband? "

"Oh, don't worry. Dead 15 years. Three-packs-a-day. High blood pressure. The works. He was walking out of a McDonald's holding two happy meals and I watched him go face first into the parking lot and that was that. I guess it's a blessing that he died before he ate. Would you want your last meal on earth to come out of a paper box with a clown on it?"

Buster thought that was funny, but he didn't laugh. He wasn't a laugher. Instead, he felt the heat easing in his belly. For the past couple of weeks, while pretending to ignore her, he had watched this woman surreptitiously, tracking her daily routines, like she was one of the deadbeat gamblers he'd once been hired to smack around.

He liked the lean, simplicity of her face, the green of her

eyes, the touch of coral on her lips, the teeth so white he was almost startled when she smiled. While the other widows at Our Lady favored cotton candy helmets from the in-house salon, Angie pulled her thick gray hair back into a ponytail that fell below her shoulders. She reminded Buster of a schoolteacher or maybe, a nurse.

Close to her now, he breathed in a hint of orange blossoms. His nose was not reliable, after being broken so many times during his "career" as a low-level muscle guy for Tampa mobsters. But the fresh fragrance of this woman thrilled him. Buster wasn't sure what kind of body she had under the cardigan that planked all the way to her thighs. Her face was unlined. Her ankles, visible below the hem of her draw-string cotton pants, were slim and pale. He liked that. What the hell, he thought. The turnover warmed his nose as he took a bite.

CHAPTER 7

It was the end of her Rough Riders shift, and Katrina loaded glasses into the dishwasher trays, swept up, and stashed the hard liquor in cabinets with locks. Her bustling efficiency was a charade to keep her from staring at the man sitting at the far end of the bar. Don't look over there, she silently scolded herself. But her eyes kept straying to the aspiring writer from open mic night. He was nursing his fourth club soda and lime. Instead of the scruffy stoner look, he wore a pale blue polo shirt with the alligator logo. His sandy blond hair was clean and combed straight back, curling slightly just above his shirt collar.

When she'd taken his order, Katrina was casual. "I don't think I've seen you in here before."

"But you have seen me before, right?" he asked.

"Well, um…Yes. Of course…I mean, sure." Flustered, she looked quickly around at the other customers ringing the bar.

"I'm Trip and you're?"

"Busy." She offered a tight, "I'm-just-your-waitress" smile. "Okay, better get to it."

Nestled in a ground floor corner of a repurposed Ybor City cigar factory, Rough Riders was named for Teddy Roosevelt's battalion, which had bivouacked on the other side of town, as they prepped to invade Cuba. The square bar was all dark wood, with a brass foot-rail and tall stools that screeched across the concrete floor when someone got up. Downtown office workers and community college staff filled the tables and chairs on the main floor at lunch, but the nighttime crowd—a tribe of post-graduate artists and leftover hippies, clustered around the bar.

Katrina loved the bohemian gaggle, but she could see

through all their non-conformity. The men wore blue jeans and T-shirts, some stained with oil paint, their shirts adorned with images of Groucho Marx or John Lennon. The women chose one of two options: '50s space-age glasses, thrift shop sundresses and no makeup; or tight jeans and striped, boat-neck tops, accessorized with black lipstick and raccoon eye shadow. The boho crowd came to eat, drink and socialize, but always kept an eye on the bill. The financial exuberance of the 1980s had not trickled down to Ybor's artists.

Glancing at the man with dimples, Katrina saw that he was reading a slim paperback with a gray cover. It looked strangely familiar. God, he's adorable! Katrina tried to shake that thought from her head. Stop it! Stop looking at him!

Each time she glanced over, he stopped reading and looked up, offering the cocky smile she remembered from open-mic night. She pictured his face pressed against her neck, his meaty hands pulling her close. Spinning around, lost in her revery, she knocked two beer mugs to the floor behind the bar. They bounced harmlessly off the cross-hatched rubber mat.

Damn, she thought, as she bent to retrieve them, why won't he leave? He's going to ask me out. I can feel it. After I've been so careful. Damn! Damn! Damn!

Just before last call, she loaded the big dishwasher and went over her plan. A midwestern girl, she tried to avoid conflict and play nice with others. But working in bars and restaurants in Ybor, after her break-up with Brian, had changed her. She was still nice, but she spoke her mind. I'll just tell him, she had decided. I won't be mean, but I'll cut off this dangerous mating ritual before it starts.

Katrina examined her face in the chrome mirror hanging on the back door of the kitchen. She had never really liked her reflected image. She thought her features were too sharp, her lips too thin, her forehead too high. And she wasn't crazy about how she looked in her work uniform—khaki pants, with red suspenders, over a blue denim shirt with the Rough Riders logo—Teddy Roosevelt on a bucking horse. Mirrors didn't show her what everyone else saw—a lean, long-legged young woman with dark, thoughtful eyes, and Joan Baez hair, wrapped in a loose bun, held by a single chopstick.

Staring at her image, Katrina yanked the chopstick and shook out her hair. Reaching up to fluff her curls, she stopped herself. She slapped both cheeks with open palms. *Dammit! You're primping for him. Stop this foolishness. Now!* She twisted her hair back into a bun and secured it with the chopstick.

When she returned to the bar, the burly poet was her last customer. The rest of the Ybor gang had left meager tips and headed off to their lofts and second story apartments for card games or sex, both served with sides of late-night intoxicants best consumed behind closed doors. She walked up to Trip, offering a passive *you're just another customer* stare.

"Closing time. You need anything else?"

"I was hoping I could talk with you for a few minutes."

Katrina shook her head and raised her palm into a STOP sign. "Before you do, I need to tell you something. OK?"

Trip's eyes widened. Katrina lifted his glass and wiped the counter in front of him. She kept her eyes focused on the bar and the rag. *No eye contact,* her inner voice shouted. *Too dangerous!*

"I don't date. I spend my spare time writing. I'm not sure how much longer I'll be in Ybor. And I've sworn off men. So, there you go. That's my story."

She set his glass down and Trip picked it up. Katrina let herself stare. He sucked the straw with moist pink lips that looked incredibly kissable. His blue eyes were rimmed by sand-colored lashes and thick eyebrows, and the whites were clear, not a red line anywhere.

Trip set down his soda. "I don't really date either. I'm not here for romance or sex. So don't worry about that. I want to talk about something else."

"You do?"

"It's about my writing. I'd like to get better and I'm thinking you might be the right person to help with that."

Caught by surprise, Katrina took a step back. "You know there are schools for that. And correspondence courses. And how-to books in the library."

"I tend to work better with a tutor. And I'm willing to pay for your time."

"And why me? You've never read my writing."

Reaching into his back pocket Trip pulled out the thin book he'd been reading at the bar—*Down in the Quarter*—poems and a short story Katrina had written about her time in Ybor. No wonder I recognized it, Katrina thought. He was reading my book!

Down in the Quarter was a breakup book. There wasn't a happy word on any of the 40-odd pages. She had run off a dozen copies in the art department at Hillsborough Community College, where a friend worked. She added a hand-drawn gray cover and left a stack in Three Birds Bookstore and on the front table at Goo Foo Pottery, not expecting anyone to pick them up.

"These poems are good. Sad, but good. And the short story made me cry."

Katrina hadn't seen this request coming. "Oh..." It was all she could manage.

Trip took up the slack. "Listen, I live a few blocks away. North Ybor. You?"

"I'm in Ybor, but the other direction." She still did not want to give too much away.

"Then, we're almost neighbors. My name's Trip. How about we talk about this while I walk you home?"

A terrible, dangerous idea, Katrina thought, but she was unable to speak just then. When she did speak, she was shocked by the words coming out of her mouth. "I close up in 15 minutes, if you don't mind waiting."

He smiled. "I'll be right here."

* * *

Trip liked how it felt to walk beside Katrina. Since that open-mic night when she had ripped apart his poetry, this willowy, melancholy woman, had lingered in his mind. She had told him to write something real. Something that wasn't "artificially sweetened." He knew she meant he needed to get sober, then see what he could do.

After going face down in the alley, Trip had bandaged his bloody forehead and cleaned up his act. He sold off his "inventory" but stashed a single jelly jar of mushroom tea in the back of Charlie's refrigerator, with a sign reading: NOT FOR HUMAN CONSUMPTION. He told himself he'd kept it in case he needed quick cash. But he knew it was there in case he changed his mind about the whole sober thing.

So far, he'd not been tempted to return to the stoner life. He missed watching the sunset while smoking a joint, but he got over it. He'd sold the motorcycle and avoided the lake country north of town, where the magic mushrooms sprouted. He drank club soda and lime when he was out with Charlie. When he wasn't driving his boss around, he thought about the woman from the poetry reading. Trip had never expended any real effort on a woman before. Now, he was flexing muscles he didn't know he had. Something about this woman seemed worth the effort.

Walking with her through the old district, Trip was happy. The March air was cool. Fog lingered around the wrought-iron balconies above the sidewalk. The neon glow of the Ritz marquee painted Katrina's face aqua and blue. Trip had to remind himself not to stare.

"Are you doing any more writing?" she asked.

"That's what I want to talk with you about. My new boss is kind of legendary. And tells me a million stories, mostly when he's drunk. I'm writing them down and I think there's something there. A short story. Maybe a book. I don't know."

Katrina stopped in front of a set of wooden double-doors. "I like that idea. Write something that's real." She nodded toward the doors. "Anyway, this is me."

Katrina's fingers brushed his forearm, igniting a sizzle that raced down his spine.

"Wait here. I've got something for you," she said.

She disappeared up the wide staircase. The street was empty. The fog gauzed over the globe streetlights. The hex block sidewalk beneath Trip's feet was steely in the pale light. The quiet street scene reminded Trip of the plays his mother had dragged him to before she disappeared. His favorite part had been the look of the stage set before the lights went down. Maybe I'm at the start of something here, he thought.

Katrina reappeared. She handed him three paperbacks, the covers wrinkled, the corners bent. These books had been read. He squinted at the titles in the streetlight—*On The Road, Great Expectations* and *Slaughterhouse Five.*

"Read these and write something real," Katrina said. "Something about you. Or about your crazy boss."

Katrina stepped back into the open doorway. "I spent four years in Ann Arbor in a big-time writing program. I've read the right books. Met the right authors. But teaching people how to write is a sham. If you've got some talent, there are only two things that will make you a writer..."

She looked angelic; her hair haloed by the hanging bulb that lit the staircase.

"And what are those things?" he asked.

"First you read a lot, then you write a lot. That's it. That's all I got to offer."

"I think you might have more to offer but thanks for these," Trip held up the books. "Can I see you again sometime?"

"I'm around." She smiled at him. An encouraging smile, Trip thought. She slipped inside.

He lingered on the sidewalk, remembering what it felt like when her fingers brushed his arm.

CHAPTER 8

Getting stories out of Charlie wasn't hard, especially on their drives home each evening. After a few drinks at The Turf or Licata's, Charlie's adventures just spilled out. Trip couldn't take notes, but after his boss stumbled off to bed, he recorded everything he could remember on yellow legal pads.

People always asked Charlie about his criminal career. Trip wanted to work up to that. He asked about Charlie's childhood and learned that he and his boss were not so different. Both loved their birth mothers and lost them early. Both had bad experiences with stepmothers. Talking about his mother brought up all kinds of emotions Trip had carefully filed away. He was happy that Charlie didn't ask too much.

Working from his notepads either late at night or first thing in the morning, Trip wrote a few chapters. He didn't like the results. In third person, Charlie's stories sounded clunky. Trip hadn't read a lot of fiction, but he liked how *The Catcher In The Rye* was told in Holden's own anxious voice. He decided to let Charlie tell his own story.

* * *

I wasn't born mobbed up. No way. My baby rattle was solid silver. My family home on Ross Avenue in Tampa Heights stood three stories, wrapped by a wide porch. In my baby pictures, I'm wearing lace, my hair all Lord Fauntleroy curls, my little-boy feet wrapped in silk socks and strapped into tiny white sandals.

In turn-of-the century Tampa, the Walls were royalty. Still are. We're cousins of the McKays and the Lykes. We partied with the Hendersons and the Knights. At five, I was a page at the second Gasparilla coronation, the queen's gilded crown rested on a sequined pillow in my hands.

The Walls made their first money shipping oranges north by steamship and rail, but like their friends, they got rich buying, selling or subdividing stands of scrub and pine around Tampa's fledgling downtown. My pop was a quiet guy. Never cracked a joke, that I heard. I think he was handsome, but it was hard to see his face behind a thick brown beard, already flecked with gray. It was my mother who made our family fun. She was tall, with thick, copper hair that fell in waves around a face you might see in silhouette inside a locket. Mostly, I remember her hands—her long fingers, coated in clear polish, dancing across the keys of our upright piano, as we kids sang "Alexander's Ragtime Band." My pop was a lot of things, but singer wasn't one of them. Instead, he clapped out a beat and beamed at us from the couch.

I don't know much about their courtship, but my parents had what people called a "mixed marriage." My father was Episcopalian, and a rising star in Tampa society. My mother was Southern Baptist, the daughter of two schoolteachers. Local gossips said she married up, but I swear it was my father who got the better end of the deal.

For almost five years they were childless, but then the babies came. I was born three months into the new century. Three more children, Benjamin, then Adele, and Fiona, came over the next four years. My father insisted that his children be raised in the Episcopal Church, and mother agreed, but she never cut ties with the Baptists. About once a month, Mom hauled us to Sunday service at Riverside Church, just north of downtown, where a minister known as Brother Abernathy got worked up and red-faced, railing against the devil. He finished his long sermons planted atop the empty front pew, a black bible raised above his head, shouting "the wage of sin is death! Rise up, come down this aisle and be saved!" All that yelling, Mom told us as we walked home, was "a Baptist thing. Don't let it frighten you."

Before her marriage Matilda Carter had sung in the choir

and I think it was the Southern Baptist hymns that moved her. They were so much more soulful than the Episcopalian dirges we endured most Sundays. Each night, as I lay in bed, I got a hymn, in my mother's warm alto, her long fingers on my cheek. It was always the same verse: "Just as I am/though tossed about/with many a conflict/many a doubt/ fighting and fears within without/Oh Lamb of God, I come. I come."

I don't brag about this, and I never tormented my brothers and sisters about it, but I was always Mother's favorite. I was firstborn, there's that, and I had her fine features, her stork neck, but it was something else. Some rebellious spark. Something we knew about each other every time our matching gray-green eyes locked.

* * *

I remember it was a sunny summer morning, and my father had left for work. Mother left my younger siblings with the housekeeper, and we took the streetcar to the end of the line, a mile or so north of our house. I was six but felt completely grown up as we rode north together. She had dressed me in all white but carried a change of clothes for me in a canvas satchel, along with a picnic lunch. At the end of the line, we walked to the west, where the Hillsborough River narrowed and the thick grass ran down to the brown water.

"Don't tell your father or your brothers and sisters about this. It's a secret. Something for just you and me. Okay?" I was happy to share a secret with her even though I had no idea what it would be.

Brother Abernathy was waiting for us at the river. Instead of his baggy Sunday suit, he wore a blue work shirt and black rubber overalls that covered his khaki pants almost up to the belt. "Where's your fishing pole?" I asked when he greeted us.

"Today, I'm a fisher of men." His cheeks were dimpled, his smile wide. I thought of him as old, but looking back I know he was probably 50 at the time. A round, jolly fellow when he wasn't preaching, I always considered him my extra grandfather.

The grassy riverbank was shaded by regal water oaks, their thick branches bent and hung with moss. A few houses were visible in the distance, but we were on the edge of the city, beyond the original neighborhoods. Across the tannin-tinted river, a stout negro woman and a boy about my age sat on a sandy bank, their cane poles arcing out, two red bobbers riding the river's rolling current. I could hear birds clucking and whistling in the oaks, and the rustle of the slow-moving river, as it bubbled over ridges of limestone.

While my mother waited on the grass, Brother Abernathy took my hand and led me into the river, the bottom squishy under my feet. The preacher wasn't a tall man, but he was taller than me. We stopped when I was chest deep in the water. The current tugged at my ankles. Maybe it was fear or cold or both, but I was shaking, my eyes moist with tears but I steeled myself. I was not going to cry.

"Charles, we're all sinners. Even an innocent child like yourself. And for a sinner to enter the kingdom of heaven, to earn the grace of Jesus Christ, he has to die and be born again, just like our Lord Jesus died and on the third day rose from the grave. You know that story, don't you?"

I couldn't answer. My efforts to hold myself together failed. I felt the warm tears on my cheeks. My hand, held tight by the preacher, was trembling, out of my control. I shot a terrified look at my mother.

"It's okay, baby. It's okay." She called from the bank. "Be my brave man and this will be over in just a minute. You'll be fine. Then we'll sit down here with Brother Abernathy and have a nice picnic."

I wanted to scream and run from that river, but more than that, I wanted to be my mother's brave boy. The one she shared secrets with. The one she loved best. I nodded up at the preacher. "I know the story. I love Jesus. I want everlasting life."

"That's a good boy," he said. "Now when I say it's time I want you to reach up and hold your nose. Hold it tight and close your eyes. Then, I'm going to put my arm behind your back, and bend *you over into the water. Just for a tiniest second, then I'll bring you up. Okay?"*

I was steel now. Determined. Brother Abernathy looked at me and smiled. "Are you ready?"

I felt his arm on my back. He raised his other arm over my head. "Charles Wall, I baptize you in the name of the Father, the Son and the Holy Spirit. You'll be forgiven for all your sins and transgressions. Your old self will die, and you'll be born again into everlasting life as one of God's chosen flock."

My fingers gripped my nose, and my eyes were pressed shut. He bent me back into the warm river and just as quickly, I was coming up, water falling from my hair and shoulders. Brother Abernathy lifted me into his arms and carried me from the water. He didn't seem to mind that I was wet. He stepped onto the grassy bank and set me on my feet, right in front of my mother.

"Matilda, your son has been born again into eternal life. May God bless young Charles on this day and all the rest of his days. Amen."

"Amen," my mother replied.

Alive forever. I liked that thought. It was worth a few moments of terror. My mother wrapped me in a towel, then picked up the bag. She led me behind an oak tree and dried me off, then helped me into the clothes she had packed. I loved her fiercely at that moment. Her fiery hair cascading around her face. Tears stained her pale cheeks, but she was smiling and singing softly into my ear. "Just as I am though tossed about..." Standing on that riverbank, I let myself drown in the sweet smell of her.

* * *

Trip stopped typing. It was almost midnight. Time to go.

Katrina worked night shifts at Rough Riders and at the end of each shift, Trip was waiting. On their six-block walk they talked about writers and books. About once a week, he drove Charlie's Cadillac to the downtown library to check out the novels she had recommended.

Reading was a muscle Trip was just learning to flex. His high school English teacher, Mrs. Jackson, had encouraged him to check out Dylan Thomas and J.D. Salinger, (Trip learned from Salinger's *Nine Stories* that there was such a thing as a short story). He liked the wordplay in the songs of Bob Dylan, but he'd spent most of his childhood outside—smacking golf balls or shooting hoops.

Now, at Katrina's urging, he was devouring Charles Dickens, and her favorite Russians—Dostoyevsky with his anxious, often desperate characters, and Chekhov's short stories, where nothing happened and everything happened, all at the same time.

He simplified his life. He stayed sober and didn't seek out his old druggy friends. The highlight of his days were walks with Katrina and the hours when he sat at the typewriter, organizing Charlie's tales into a narrative. A life story.

CHAPTER 9

It was May of 1915. Summer had arrived and we were sleeping with the windows open. Things were going to hell in Europe. A German sub had sunk the Lusitania, sending more than a thousand passengers and crew to the bottom of the Atlantic. A feeling of dread soured my 15-year-old gut. I thought trouble would come from somewhere across the ocean. But I was young. I hadn't learned that real disasters happened closer to home.

Five months into a troubled pregnancy, my mother was confined to her bed. Once a day we were allowed in, my younger siblings jostling, so the tips of mother's fingers could brush their cheek. I stood back, too grown-up for childish bustling. Mother gathered my siblings into her arms and whispered—"My babies." Then, she sent them out and patted the bed, I came close. We sat together, shoulders touching, my hand wrapped tightly in hers.

She got sicker. I sensed her light dimming, her softness hardening. One afternoon, the maid led me to her bedside. Mother struggled to sit up; her belly huge inside a white lace nightgown. Her face had lost its color, her once radiant hair was limp and flat, her eyes lifeless. I was terrified, but I kept a thin smile on my face. She patted the sheets, and I climbed in beside her. She smelled of lilacs and rubbing alcohol.

"You are my brave young man." Her voice was a hoarse whisper. "I have some things I need you to do."

She took a ragged breath. "Always be nice to your brothers and sisters. Help your father when he needs it. And this is the most important thing—don't let people tell you how to live your life. You decide. You, not somebody else."

I nodded solemnly, not sure what I was supposed to say. Getting that promise from me seemed to steal her strength. She kissed my forehead before slipping down into the thick bedclothes. It was the last time we were alone together.

Before this troubled pregnancy, I had spent hours after school running the streets with a gang of rich misfits. We rode the streetcar to downtown and loitered outside bars and gambling houses. In Ybor City, we hid in red brick alleys, shouting taunts at the hookers when they came down from their second story rooms to pick up the afternoon paper from a newsboy. They were the most exotic women I'd ever seen, draped in red feather boas, their dresses cut low to reveal fleshy breasts. When their pimps came after us, hair slicked back and parted down the middle, wearing flashy suits, with silk ties and flowers in their lapels, we raced into the maze of Ybor alleys. There was no way the pimps, in their tight leather shoes, could keep up with boys running full tilt.

Mother got worse. I stayed close to home. After school, I spent most days in my bedroom reading Treasure Island and Dr. Jekyll and Mr. Hyde. On a blazing afternoon in July, I heard my mother scream. It was the maid's day off and my father had spent the day at mother's bedside. I dropped my book and raced into the hall where my brother and sisters stood crying. My parents' bedroom door flew open, and my father emerged.

"Charles. I need you!" He grabbed me by the shoulders and spun me around. His face was sheened with sweat, his eyes red. "Keep an eye on your brother and sisters. I've got to go get Dr. Mills. You're in charge until I get back. Don't let those kids into your mother's room. Got it?"

I nodded, and my father ran from the house.

Fear tightened my throat. I fought to hold back tears. I padded between the living room and the kitchen, trying not to hear my mother's screams. It sounded like someone was ripping out her fingernails, one every two minutes or so. Her cries chilled me, but I was the oldest, and my job was to comfort my brothers and sisters. I told them mom would be fine.

My father returned just as the sun was setting. He raced upstairs but stopped halfway. "Charles!" he shouted. "Man the front *door! People are coming!"*

I did as I was told. I opened the door first for the chubby, red-cheeked midwife, who hurried upstairs with a cloth satchel. Dr. Mills was next, in white shorts and pull-over shirt, looking like he was fresh from the tennis court. He was followed moments later by his nurse, Mary, in her uniform, a tiny, folded cap pinned into her hair. I had barely closed the door when Mr. and Mrs. Touchstone, my parents' best friends, knocked. Right behind then was Brother Abernathy. He didn't stop to say hello or pat my head. Like all the other guests that day, he rushed upstairs, his face looking like it had been carved from stone. I didn't know a lot, but I knew a preacher arriving after dark wasn't a good sign.

My brother fled the house for his A-frame wooden fort out back. In the twilight, he aimed his toy musket out the window, hoping he could kill the invisible intruder who was hurting our mother. A few minutes after the doctor arrived, my father came downstairs and sat at the kitchen table. The smoke from his Pall Mall looked like steam as it escaped his beard. My sisters stood at his side, their hands on his shoulders. Across the table was Mr. Touchstone. There were highball glasses and an open bottle of whiskey on the table.

We heard mother's screams, followed by the quiet, then more screams. I don't know how much time passed before we heard one horrible, plaintive wail. After that, the only sound in the house was the metallic ticking of the grandfather clock in the living room.

At some point all the people I had let into the house came down the white-railed staircase. The nurse was in front, carrying towels and sheets, red with blood. Behind her was the fat midwife. There was something inside the gray towel she pressed to her chest. Dr. Mills was next, shaking his head, wiping his wet hands on his shorts. Brother Abernathy clutched his Bible; his cheeks stained with tears. Mrs. Touchstone looked like she'd seen the devil up close.

The midwife and the nurse turned toward the laundry room. Mrs. Touchstone's hands settled on my shoulders. My sisters draped their arms around father's neck. They sniffed back tears.

Everything about that moment was wrong. There was a Baptist minister in our kitchen and a bottle of whiskey in plain view on the table. My mother would have never allowed it.

Dr. Mills whispered something to my father, then looked at the minister. Brother Abernathy pulled a handkerchief from his back pocket and wiped away his own tears. Mrs. Touchstone eased my sisters away. The minister leaned down, his hand on my father's shoulder, his mouth near his ear. He whispered something none of us could hear.

When Brother Abernathy stepped back, my father stared blankly at him. He rose slowly, holding a full glass of whiskey. He tossed it back. The empty glass slipped from his fingers and shattered on the gray-tiled floor. Like a condemned man at the gallows, my father climbed the stairs.

* * *

For the next few days our kitchen was full of casserole dishes and stewpots delivered by neighbors, or by my parent's friends from the Krewe of Gasparilla, or women from the Baptist church, or St. John's Episcopal. There was always someone at the door with a covered dish.

On a Thursday afternoon, maybe a week later, the five of us sat in the front pew at Riverside Baptist. My mother, dressed in her best silk nightgown, was visible from the waist up. The rest of her was hidden inside a dark wood box. Beside her coffin, atop a carved oak pedestal, was a small, closed box, holding a sister I would never meet. Brother Abernathy told us their souls were in heaven.

There was another few days of casserole dishes and stew pots. But then the church folks, the neighbors, and my parent's friends took home their cookware and the house was quiet. We ate meals the maid had left, the five of us trying not to notice the empty chair at the dining table. My father pushed his food around the plate, asking what we had learned in school that day.

During those months, I must have cried, but I can't remember it. My brother Ben and my sisters cried enough for all of us. I returned to the streets, hungry for trouble. Trouble felt natural to me now. I switched from shorts to blue jeans, rolled at the cuffs. Shirts stolen from my father's closet hung untucked around my bony body. The fabric hid the pearl-handled pistol I had found in my father's armoire. It was small but held a kind of power. That power was transferred to me when I carried it. When an Ybor City pimp confronted me one night, I pointed the pistol at his chest. The big man's arms came up—his hands open—and he backed away, blubbering like a baby.

"Sorry, kid. Really, sorry. You boys do what you like, just don't shoot that thing, okay?" He turned and ran. After that, I kept the pistol with me when I was out with my friends. When I slept, it was tucked under my mattress.

Fall came. We went back to school. On a miserable day in November when a cold front brought shrouded skies and a chilling rain, she arrived.

"Children, this is Aunt Katherine."

My father had gathered us all in the living room. Beside him was a slender woman, not too tall, her dark hair pulled back into a bun. She looked young to me, like a girl about to go off to college. I remember thinking she was pretty, though not like the beauty my mother had been. Her dress was long and gray, with lots of buttons. Above her lace collar, a single gold chain held a small cross. Her hands were veiny and too big for her body, the fingers thick and stubby, clearly no good for piano playing. "Aunt Katherine will be living here with us, and I know you'll make her welcome."

I didn't know we had an Aunt Katherine.

I remember a small service at St. John's, the Episcopal Church in Hyde Park. She and my father stood before a minister, who wore a long robe. When the minister stopped talking, my father kissed Aunt Katherine. After the ceremony, my father was gone for a few days. The maid stayed with us and the Touchstone's spent every evening in our living room. They played board games with my brother and sisters. I played a few games, then went upstairs. I arranged the pillows under the covers, so anyone looking in would think I was asleep, then I slipped out my bedroom window and ran the streets.

When my father returned home, Aunt Katherine was at his side. Men brought in suitcases, a large wooden chest, and a dozen hat boxes. My father told me to help the workmen carry Aunt Katherine's things up to my mother's bedroom. I shook my head and ran out the front door, slamming it behind me as my father shouted my name.

When I came home, hours later, he was waiting in the upstairs bathroom. He sat on the closed toilet at the far end of the narrow room. The spanking board-—a long-handled slab of polished wood—was in his right hand. He told me to lean over, with my palms on the tile countertop. The blows were hard and went on longer than any spanking he'd ever delivered. My backside was on fire, but I refused to cry out. The whipping didn't change my attitude. I hated this new reality, and no amount of paddling would change that.

None of us kids liked Aunt Katherine, but her fights with me were especially loud, and ugly. No fists, or spanking boards. Just words. Sometimes the words were dark and somber. Sometimes they were screamed, and wet with spittle. Sometimes porcelain was shattered or chairs tossed.

Okay, maybe it was me who spit the words, smashed the vases, and tossed the chairs. Aunt Katherine's face remained placid. She knew she had the upper hand.

I refused to accept this new reality. Aunt Katherine might be sleeping in my mother's bed, but she wasn't my mother. She was the enemy. My father meted out nightly punishment, bringing the paddle down on my bare bottom. I refused to cry out or ask him to stop.

After those spankings, I climbed out of my bedroom and scrambled down the limbs of the massive live oak. The pistol was stuffed in my waistband, secured by a leather belt. In the small hours of the night, I experienced the Tampa most people didn't see—where products were offered that you couldn't find by day.

One night, as I made my escape, I saw a girl in the second-sto-

ry window of the house next door. I waved. She bent and raised the window. On all fours, I crossed the wide limbs and slipped into that open window. It was Ava's room.

But that's a story for later.

* * *

Trip stopped typing and realized he was wiping away tears. Writing about Charlie losing his mother brought him back to the early morning when Trip was seven.

It was just before dawn and Ronnie Armstrong was asleep in the bottom bunk, his five-year-old brother Doug asleep above. The room was dark, but the wide curtains, covered in cowboys on bucking broncos, were framed by a pale strip of morning light. His mother leaned close to him, her face and figure shadowed, her voice a whisper.

"You know I love you, right? You and your brother."

She seemed to be speaking as much to herself as to him.

"I really thought this was the right thing. But I'm just not good at it."

He wished he could remember what else she said, but he was young and half-awake. Instead, he recalled that her girlish face was stained with tears. She wore blue jeans and a white blouse buttoned to the collar, and her hair, in a ponytail, was thick and blond, just like his.

When she stopped whispering, his mother kissed his forehead. She smelled fresh from a shower. She stood on tiptoes and kissed his brother. Trip fell back into boyhood dreams.

When he emerged later that morning his mother wasn't in the kitchen. Two bowls of cereal were on the table, along with a pitcher of milk. Celia, the Cuban housekeeper, was at the sink, normally she didn't arrive until after they left for school. Celia was squat and soft, and made up for her shaky English by pinching the boys' cheeks and pulling them into fleshy hugs they pretended they didn't enjoy. That morning, she was solemn. She cleared the breakfast dishes and hugged both boys and sent them off to school.

At 3 p.m., his mother still wasn't home. His father, who was never home before dinner, sat in one of two high-backed, brocaded chairs in the living room, across from an overstuffed couch, set with pastel pillows. There was a drink in his hand. A cigarette smoldered in a butt-filled ashtray on the glass coffee table.

Celia led Trip and his brother in, then slipped out. The boys stood like miniature soldiers in front of Ronald Armstrong Jr.

"Your mother is taking a vacation." His father looked off, over the boy's heads. "She needs to sort some things out. In the meantime, we'll continue doing what we do. I need you boys to help me and Celia keep this household in order. Can I count on you?"

Ronnie had nodded, though he was confused about what his father meant and what he was supposed to do about it.

His mother never returned from the vacation. A year later, the boys sat in the front row at St. John's Episcopal, watching his father marry a slight, quiet woman named Lynn.

After that, whenever Trip asked his father about his mother, he always got the same answer.

"Lynn's your mother now and she loves you boys like you were her own."

Lynn tried to be a mother to the Armstrong boys, but Ronnie didn't make it easy for her. He didn't need a new mother. He wanted the old one. He looked for her in restaurants and department stores. He wrote her letters filled with rambling stories about his school, his brother, his father, and anything else that came to mind. Writing the letters made him feel like he was talking with her. But he had no address for her. No phone number. He dropped his letters into a shoebox he kept on a shelf in his closet.

Trip shook the memories from his head. He thought he was writing a biography, but he kept discovering strings that tied him to Charlie.

Beyond their mothers and stepmothers, the old gangster

knew Trip's father. He'd probably handed envelopes stuffed with cash to his grandfather, who had been chairman of the Hillsborough County Commission. Maybe the main character was a stand-in for Trip himself, another privileged man-child who'd made his own way, outside the rigid boxes of society.

And like him, Charlie's love life had focused on one very special woman.

CHAPTER 10

The Corrals and the Walls lived side by side in a wealthy neighborhood just north of downtown. Our houses were Victorians, built in the late 1890s, with wrap-around porches, lattice trim and grand interior staircases. The neighborhood was thick with stately live oaks, like the one growing between our houses. One of the oak's muscled arms stretched to my bedroom window, a perfect escape route for a prodigal son. Another flexed within six inches of a second story bedroom at the Corrals.

Every night, for more than a month, just after my 15th birthday, I fled the world of Aunt Katherine by climbing across the thick branches to the window of Ava Corral's bedroom.

Ava's father and his brothers owned cigar factories, and tobacco farms in Cuba. His money bought him access to Tampa's "white" society, not that there was that much society in 1915. Enrique Corral could afford a stately house in Tampa Heights, the city's most expensive neighborhood.

On our nights together Ava and I didn't talk much. As children, we'd often climbed out onto the spreading branches of the old oak and talked for hours.

But we were older now. When we spoke, we whispered, so her sleeping family wouldn't discover us. We used our mouths for other things. Ava was tiny, her face a perfect mix of ovals and angles, with thick eyebrows and long black lashes. Her eyes were yellow gold, the color of the flan de leche they served at the Columbia Restaurant.

We stood in her pastel bedroom, next to the four-poster bed, learning how it felt when lips pressed together and what happened when tongues collided. I loved the orange blossom smell of her neck and the tautness of her skin. Each Easter, in the flower beds around our houses, the lilies blossomed. I thought of Ava like that. One minute she was a stalk of a girl and the next she was flowering. I was tall, skinny and clumsy, worried that my breath smelled of garlic, or that the pimple on my chin might burst while we kissed. Ava noticed none of this. She was warm and willing, as long as my hands stayed pressed to her back, caressed her neck, or gathered up a knot of black curls. I didn't push things any farther. It was all new to me and I was fine with whatever she was willing to give. When our lips and tongues started to ache, I said goodnight and slipped out the window.

Eventually, I convinced her that we could kiss longer if we stretched out across her wide bed, under the silk and lace canopy. I came to her room in a pin-striped nightshirt that fell to my calves. She wore a pink nightgown of wispy silk. Nights passed and things heated up. I found my body on top of hers, the buds of her breasts against my chest, my knee pressed against her most secret parts. My hands were still not allowed to stray too far.

The kissing, the slow press and release of our bodies, was magical, intoxicating. One hour stretched to two. One night, feeling her breath soft and steady against my face, I fell asleep. I awoke at dawn to the sound of Spanish curses. Enrique Corral loomed in the doorway, in a white nightshirt, his hair wild, his usually waxed moustache drooping at both ends. He had the arched nose of a bird of prey.

Mr. Corral jerked me off the bed and dragged me across the oak floor toward the door. He tossed me into the hallway. I leapt up. He stomped closer, cursing me, my family, and all my ancestors. I had just reached the top of the carved mahogany staircase when his open hands slammed into my back. Rolling and bouncing, I tumbled down to the landing, dazed but unhurt. He continued to shout from the top of the stairs. Dolores Corral stood behind him, in a thick white robe, her hair knotted and pulled back. She had fed me, tended a scraped knee, kissed my forehead. But that was years ago.

I got to my feet and ran, in my nightshirt, until I couldn't run *any longer.*

I had to go home at some point, and when I did, my father was waiting with the paddle. I got the worst beating of my life, then he locked me in my room. For the next few days, the maid left trays of food outside my door. I was allowed out once a day, so my father could bruise my behind with the paddling stick.

When I returned to Hillsborough High a week later, a girl told me that Ava was no longer at the all-girl Academy of Holy Names. She'd been sent to a Catholic boarding school near Boston. My father made plans to send me to a military academy in Georgia. But he never got the chance.

I've tried to push it from my head, but the truth is, what happened on my last afternoon at home is crystal clear. It was May, six months into our life with Aunt Katherine, and a few days after Ava was sent away. My father wasn't yet home from work. We were in the living room, next to a curio cabinet. I remember Aunt Katherine screaming at me, as she held the remains of a tiny porcelain shoe I had just smashed on the floor. We had fought before, but this time, my anger boiled over. The room disappeared into an ocean of red. I hated Aunt Katherine for ruining my life. I hated my father for letting her do it. I hated Ava's parents for sending her away. More than anything, I hated God for taking my beautiful mother.

My father's pistol was stuffed into my pants. I'm not a violent person. Never have been. And I've never harmed a woman. But when everything went red, I felt my fingers wrap the pearl handle. I pulled the gun. Aunt Katherine, staring into the dark chasm of the barrel, went silent, her mouth open, but no sound escaping. I yelled something I'm not proud of—something like: "Die, you witch!" What I was doing wasn't right or wrong. It just was. This woman needed to be shot. I was the one to do it. Simple as that.

I squeezed the trigger. Fortunately, for me and Aunt Katherine, I'm a terrible shot. The bullet missed wide, shattering some molding in the dining room. Aunt Katherine dropped to the floor, sobbing. My brother and sisters stared down from the staircase. I let the gun clatter onto the floor and climbed the stairs, not acknowledging my siblings.

I had packed a bag in case I needed to make a quick escape. I took one last look around at my childhood bedroom, but it wasn't mine anymore.

I heard my father shouting my name. I grabbed the bag, scrambled down through the limbs of the oak tree and ran south, stopping only when I was deep in downtown. I didn't have a plan, but I had a destination in mind.

CHAPTER 11

Through Charlie's stories, Trip's hometown, the port city called Tampa, wasn't the repressed and boring place Trip had thought it was. Charlie's Tampa wore respectability like a mask; underneath, it throbbed with vice, corruption and ethnic and racial tension.

For most of the 20th Century, there was a white city, a black city, and an immigrant city, populated by Cubans, Spaniards, Sicilians and Jews. The three Tampa's were separate and unequal. White Tampa owned the banks, the cops and city hall. Black Tampa was poor, but had its own shops and schools. Immigrant Tampa was the economic engine that propelled the city's economy. In Charlie's day, immigrants didn't get white jobs. They didn't win elections, and the clashes between white Tampa and immigrant Tampa, often got ugly. Ybor City teenagers kept rolls of coins in their pockets, ready to wrap them in their fists when they fought with cracker teens.

But the generation that came of age after World War II began to push for reforms. Children and grandchildren of the original immigrants went to school with the cracker kids. Nick Nuccio, then Dick Greco, were elected mayor. By 1985, the low-slung downtown, built to handle the river and port trade, had sprouted some silver-skinned skyscrapers. In this new order, the brothels became strip clubs, the bribes were called campaign contributions, and the Chamber of Commerce touted Tampa as "America's Next Great City."

But had the city really changed all that much from Charlie's day to Trip's?

* * *

In many ways, I'm like my hometown, part saint, part sinner. Tampa, in the first few decades of the 20th century, was full of churches and brothels. White men got their hands dirty working the banana docks and the riverfront warehouses. Immigrants labored over the cigar rolling tables, or peddled vegetables from horse-drawn carts. Good Christian girls got knocked up. Pious wives stitched their Sunday dresses and patched their children's torn trousers, while their husbands drank brown liquor on Saturday night and toted black bibles on Sunday morning. People of all races peed and puked and prayed in trash-strewn alleys, where fresh shoots of ivy, green as Eden, sprouted from the mortar of the red brick walls.

Thanks to all my nighttime rambles and adventures, I knew this gritty port town as well as anybody. The night I fled Tampa Heights and Aunt Katherine I had a destination in mind. A place I thought I could get a bed and some work.

Dirty Joe's was a bar and gambling house on the north end of downtown, where brick warehouses along the river provided storage for bananas and tobacco bales, unloaded from rusted, barnacled ships. Others stored cigars until they were shipped out. A few of the buildings offered diversions for the crews and the locals.

Dirty Joe's had no sign. Sailors and gamblers don't need a sign. That night, I lingered on the sidewalk outside the swinging doors. A guy in a dirty undershirt pushed through the doors, holding a broom. He flipped a nickel in my direction and barked—"Move along kid. This is a grown-up joint."

He started sweeping the sidewalk.

"I heard this place was called Dirty Joe's." I was a gutsy kid at that point. "Are you Joe?"

"In the flesh." He pulled the wet cigar from his mouth and smiled, showing off some tar-stained teeth. He shouted something through the swinging bar doors and a few minutes later, a curly-haired waitress brought me a cold bottle of Coke.

"Does your momma know you're running loose down here?" He was somehow able to talk around the fat cigar in his maw.

"My momma's in heaven." I tried to sound like a tough, street-smart kid.

"And mine is residing way south of there." He choked out a laugh. "They probably both got what they deserved."

The bar's real name was The Franklin Club. The owner was a fireplug of a man, who wore grimy undershirts—now I think they call 'em wife-beaters—and shaved once a week. Up close, Joe smelled like the hallway outside a public bathroom. I tried not to get too close.

I told him I needed a job. Instead of a resume, I described the small-time bookmaking operation I'd run at Hillsborough High, taking quarters, dimes, and nickels from schoolmates eager to bet on high school football games. He snickered, choked briefly, then handed me the broom.

"Let's see what you can do with this," he said.

After I'd swept the sidewalk, he led me inside. Dirty Joe's was a bare bones joint with red-brick walls, a sawdust floor and battered pine bar, set with backless stools.

"Get to it kid! The floor ain't gonna sweep itself." Joe slipped behind the bar and started wiping beer mugs with a smudged rag.

When I finished, he led me through a set of double doors to the private room in back. Unlike the bar, this room was wallpapered in gold brocade, and the green felt of the gaming tables glowed in the light from a chandelier, with bulbs shaped like candles; crystal droplets dangled like swollen raindrops. I felt like I'd stepped from a shrimp boat onto a yacht. It was late afternoon, and the room was empty, the chairs upturned on the tables, the cards and chips neatly stacked. The bar was mahogany, with a mirrored wall behind, and glass shelves that held whiskey bottles and cut crystal glasses.

"You'll work nights. You see somebody put down a drink that's more than 3/4s empty, you pick it up," Joe spoke in a growl that could have come from a bulldog. "You see empty glasses on a blackjack table, you clear 'em and you send Kitty over. Gamblers like women fetching their drinks. They don't mind a little dickwad like you picking up the empties and cleaning up the messes, but that's it. And keep your lips sealed. When you're working here you see nothing except those empty drinks and messy tables and floors. You got that?"

I was almost a foot taller than Joe, so I was looking down at him during his monologue. I nodded—"I got it."

Thinking back on it, the grime, the gruffness, the barked orders, were a facade, that hid the fact that Joe was a gentle man. He kept a baseball bat behind the counter in the front bar and pulled it out when a sailor got nasty or rowdy, but I never saw him swing it. His staff in the gaming room were well-dressed and genteel. Joe seldom set foot inside the back room, except at the start and the end of each night. He was the bartender in the front room, where sailors and working men from the port or the riverfront warehouses came for cheap beer and boiled peanuts.

I bunked in a narrow room upstairs, with a vile, but working bathroom down the hall. There were other rooms on the second floor, with female tenants. At night, men walked the hallway. I learned to ignore the sounds I heard from those rooms late at night. My new place wasn't anything like my family's Tampa Heights house, but when I stretched out on the narrow bed that first night, I felt like I'd found my real home. I didn't know where I was headed, but I knew it wasn't off to college, to the alter, or to a job in some office like my father and his friends. I never could picture myself living that way.

After three months of sweeping and clearing empties, I was fitted for a tuxedo and promoted to dealing blackjack. A year after that, I was managing the place for Joe, who was spending more days sprawled across a ripped-up couch in his office, a needle stuck in his forearm.

Except for the "business women" who worked in the upstairs rooms and sometimes lingered by the back bar in tight dresses and heels, Joe's customers were all men, including some of my father's society pals, who looked stricken when they recognized me. I'd shake my head and wink at them. They got the message—my lips *were sealed. I hoped they would do the same if they saw my father.*

Before the needle really got hold of him, Dirty Joe became my smelly, surrogate father. He taught me the tables—blackjack, roulette, craps—and showed me the ropes of the small-time Bolita throw he ran. Bolita, a Cuban version of a lottery, (the Spanish translation is "little balls"!) was technically illegal, but in Tampa, even the cops played the numbers. Most people placed bets with the door-to-door Boliteros, but some folks bought at laundries, restaurants, and outside bars like Dirty Joe's. Each afternoon, before the night customers arrived, I sat under the awning outside, taking pennies, nickels, dimes from Christian folks—working men and women—who would never think about setting foot inside a bar or gambling house. They liked handing their meager coins to a boy barely old enough to shave. I wrote down their whispered numbers in a notebook and gave them a written receipt. At 6 p.m. every night, Joe threw the bag—a black velvet sack with a drawstring on top and 100 ivory balls inside.

A Bolita throw is just that. The bag holding numbered balls gets shaken and tossed from one catcher to another. I was one of the catchers, along with Nick, the gaming room bartender, with his waxed moustache and pomaded hair, and Kitty, the tiny twig of a waitress, who was always smiling from under a helmet of blonde hair. Most nights, I was the final catcher. The catcher's job was to tighten his fingers around a single ceramic ball inside the velvet bag. I think Joe liked the idea that an innocent kid chose the winning ball. When I had snagged it, Joe would tie the ball off with string, pull a switchblade from his back pocket, cut the fabric and remove the winner. Then he'd scrawl the ball's number—anything from 1 to 100—in chalk on the tiny blackboard outside. When the folks who had bet that number showed up the next day, Joe handed over their winnings.

"Never welch on a bet," he told me after one of his throws produced so many winners it put him deep in the red. "Pay off your winners. Period. Then, the housewives and the working stiffs will know you run an honest game, and they'll continue to believe that tomorrow is gonna be their day."

That was Joe's best lesson. In the gambling trade, your reputation is everything. A good bookmaker always pays off, even if it breaks the bank. I was in the business for almost 35 years, and nobody ever said Charlie Wall didn't pay off.

CHAPTER 12

Trip's life with Charlie had a predictable routine: On their 6 p.m. drive to his boss's downtown hangouts, Charlie was a sober and anxious passenger, scanning the streets for a sedan full of heavily armed hoodlums that never appeared. On the drive home, with a few old fashioneds in his belly, Charlie told stories from his glory days or talked trash about one of the human antiques he'd chatted up in the bar. No matter how much he drank, Charlie's antennae went up for the walk from the car to the house.

"This is where it's gonna happen. A man coming home, maybe a little sauced, thinking he's safe. And then..." He aimed a finger gun at Trip's temple. "...BAM! You're dead."

Part of Trip's job was to follow the rituals of a mob bodyguard. Stepping from the car, he scanned the street and sidewalks. If all was clear, he slapped the roof with his open palm. That was the sign Charlie could emerge. The pair would walk slowly to the house, Trip one step behind his tottering boss, ready to spring into action if a hired killer appeared. None ever did.

Inside the house, Charlie would release a long, guttural burp, then he would bow, like a maestro who had just conducted Beethoven's Ninth. Without waiting for applause, he would turn and disappear down the hallway to his bedroom. When the hallway door was closed, Trip was not supposed open it.

"I've got a big gun down there with me. Stop a rhino." Charlie told him more than once. "You come down that hall uninvited, and I'll shoot first and won't even worry about asking questions later. You got that?"

"I got it." That old school paranoia was what made his boss such a great character, Trip thought.

Most mornings around nine, Trip stumbled, half-asleep, into the kitchen, where the wide windows lit the icebox, the gas stove and the wooden countertops. In the cast-iron sink, he cleaned and prepped the stove-top percolator and set it on a burner. He poured milk into a saucepan and turned on a second burner. When things were steaming, Trip poured the mix together, adding a spoonful of sugar. He carried his cup to the front yard and picked up the newspaper. Back at the kitchen table, he'd turn through the pages, but he always put the paper back together, just as it had arrived, and left it folded for his boss. The coffee and the milk stayed on the stove, kept warm by the pilot light.

Charlie made his initial appearance at noon. He took his coffee and the newspaper back to his bedroom. Most days, Trip didn't see him again until 6 p.m., when he emerged dressed for an evening out.

These rituals were altered only on Sunday, Trip's day off, and Monday, when Zennia, the maid, arrived.

Zennia, another tottering relic of old Ybor, let herself in with her own key every Monday at 11. She was a stern-faced woman, who brought her own radio and kept it tuned to Spanish talk radio. She might have been thin once, but now her flesh challenged the seams of her white maid's uniform. Zennia arrived with the week's meager essentials—Naviera coffee (roasted in Ybor), milk, butter, Cuban bread, some guava pastries, whatever fruit was in season, a six-pack of Coke (for Trip), and toilet paper. They didn't need much. Charlie ate one meal a day at one of his watering holes. He paid for Trip's dinners on work nights. Trip supplemented his diet with peanut butter, strawberry jelly, Wonder Bread, and eggs and bacon, from the Blue Ribbon grocery store a few blocks from the house.

While Zennia cleaned his wing of the house, a silent Charlie, still in his bathrobe and with an unlit cigar in his mouth, read the paper on the living room couch.

On a Tuesday afternoon, three months into Trip's life with Charlie, the old man didn't appear at 6 p.m. Thirty minutes ticked by. No Charlie. At 7, Trip stood outside the closed door that led to Charlie's wing. He wasn't always sure when Charlie was telling him the truth, but he was certain the old man was serious about shooting anyone who came down the hallway.

Trip knocked four times. When Charlie didn't answer, he eased the door open a crack. "Hey Charlie! It's Trip. Time to go!"

Trip's fear that Charlie would shoot him was slightly less than his fear that the old man had suffered a heart attack or a stroke and was lying helpless in his bedroom. He eased into the dark hallway. "Charlie? Mr. Wall? It's Trip. Are you okay? Can you answer me?"

He groped for the light switch. The bare bulb, dangling from a black cord, revealed walls yellowed by decades of cigar smoke.

Trip took one small step at a time, his head on a slow swivel. A room on the left was stuffed with boxes, old hard-sided suitcases, and a steamer trunk. Built-in bookcases along three walls, were thick with hard-cover books. Another step revealed a linen closet. It smelled musty, but thanks to Zennia, the towels, sheets, and pillowcases were clean and folded. Trip grabbed a white pillowcase. Through another open door, he saw a sub-way-tiled bathroom.

That left the closed door at the end of the hallway. The door to Charlie's bedroom. He's in there, Trip thought, and he's aiming a gun at the door. He took a step and the old floor creaked. He wrapped shaking fingers around the doorknob and called Charlie's name.

The hallway was dead quiet.

Trip took a long breath, then eased the door open, just enough to insert the pillowcase, which he waved like a white flag.

"Charlie? It's me, Trip! I come in peace. Are you okay? Listen, I'm coming in."

Trip pushed open the door, expecting to be greeted by a gun barrel or a dead body. Instead, Charlie sat motionless in a high-backed chair by a side window, his head and shoulders lit by a standing lamp. He was still in his paisley robe and house slippers. One arm hung down; bony fingers clutched a single sheet of newsprint.

Trip stepped closer. Charlie's tears had left tea-colored rivulets through spikes of gray stubble.

"You okay? Charlie? I'm worried about you. Can I do something?"

Charlie raised his arm and let Trip take the newspaper. It was the *Tampa Tribune* obituary page, narrow columns with short descriptions of the day's dead. Scanning the page, Trip saw a black and white photo of a round-faced Spanish beauty, young and beaming. *Ava Corral Merrill, 85, was a native of Tampa, a resident of Boston, a wife, a mother. She is survived by her husband, two children and four grandchildren. Services are pending in Boston and Tampa.*

"I'm so sorry, Charlie." Trip set the newspaper on the bed.

It was a full minute before Charlie spoke. His voice was soft, with none of the bravado Trip had come to expect from his boss. "There comes a day when you realize you can't start over. Can't go back. You don't have another try. You're just done. Done and forgotten."

Charlie drew a splotched and veiny hand across his face. Trip was not sure what to say.

Charlie looked off toward the open window, through the metal burglar bars, at the neighborhood in the distance. "You're still young. You don't know that day. Not yet. But it will come. It comes for everybody and that day, my friend, is not a good day."

Trip waited for Charlie to say more, but he didn't speak again.

Over the next few days, the old man rose for stumbling treks to the bathroom but always returned to the chair. The food Trip brought sat uneaten. *Café con leche,* delivered at noon and three, turned gray and jellied in the cup.

Trip tried anything that might break the dark spell holding his boss prisoner. He told dirty jokes, but Charlie never laughed. He raided the bookcases and read aloud from novels by Hemingway and Steinbeck. No reaction. He delivered the raciest passages from Dashiell Hammett and Mickey Spillane—Charlie had a large collection of both writers—but still nothing. Trip thought a spoonful or two of magic tea might do Charlie some good, but he decided against it. He might be tempted himself. And what would Charlie be like on 'schrooms? Trip didn't want to picture it.

At first, he didn't share the news about Charlie's depression with Katrina, thinking it would pass, but after a week, Trip needed a second opinion.

"He saw an obituary and now he's depressed." It was midnight. He was on his regular stool at Rough Riders. Katrina, in her work uniform, was on the other side of the bar, wiping an already clean counter.

"There's no family to call. They've all disowned him. Most of his friends are dead. If someone comes to the door, he makes me send them away. I've tried television shows. Dirty magazines. I'm out of ideas."

Katrina was gathering her thoughts. Trip had spent enough time with her to know he shouldn't interrupt. She carefully folded the bar towel, then looked up at him.

"He needs something to give him a burst of joy. Something that makes him feel like his life still means something. Figure that out and you might get him back."

* * *

The next morning, Trip was on the porch swing reading *Great Expectations*, a Katrina recommendation. In the shadowy sitting room of a ruined mansion Pip was meeting the eccentric Miss Havisham for the first time. Looking up from the book, Trip saw the hole, about three inches below Charlie's front porch light, a half-inch wide, the finger-sized shaft choked with a spider's web.

Charlie had told him the story a few weeks earlier.

"That's the first one." Charlie's skeletal index finger disappeared into the hole. "It was two a.m., Friday, Dec. 16, 1931. Sniper shot. Scarface Johnny thought it must have been someone with military training but that didn't make sense. Mob hitters do it up close. Anyway, it missed my head by two inches. That was an exhilarating night!"

"What did the cops say?"

Charlie spoke like a tired teacher giving a lesson to the slowest kid in class. "Son, in my business, you never call the cops."

Another day, Charlie explained the spray of holes on the north side of the house, a few steps from what was left of the garage.

"That was Feb. 12, 1936, 2 a.m. A 12-gauge from close range. The buckshot grazed my shoulder. As my friend used to say—it just glimpsed me. The garage was still standing then. I had a guy hang pressed steel on all the walls. Once the garage door was down, it was like sitting in a giant bullet-proof vest."

Charlie was always happy to talk about the big one. The night in 1955 when two assassins came to his front door.

At the library where they kept microfilm copies of the local newspapers, Trip had read about that night. Charlie Wall showed up in lots of stories in the *Tampa Morning Tribune* and *Tampa Daily Times*. There were stories about gambling, allegations of bribery, a prostitution bust at the El Dorado, his Ybor nightclub, and a drunk driving arrest in 1974, after a four-car pileup on Columbus Drive. But the biggest story was dated April 19, 1955. The *Tribune* front page included a four-column, black and white photo of Charlie in a paisley bathrobe and house slippers, talking to three uniformed police officers and a detective in a dark suit:

Gambling Kingpin Survives Gun and Knife Attack

TAMPA – Charlie Wall, a Tampa nightclub owner, and reputed head of a major gambling syndicate, was unhurt Thursday night after two assailants, armed with a shotgun and a switchblade, tried to force their way into his Ybor City home.

One of the alleged attackers was dead at the scene, shot in the head by Wall, police said. A switchblade was recovered from under the body. Police identified the dead man as Jackie Aprile, 41, whose criminal history includes convictions for armed robbery, assault, and arson. The other alleged attacker, whose identity remains a mystery, fled and had not been apprehended by press time.

Wall told police he'd been expecting guests, but on opening his front door, was confronted by two strangers, both armed. Wall told police one assailant's shotgun misfired, giving him time to draw his revolver.

"I'm just an ordinary citizen, spending a quiet night at home, and I'm forced to defend myself against two deadly assassins. What has this town come to?" Wall said.

Speaking off the record, a police source told the Tribune that the attempt on Wall's life was likely delayed retribution for his testimony to the Kefauver Crime Commission in 1950. Wall, who told the panel under oath that he had shut down his gambling enterprise in 1948, was given immunity in exchange for his testimony. Although the testimony remains sealed, there was speculation that Wall testified extensively about the operations of the Antinori and Trafficante crime families and their alleged involvement in gambling and prostitution.

When he asked his boss about that night, the normally hunched old man stood up straight and smiled. "I got copies of the stories in my scrapbook if you want all the details. Let's just say I was attacked on the porch of my own home, and I defended myself. I've had a lot of fun in my day, but April 18, 1955, that's gotta be the hands down best night of Charlie's Wall's long and crazy life."

"They tried to kill you!"

"Your generation had it too soft. You don't get it. Those moments on my front porch, two guys trying to take me out, I was never more alive than that! I still remember every second: The dead snap of that shotgun as it misfired; a wisp of smoke rising from the barrel; that fat fart falling dead at my feet. And the other one, the frick-frackin' dago Neanderthal, running off down the street like a scared cat. God, I loved that!'

He had tapped his forehead. "It's all in here like it was yesterday. What's that song? Oh yeah, 'Precious Memories.' That's what I got."

Only Charlie Wall would consider the night of his attempted assassination the best night of his life, Trip thought.

Back on the porch swing, with *Great Expectations* open on his lap, Trip took a fresh look at the bullet hole by the front door. It was like that moment in a detective story when a minor character says something unrelated to the case, and those innocuous words help the gumshoe stitch together the threads of the mystery. Rising from the swing, he slid his index finger into the hole. And just like that, Trip knew how he could free Charlie from the gravity of depression.

CHAPTER 13

Trip's scheme to get Charlie out of his chair—and his funk—didn't start with anything as dramatic as an arrow. The bedroom phone had a long cord and Trip set it on the small table beside Charlie's chair. He asked Katrina to call Charlie's number, wait until someone answered, then hang up. She hadn't met Charlie, but she knew his past.

"What's this about?"

"I'm following your advice. That's all I should say. And that you're doing me a big favor."

She dialed Charlie's home phone twice a day for a week, letting it ring until Trip picked up and said, "Wall residence."

Charlie did not acknowledge the ringing phone.

"Same thing." Trip set the phone back in the cradle. "Somebody breathing on the line, then they hang up."

Charlie didn't speak, but his head rotated from the window. He stared grimly at the phone. Late one afternoon, Trip dialed Charlie's number from an Ybor City pay phone. It took 15 rings for Charlie to pick up.

"Yeah?" Charlie's voice was barely a whisper.

"This Charlie Wall?" Trip had wrapped the phone with a bandana and spoke in muffled tones.

"Who wants to know?" Charlie's voice held none of his former swagger. Trip slowly breathed in, then waited a long beat, before breathing out. He never spoke, allowing a few more seconds tick away before he slammed down the phone. For the next three days, he repeated the process. By week's end, his boss answered the phone on the first ring. At the same time, Charlie started sipping coffee and taking a few bites from the sandwiches Trip left on a tray. Bringing in coffee the following morning, Trip saw a Colt .38 on the table next to Charlie's chair.

At Rough Riders that night, he used his left hand to scrawl a note on a bar napkin. The words were loopy, as if the writer was both uneducated and in a hurry. He repeated the scrawl on the front of an envelope and licked a stamp. When the letter arrived two days later Trip stood beside Charlie's chair, holding out the envelope.

"A letter for you."

Charlie waved it away.

"How about if I read it to you?" Trip tore open the envelope.

"Prepare to die you fucking snitch." Charlie raised his hand and Trip gave him the letter. Charlie held it close to his eyes, so he could read it without his glasses. He smiled. Trip hadn't seen his boss smile since he got the news about Ava.

That night, from another phone booth, Trip dialed Charlie's number. The old man picked up.

"What?" he snapped.

"Prepare to die, motherfucker!"

At 6 p.m. on April Fool's Day, just two days after that call, Trip was startled from a nap by a pounding on his door. He opened it to find the old man dressed in seersucker, the straw boater in his left hand.

"We going out or what?" Charlie asked.

Rising from his bed, Trip smiled. "So, everything's okay?"

"Nothing's okay, but I'm thirsty and hungry and I'm paying you to drive me where I want to go."

"Let's go, then," Trip tried to hide his smile. "Just give me a minute to get ready."

At that point, Trip had already located Danny Hernandez, the star of the Jesuit archery team. Even though his boss was up and around, he decided to go ahead with the final phase of his Charlie Wall restoration project. The arrow would be sort of a booster shot, to keep Charlie on his feet.

Two nights later, Danny's arrow sliced just above Charlie's head. Alone in his bedroom that night, Trip allowed himself a satisfied smile. He'd done it. Charlie Wall was back! To celebrate, he slipped a fresh sheet of paper into the typewriter.

* * *

Early one evening, after I'd been working maybe a month, Joe pulled me aside. I was still a front-room kid, sweeping up, washing glasses. Joe hadn't started with the junk yet, but he was always a little drunk after the sun went down, his daily panatela just a wet stub, flecks of tobacco impaled on the stubble around his lips and chin.

"I need you to put down the broom and go up to your room. Somebody's gonna knock. You open the door. Got it?"

I nodded down at him like I always did—"I got it."

My room, with a single window looking out onto the brick warehouses on the opposite side of Tampa Street, was too small for anything but a wooden dresser and bed frame, with a single mattress. I heard a soft tapping and opened the door to a waif of a girl, in a clingy gold dress. Her dangling rhinestone earrings emerged from an explosion of curly red hair.

"You Charlie?" She spoke with a breathiness that I think was her attempt to sound sexy.

"Yeah, I'm Charlie." I clutched the doorknob. My heart knocked away in my chest.

"My name is April. May I come in?"

Her face was fine-boned, precise, and like her arms and hands, sprayed with khaki-colored freckles. Her dress, made from some cheap, glittering fabric, fell just above her knees. Patterned hose left a checkerboard across her thin calves and ankles. She wobbled atop a pair of gold high heels.

"You want to come in? Here?" I should have known what was happening, but I was still a kid—not yet 16—and while I had done a lot of kissing with the Ava Corral, my first and, so far, only love, I was still a certified virgin.

"I'd like to come in, if that's okay with you. Joe said you might be a little shy."

I stepped back and the tiny, coltish creature, smelling like tobacco and cinnamon, pranced into my room on those crazy heels. April seemed to be new to the game. For the next hour or so, she made me feel like we were learning things together. Years later, when I heard Sinatra singing "I Remember April," I'd feel her icy fingers sliding over my skin, I'd see her nervous smile as she looked up at me in that noisy, narrow bed, her pink lipstick smeared by my kisses.

A knock woke me around midnight. April was gone, but I could still smell her on the sheets. Grabbing my robe, I rushed to the door thinking she was back, but it was Dirty Joe, his evening cigar chewed down halfway, a copse of chest hairs bristling from the collar of his undershirt. He looked me up and down, then extended a beefy hand. I shook it.

"Welcome to the grown-up world kid. Now, get dressed and get to work. We got a good crowd downstairs tonight."

CHAPTER 14

When he heard a knock on the front door at 10 a.m. on a Wednesday, Trip was surprised but not anxious. Charlie didn't really need a bodyguard. The only person trying to kill the old man was Charlie himself, with the booze and the rare steak dinners and all that gorgonzola dressing blanketing the iceberg lettuce and cherry tomatoes that passed for salad in his favorite haunts. Still, Charlie had rules and one of them involved someone knocking on the front door.

"Visitors are too dangerous." Charlie repeated this line at least once a week. "I thought I was opening my door to friends back in '55. Instead, I was staring down the barrel of a gun."

Shaking his head to clear the first-thing-in-the-morning fog, Trip primed himself to brush off an eager siding salesman, or a security system rep. Peering into the peephole, he saw something more dangerous than a mob hitman or a door-to-door salesman. The morning visitor was a *Tampa Tribune* reporter Trip knew from the Ybor poetry scene. Daniel Hebert had done a couple of open mic poetry nights when Trip was also on the bill.

"Who is it?" Trip didn't open the door.

"Hey, it's Danny Hebert. From the *Tampa Tribune*. Want to talk with Charlie."

"Charlie's asleep."

"Then, how about I talk with you?"

Trip eased open the door. On the porch stood an Ichabod Crane character, all bones and sharp angles, with a swatch of unruly hair that no brush could tame. Hebert wore the standard young reporter uniform—khaki slacks, a blue button-down, and a skinny tie.

"Like I said, he's still asleep." Trip started to close the door.

"Wait! Don't I know you?" The reporter cocked his head. "Ybor City, right? Trolley Stop Cafe. I saw you read one night. You live here?"

Trip nodded, offering no more information. "Okay, look, I want to do a story. Charlie's a legend, but nobody's written about him since 1960. It's time for a feature. If he's willing."

"And why should I talk to a gal-darn Tribune reporter?" It was Charlie, in his silk bathrobe and slippers, unshaven, his hair a rat's nest. Trip had never seen the old man up this early. His voice was raw, almost choked, like he'd just swallowed a cigar.

"Ronald," he said to Trip. "I got this."

"Get in here," Charlie barked to the reporter. "I don't like open doors."

Hebert stepped in and Charlie flipped the bolt lock. He didn't invite the reporter to sit down. Instead, they faced each other. Trip lingered in the kitchen, close enough to hear the conversation.

"I'd like to interview you." Hebert handed Charlie a business card. "Do a feature story. It's been a while, and I think folks would like to know how you're doing."

Charlie snorted, then cleared his throat. "Folks long ago formed their opinion of me. One story isn't going to change that."

"Look, to me, you're a living legend. We don't have many of those in this town. It would be an honor to write about you."

"Back in the day I never trusted a reporter." Charlie squinted at the business card. "They bugged me even more than the honest cops. So, why should I trust you?"

"This isn't what you'd call an expose," Hebert said. "I mean, what we're talking about is all ancient history, right?"

Charlie slowly lowered the business card. "I'm historical, but I'd prefer if you didn't use the word ancient. I'm single and still trying to impress the ladies. Ancient ain't sexy. Am I right?"

"I'll be gentle," the reporter said. "I have a feeling the ladies will be impressed after reading this story."

Like a cat coughing up a hairball, Charlie struggled to clear some early morning phlegm from his throat. He pulled a tissue from the pocket of his robe, spit into it, folded it and slipped it back in his pocket. "There may be a story or there may not be a story. I need to talk with someone before I agree to anything with you and your newspaper."

"Hey, there's no time element."

"At my age, there is always a diddly-dong time element!" Even this early in the morning, Charlie was creative about his cursing. "Come back here in one week. And don't come this early. I only heard you because I was up taking a very urgent pee."

The reporter left and Charlie appeared in the kitchen. Trip handed him a café con leche. "You gonna talk to him?"

"That's my business. But maybe, I will. What did I tell you about opening the door to strangers?"

"You told me don't do it. But I knew this guy. Seen him around. Figured he was harmless."

"Nobody is harmless. Especially a reporter. Don't open the door even if it's your mother on the porch. She might be the one sent to blow your head off. Can you remember that?"

A plug of acidic bile clogged Trip's throat. Talk of his mother always set him off. His father had torn up all her pictures, but Trip kept dozens of images of her in his head. Charlie's words brought them all back.

"You okay?" Charlie asked, seeing Trip in some kind of emotional distress.

"I got it. Don't open the door. Sorry."

Charlie nodded gravely, then turned toward his bedroom, slamming the hallway door in Trip's face.

The day was young and there were hours to fill until 6, when Charlie would need a driver and companion. Trip made a strong cup of *café con leche* and sat down at his typewriter.

* * *

I was sprawled atop a stone outcrop deep in a jagged crack in the earth. Rivers of molten magma coursed through my veins.

"Charles, are you in there? Can you hear me?"

Something moist and cool brushed my forehead, before sliding gently across my eyelids and down my neck. The words seemed to float down from somewhere far above.

"Now try opening your eyes." It was the same tender voice. Somewhere between a girl and a woman. I pictured a beautiful angel, all in white, lifting me from the shadowy pit toward a brilliant, crystal light.

I got one eye open, then another.

"There you go! Welcome back!" A face emerged from the glossy brilliance. My mother! Her sharp features softened by a cascade of auburn curls, her teeth so white they glimmered.

"Mother..." I whispered.

"Charlie....?"

The voice again. But it wasn't my mother. I blinked furiously. A new face came into focus. Darker than my mother's, angular and round, the nose and mouth hidden behind a white medical mask.

"Who...?"

"Hello, Charlie. I thought we'd lost you."

Those eyes were so familiar. I struggled to think but my brain was bobbing in an undertow. I closed my eyes. Another few seconds and the whirlpool slowed. When I opened my eyes again, I knew her name.

Ava!

I hadn't seen her since the night two years earlier when her father found us in her bed.

"Hi Charlie."

I opened my mouth, but I couldn't form a word.

"Easy. Take your time. I'm not going anywhere."

Eventually, some hoarse words emerged. "Where ... where am I?"

"You're here. With me. Right where you need to be."

I was on a narrow plank, my body swaddled in soaking-wet fabric, under a khaki-colored sky. I felt hot and damp at the same time. Ava stood and waved her arm, like an eager student with the correct answer.

"He's awake," she shouted at someone I couldn't see. "His fever broke."

With her surgical mask off, she was as beautiful as I remembered.

A tall, gray-haired man, his nose and mouth covered by a mask, walked into my field of vision. A silky white gown hung from his shoulders like a cape, his khaki trousers visible below the hem. My eyes focused and I saw that Ava was wearing a white uniform, buttoned to her collar, a nurse's tri-cornered hat pinned atop thick, black hair pulled into a bun. The tall man whispered something to her, then he knelt and pressed a stethoscope to my chest.

"Breathe in," he said. "Now out."

Too weak to resist, I did as I was told. My breath rose raggedly. The khaki-colored sky was really the ceiling of an Army tent. There were cots around me, people stretched out under white sheets. Pulling back the stethoscope, the man gently wrapped my jaw with his fingers and eased my face to the side, so I looked directly into his tired brown eyes.

"You're a very lucky young man. I was sure we'd lost you, but this nurse never gave up hope. She was right. I was wrong." He stood and turned to Ava. I felt like I was listening from the bottom of a well, but I heard him say—"Get him some fresh sheets and a dry pillowcase. And make him drink. Make him drink a lot."

I remembered why I was here. The Spanish flu. A pandemic is what the Tampa Tribune called it. Some of the gamblers in Dirty Joe's wore paper masks, tied with string behind their heads. People were dying but I was 17 and immortal. On the lawn of the courthouse downtown, I had gathered with a thousand others at a memorial for the crew of the Coast Guard Cutter Tampa, sunk by a German sub a week earlier, 16 local sailors among the dead. By nightfall, I was coughing, alone in my bed above Dirty Joe's. The next morning, I awoke feeling that molten magma oozing inside me and the world went blank.

Now, on a cot, under a canvas tent, I was back among the living.

Ava peeled away the wet sheets, then removed the cotton gown that was soaked with my sweat. She brushed my naked body with a moist cloth. I should have been embarrassed. Instead, I sank into a deep sleep. I'm told I slept for another full day and night. I awoke exhausted, like a traveler at the end of a long journey. I sat up, looking around the tent hospital for Ava. I had so much to tell her. I spotted her at the far side of the tent, wiping the forehead of another feverish young man. Crushed in my fist was a carefully folded piece of paper. Lifting it to my nose, I smelled an orange blossom. The three-line note was written in a delicate cursive.

"Get better.

I'll find you when this is over.

Ava."

CHAPTER 15

The morning after the reporter's visit, Trip awoke to find Charlie framed in his doorway, freshly shaved, and decked out in a steel-gray suit. A silk handkerchief flowered in his breast pocket and he was carrying a black homburg, belted by a matching silk band. Trip thought his boss could pass for a regal South Tampa businessman of a certain age, not a broken-down ex-crook.

"I've got a date with my shyster," Charlie drawled from the doorway. "You might enjoy it. Good for that secret book I know you're writing."

Thirty minutes later, they stood on thick Berber carpet in an ornate Hyde Park mansion, as a slender, perfectly coiffed woman approached. Trip couldn't tell if she were 30 or 60. Her cheeks were softly powdered, her lips pale pink, her lashes thick, though none of it seemed like actual makeup.

"Sylvia, this is Trip," Charlie barked. "Bodyguard. Not great, but he's learning on the job. Tampa's still a dangerous town if you're Charlie Wall."

Concern shaded Sylvia's elegant, unlined face. "Charlie, you be careful, okay?"

"What can I say? I'm a human target. Who'd want to kill me anyway? Everybody knows I'm as harmless as a pussy cat."

"I'm not sure I'd use that description, but don't take any chances. We don't want anything happening to you." She turned to Trip. "Please keep an eye on him. I've always had a little crush on Charlie." Her long, lacquered fingers slid across Charlie's shoulder. "But, of course, I'm not alone. Charlie, you want the usual?"

"Ah, Sylvia, you know how I like it. And my boy here will have a Coke. You got a Coke?"

"Anything for you, Charlie. You know that."

Then, like a Shakespearean sprite, Sylvia disappeared. Charlie nodded toward a tall, carved wood door. Trip followed his boss into the office where John D. Barnett stood behind a mahogany desk, wide enough to land a small airplane.

Barnett stood as Charlie approached. The lawyer was tall, his wavy hair touched with gray at the temples, his starched dress shirt pinstriped, capped by a white collar and carved by a pair of red suspenders. A jacket hung on a hat rack beside the desk. The wall beyond held three framed certificates. Trip couldn't make out the cursive script but the heading on one read: "HARVARD UNIVERSITY."

"Charlie!" the lawyer said. "You're looking especially good today, my friend. Eddie here says you two haven't met, but somehow, I can't quite believe it."

A man rose from a high-backed leather chair. He was a foot shorter than Charlie, but his voice was deep and masculine. Eddie Lanker seemed genuinely excited to meet the old man. "I grew up in Tampa. I'm...what can I say...I'm a fan."

"My reputation precedes me," Charlie said with as much false modesty as Trip had ever heard him muster. "That was long ago. How did the old mobster say it in that movie? 'I'm a retired investor, living off a pension.'"

Both men laughed. Trip wasn't sure if the men were laughing at *The Godfather* reference or Charlie's poor attempt at a Hyman Roth accent.

"Eddie Lanker?" Charlie asked. "Haven't I heard of you? The strip club king?"

It was Eddie's turn to smile. "As my mom tells her girlfriends—my son's in the entertainment industry."

"And people do like to be entertained," Charlie said. "I labored in that sweat shop for a while myself."

"The El Dorado," Eddie said reverently. "It's almost as legendary as you."

"I made a few bucks. Still miss it sometimes. Let me tell you, there were nights…" Charlie seemed to drift off, but he caught himself. He turned toward Trip. "Oh…this is Ronald Armstrong, whom I've employed as a driver and bodyguard. He's a good driver, but so far, just a passable bodyguard. I'm not certain what he'll do when the poop hits the propeller, if you know what I mean." Charlie chuckled, as he waved a veined-striped hand in Trip's direction, his way of saying, "I'm kind of kidding."

"He's one of those upstart artists who've taken over the Latin Quarter," Charlie continued. "A future Hemingway or Steinbeck, I'm not sure which, but he apparently finds me a worthy subject. I'm his Gatsby or maybe that Dickens one. What's his name? Fagin?"

"Or maybe you're his white whale." Barnett said.

There were two brown leather chairs across from Barnett's desk. Eddie slipped back into his and Charlie collapsed into the other. Trip sat on a couch which offered clear views of all three men. He'd forgotten his notebook, but he promised himself he'd remember what he heard.

Barnett leaned forward, elbows on the desk, his gold cuff links were the size of kernels of popped corn. "Charlie, if there's anything you want to talk about in private, we can step into my back office. But Eddie's a client and you can trust him, mostly."

"When John told me you were visiting today, I asked if I could get an introduction," Eddie said.

Charlie nodded at Eddie Lanker, then turned back to his lawyer. "I got a question, but it won't require a private conference. There's a *Tampa Tribune* reporter who wants to write a feature story about 'Tampa's last mobster,' or some stale baloney like that. Should I talk to him?"

"Do you want to talk to him?"

"I don't mind. Be nice for the scrapbook. Might help me with the ladies. As long as you don't think it'll get me in any trouble."

Barnett placed his palms flat on the wide desk. "I should know this, but remind me, how long since you…ah…" The lawyer raised his hands, making air quote marks—"Since you 'retired' from your various activities?"

"I mostly quit my...activities...just after the war, 1948. Though I still owned the El Dorado, 'till '61, but by then it was all legal. I've been clean as the proverbial whistle for 35 years at least."

"You quit everything?" Barnett squinted at him.

"Every dad-gone thing. That's why I'm still living in that old dump in Ybor and not a mansion in Hyde Park like my attorney."

Barnett smiled. "You're funny, Charlie. We both know you stay in that old house because you're too stubborn to move. Anyway, thirty-five years, in legal terms, that's the ancient past, so you're okay. The only crime with no statute of limitations is murder and you never killed anybody, did you?"

"Just that one bum on my front porch in 1955. Ruled self-defense."

"Then, you're fine," Barnett said. "I'd avoid too many specific details. You're already on the record in federal and state court, and with the Congressional commission. Here you are today, a retiree, enjoying your golden years."

Charlie coughed.

"I enjoyed the heck out of my golden years. But these are not them. I got piles, a heart murmur and if I do meet a woman, I'm terrified my flag will only fly at half-mast."

Sylvia appeared with a brass tray holding three highball glasses, brimming with ice and brown liquid, and a bottle of Coca Cola. She served the three whiskies, then turned to Trip. "...And a Coke."

She disappeared as quietly as she had arrived.

Barnett pulled a teak box from a desk drawer. It was large enough to hold a pair of cowboy boots. The lawyer snapped two silver latches and raised the lid. Looking inside, Charlie whistled as if Barnett's box was filled with gold doubloons.

"Real Cuban *Cohibas*." Charlie lifted one of the dark torpe-does. "The finished product of the cigar maker's art."

Charlie and Eddie unwrapped cigars. Trip waved away the lawyer's offer.

After snipping the ends, Barnett lit Charlie's cigar with a gold lighter, then lit Eddie's. Eddie took a few frantic puffs, to get the cigar fully lit, then set it in an ashtray on Barnett's desk. He pulled a pinkie-sized plastic vial from his jacket pocket.

"John, you mind if I take a little pick-me-up?" Eddie didn't wait for an answer. He unscrewed the top and dipped a tiny spoon.

"Do I have a choice?" Barnett grumbled good-naturedly.

Eddie took a sniff, then held the vial in Charlie's direction. "I'll abstain," Charlie said. Eddie looked at Trip, but Charlie spoke for him. "My friend here is as straight as the proverbial razor."

Trip nodded. Cocaine was never his drug but seeing a mound of snow headed to Eddie's nose made his mouth water.

"Well, if you guys don't mind…" Eddie took another snort. He shook his head and screwed the cap back onto the tiny glass vial. "You know Charlie, they put this stuff in Coca Cola back in the day."

"No wonder I got so much done back then," Charlie said. "Now, answer something for me. You mind?"

"Anything." Eddie wiped chalky flecks from his nose.

"That club of yours. That's it? That's freakin' it?"

"What's it?" Eddie asked, his eyes widening as the coke landed.

"Your business? The dancers? They're just naked? That's it?"

"That's pretty much it," Eddie said. "They dance on stage and guys toss cash in their direction. But it's the lap dances in the back room where the money really changes hands."

Charlie took a long drag on the cigar and exhaled before he spoke. "You got no band. No comics. No props. No stagehands. No food. No busboys. No cooks. No booze. Just sodas, and naked girls? That's it?"

"Don't forget the DJ, some waitresses, and a couple of bouncers." Eddie leaned back; his tiny frame swallowed up by the big chair. All Trip could see was the smoking tip of his cigar. "Listen, people still talk about the El Dorado, but the truth is, all that burlesque shit is as dead as disco. This is the modern world. No more pasties. No more bad jokes and out-of-tune musicians. We cut right to the chase now."

Charlie snorted. "You don't find it boring. I mean, the naked part? To me naked is boring. Where's the tease? The feathers? The slow reveal? Now that's sexy."

"Look Charlie. You did what worked back in the day. I'm doing the same thing. Giving the people what they want."

Charlie shook his head. "I guess I wasn't meant for the modern world. Just naked would have saved me a lot of money and a lot of grief."

"And let me tell you the best part." Eddie leaned forward. "The absolute best part. They pay me!"

"Who pays you?" Charlie asked.

"The dancers. They pay me to work there."

Charlie's head spun in Trip's direction. "Ronald, can you drive me to Tampa General? Right now!" Charlie's hand rose dramatically to his chest. "I think I'm having a heart attack." He turned back to Eddie: "THEY PAY YOU?"

John Barnett rocked back in his big chair, laughing. Eddie leapt up, his arms outstretched, like a kid about to take a bow in a high school talent show.

"Welcome to the fabulous '80s!" Eddie shouted.

CHAPTER 16

I awakened in my room above Dirty Joe's. The Spanish Flu couldn't kill Charlie Wall, but it left me so weak I had to struggle on spaghetti legs to get down the hallway to the bathroom, using door frames and walls for support. The table next to my bed held a basin and a pitcher of water. Joe and Kitty, the bar maid, took turns bringing up bowls of collard green soup, thickened with chunks of ham, and long slices of buttered Cuban bread. They sponged my forehead as I ate.

After the meals, I'd drift off, into vivid dreams: I'm reaching out to catch the Bolita bag, as Joe approaches with the scissors, ready to cut out the winning ball. I'm curled next to my mom in her sickbed as she whispers my name. I'm barefoot, the ridged bark of the oak tree under my feet, as I scamper across the limbs toward Ava's room. I'm with my brother and sisters, sitting in the front pew at Riverside Church, my mother's frozen face in the open coffin a few feet away.

I don't know how many days passed before I was pulled from my dreams by a series of clicks, coming one at a time, with a few seconds between. CLICK. Something hit my window. CLICK. I struggled from the sheets and blankets, the room spinning as I stood. CLICK. I parted the curtains, and my dark sickroom was suddenly ablaze with midday light. CLICK. Ava Corral looked up at me from the sidewalk. Her mane of hair pulled back and knotted behind her head, her petite frame tucked inside a pale blue sack of a dress, with bands wrapping her hips, a look that was fashionable at the time. She waved up at me. Seeing her smile was like seeing the sun after a long rainy season. I raised the window. I hadn't spoken to anyone for days and I could only stare mutely at Ava.

"May I come up?" She called from below.

I pointed to the downstairs door. In those days, it was never locked. It took me a long time to turn from the window. By the time I did, she was framed in my bedroom door, a suitcase in one hand, a straw picnic basket, covered by a pale blue cloth, in the other. Was I dreaming again? Ava set the suitcase and the picnic basket on the floor. Taking my arm, she led me to the single bed. She had me arranged under the covers and sat on the edge, her hand resting on my cheek.

"I'm a mess," I managed to mumble, in a hoarse whisper.

"You're a miracle. You're so much better than when I last saw you."

"How?" I couldn't get more out. Fortunately, Ava picked up the slack.

She told me that the pandemic had forced her school to shut down for the semester, so she had come home. Despite her father's objections, she had volunteered to work in an emergency tent hospital near Hillsborough High School. For five days, she kept a vigil by my bed, wiping my face and chest with a wet cloth, as I wavered between life and death.

"The doctor was convinced you were a lost cause, but I could feel you struggling, trying to live. And you did."

Joe appeared at the door. He was unshaven, his T-shirt stained. He pulled the stub of a cigar from his mouth. "Sorry, kid. Didn't know you had company. Just checking to see if you need anything, but it looks like you're okay for the moment."

He looked at Ava, then back at me. "Don't do anything too strenuous." His smile revealed gaps where teeth used to be.

"He cares about you," Ava said, after he left. "That's nice."

For some reason, I hadn't let myself think that this smelly old Cuban loved me. The thought washed over me, and I started to sob. Embarrassed, I rolled away from Ava. She stretched out next to me, atop the covers, and held me until the crying stopped. When I was calm, Ava got up and brought the picnic basket to my bed. Under the cloth was a loaf of dark bread, a hunk of cheese, wrapped in waxed paper, and a thermos.

"I brought food. And lemonade."

She filled the cup and passed it to me. The cold, sugary drink, seemed to shake me out of my stupor. I sat up in bed. Ava plumped the pillow behind my back. "So, you're all grown up now, living in your own place." She looked around at my bare room, so different than our lavish homes in Tampa Heights.

"It's a start," I said. "I'm learning things."

"I saw your brother. He told me where you were. He calls you the black sheep."

"I guess I am."

"They'd take you back, you know. You don't have to do…this."

My words came easier now. Ava's lemonade had flipped a switch into the ON position. "I'm not going back," I whispered, my voice gaining strength. "I'm not sure if this is forward or not, but it's where I'm going. What about you?"

"I'm supposed to be on a train back to Boston today. My family said goodbye at Union Station, but I changed my ticket for one tomorrow."

"Where are you going to stay?" I felt parts of me awaken that had been asleep for a long time.

"I was hoping I could stay here with you."

* * *

On the day of the newspaper interview, Charlie woke early. He was clean-shaven and dressed in a bright-blue pin-striped suit, pale blue dress shirt and rep tie. When the reporter knocked, he ignored his normal safety concerns and rushed to the porch and offered his hand to Daniel Hebert. A young female photographer stood behind the reporter, her cloth camera bag pregnant with the tools of her trade.

Trip lurked in the kitchen, listening. His coffee had gone cold and his stomach ached, as though he had swallowed a brick. He'd heard Hebert read his fiction at the Trolley Stop. The skinny reporter had talent, a newspaper job and an actual resume. What if he decided to do a book on Charlie?

And Charlie spilled all the beans. For two hours that Tuesday afternoon, he talked about his bolita syndicate—"Biggest in the state until the Sicilians muscled in"—about elections he fixed by paying poll workers to add dozens of ballots to the boxes they were driving to the election office downtown, about his gambling houses and finally, about his famous nightspot, The El Dorado. The interview ended with a moment-by-moment recounting of the night in 1955 when he faced two assassins on his front porch. "I put one of them down like the dog he was and the other ran like the coward he was."

Two weeks later, on a Sunday, the story occupied half the Tampa *Tribune's* front page. The "coward" quote was pulled out and set in large type next to a new photo of Charlie, on that same porch, grinning in his suit and paisley bow tie.

The night before the story appeared Trip couldn't sleep. The next morning, the front page on the table, he was relieved. Hebert had written a standard newspaper feature. Charlie came off as a colorful relic from a bygone era. Hebert hadn't set up any follow-up meetings. Trip was still the only one telling the full story of Charlie's life.

He wasn't sure if Charlie read the article, but the old man loved the attention. He sent Trip to the newsstand to buy five extra copies, and took one to The Turf, but he needn't have bothered. The regulars stood and applauded when Charlie swung open the wide front door.

"What can I say, boys?" There in the doorway of the dark bar, the late afternoon sun pouring in around him, the old mobster glowed like a saint.

"Who wants to buy a drink for a freakin' legend?"

CHAPTER 17

Someone was knocking—hard—on Buster's door.

Buster was retired, but when you had "muscle guy and hit man" on your resume, an unexpected knock was likely trouble. To make it worse, he wasn't sure how long the pounding had been going on. At 84, he didn't hear well. He was sure of one thing—someone was knocking with the butt of a handgun.

Buster was supine in his Laz-Z-Boy, his bulk wrapped in a terry-cloth robe. He'd been pulling together the strands of a plan. It wasn't easy. His thoughts were like wild horses. They didn't want to be rounded up. To develop a workable plan, he had to throw a lasso around each individual idea. Over the last hour, he had corralled a stable-full. But now they scattered, spooked by the insistent pounding.

Buster jerked the wooden handle and the burnt-orange recliner snapped into a sitting position. The sudden change in altitude set the world spinning. When things slowed down, he pressed hard against the chair's tattered arms and struggled to his feet.

Gotta remember Nick's rules, Buster told himself.

Back in the 1930s, Nick Matassini had been Buster's mentor. A low-level mobster, like Buster, Nick had seen it all and somehow survived into middle age. Buster had been the brawny new kid. Reliable, but not smart. Nobody expected he'd live very long, but Nick hoped a few lessons would increase Buster's odds.

In those days, Tampa's underworld was divided between Charlie Wall and a cadre of small-time Sicilian gangs. Violence often flared as they battled for control of the rackets. A 1931 shoot-out in an Ybor café left two guys dead. The headlines took up half a page, and the cops were out, making a show, though everyone knew the investigation would go nowhere. Mob murders never got solved. Buster and Nick had nothing to do with the shooting, but Santo Trafficante Sr. ordered them to lay low in a shotgun-style safe house on the north end of Ybor City. Nick passed the time schooling his young apprentice.

"You know how most guys get it?" Nick asked. "Do you? Huh?"

Buster played along. "I give up. How do they get it?"

Nick pointed his index finger at the front door. "Opening the door for a friend. Sad but true."

Nick was a stick figure mobster with a stork neck and mud-colored spots splattered across his jackknife face. Muscle guys like Buster didn't speak much, but Nick was a nervous type. His speech had a rat-tat-tat rhythm.

"You know the second way most guys get it? Huh? Huh? Do you?"

Buster grunted. That was all the encouragement Nick required.

"Cranking their car first thing in a morning. A car in the morning is a fucking death trap. Turn the key and KA-FRIG-GIN-BOOM!"

Nick made sure everybody knew his wife cranked his car each morning. Tampa's mob world had rules—you didn't kill wives or children. Girlfriends, especially the kind that rented by the hour, did not merit the same protection. Nick died on a summer afternoon in 1940, while his Chrysler was idling at a stoplight on Lake Avenue, his girlfriend's head in his lap. She made the mistake of sitting up at the wrong time and took some buckshot in her neck and shoulders but lived. Nick had let himself get careless. He died with his zipper down after only 55 years on the planet. Buster was convinced the reason he had survived into old age was because he had followed Nick's rules. Like the ones about how you open a door:

Never stand directly in front of the door. Stay to one side, pressing your shoulder against the doorframe, in case your visi-

tor decides to unload a spray of buckshot. Doors are flimsy, walls are safer.

When you speak, sound like you've got a gun in your hand that you are itching to fire. Remember, they are just as scared as you. Keep 'em that way.

Buster pressed his shoulder against the door frame.

"WHAT?" He wanted to sound tough, but he hadn't spoken all day. His "what" came garbled with phlegm, sounding more like "WURF!"

"Mr. Maniscalco?" The voice was female, low and silky. Times had changed, for sure, but his mobbed-up world had always been a boys' club. This woman most likely wasn't here to kill him. Still, Buster didn't veer from Nick's checklist. He continued to talk like a man ready to fire his weapon.

"Who wants to know?" he barked.

"Excuse me?"

"I said who wants to know?"

"Mr. Maniscalco, it's me, Angie. Angie Castellano, from down the hall. I brought you coffee."

Buster's door at the nursing home didn't have a lock, but he'd screwed in an old-fashioned hook and eye latch. It wouldn't stop anyone for long, but it was better than nothing. Buster lifted the hook from the eye but followed Nick's final door-opening rule.

Once you are sure it's a friend you can open the door but keep your shoulder and your shoe against it just in case your "friend" tries to kick it open.

Buster eased the door open just a few inches. He kept his shoulder and his stubby toes, the nails crusted and bent, pressed against the wood. A woman's hand slipped through the opening, hoisting a white ceramic mug. The room filled with the nutty aroma of fresh coffee.

Buster tossed a lariat around a new thought. It's that woman, the pretty one with the long gray hair, pulled behind her neck. The one who always keeps a chair open for me in the dining room, patting the empty seat when I walk by with my tray. The first few times she did it, Buster had grunted and moved on to an empty table. But lately, he'd been sitting beside her. Why not, he thought?

Satisfied he'd followed all of Nick's rules, Buster opened the door. Angie Castellano swept in, the coffee mug in her left hand, a metal cane in the other. Buster thought she might twirl the cane and toss it into the air like a baton.

"I couldn't remember if you liked one lump or two, so I just brought a couple of sugar packets and a spoon."

Buster had hoped she'd hand him the coffee and leave but Angie was across the room before he could turn around. "Um… uh…" Buster mumbled.

She set the mug on Buster's wooden dresser.

"What are you doing locked in here all morning? It's not healthy."

Buster didn't like sharing his business with anyone, especially a woman. "Thinking. I was doing some thinking."

Truth was, he had been very close to figuring out how to escape from this rinky-dink old age home and take care of one last bit of important gangster business.

"Come on. Drink it before it gets cold." Angie said.

She plopped down on his unmade bed, as if she did it every day. Buster lumbered over on achy feet. He took a small sip.

"Good, right?"

He nodded.

"Did you see the flyer? There's a trip to Tampa Theatre at two. *Casablanca*. The movie? You like Humphrey Bogart? God, I love him."

"What?" Buster never looked at the bulletin boards or the flyers. He had his routine, and it didn't involve the movies or the mall.

"It's sold out. I mean, the van is full, but I know for a fact that Marcie Ippolito is in bed with her gall bladder. You could use her ticket."

Buster shook his head. Angie's smile tightened.

"Look, nothing wrong with this place," she said. "But you gotta get out sometime. I know I do. You don't get out, you go nuts."

Getting out is what I'm trying to do, Buster thought. But he meant really getting out. Not off in the van on some supervised trip. No, he needed to get out unnoticed, ideally under cover of darkness. He had no complaints about life at Our Lady. There was hot food and a soft bed. He could sit on a wooden park bench in the courtyard and smoke his cheap Hav-a-Tampa cigars. And now there was Angie Castellano, who apparently had chosen him from among the tottering relics of manhood still walking the halls at Our Lady. Except for this one thing he just HAD to do, Buster was content to spend his remaining years here. He was old, with thick glasses, bad knees and corns on his feet. He couldn't hear like he used to. And working as muscle for the mob had not come with a pension plan. His nephew, a homebuilder who lived in a mansion in the Tampa suburbs, had moved him in here and handled the monthly payments.

He knew what this place was—a warehouse where tired travelers waited for the black boat that would ferry them to a very distant port. Buster wasn't afraid of death. He'd sent more than one man off on that final cruise. Our Lady would be his last permanent address, and he had been at peace with that, until last week, when the newspaper arrived.

Multiple copies of *The Tampa Tribune* were delivered to Our Lady each morning, and a front-page headline a week earlier had grabbed him. "Tampa's Last Mobster" loomed atop the page, above a three-column photo of Charlie Wall. Buster wasn't a man who spent time looking back at his life, but one regret stuck in his gut like no other: He had been sent to kill Charlie Wall, and he'd failed. And that failure, the only mark on an otherwise perfect record, haunted him.

Buster got the day nurse to read him the story. He was transported back to that cool, moonless April night in 1955. It was supposed to be an easy, up-close hit. A two-man job, with his partner Jackie "Mangia" Aprile.

The plan had been simple.

Charlie was alone and expecting a delivery. He would open the door himself. When he did, Buster would put a shell into his chest. He and Mangia would drag Charlie deeper into the house and slice his throat with a switchblade.

But the job had been sideways from the start. First off, there was no time for preparation. To make it worse, it was a local job. Tampa guys didn't whack other Tampa guys. You called in out-of-town pros for that. The final screw up was the shotgun Santo Jr.'s guy had insisted Buster use.

"I could use my own gun," Buster protested.

"You'll use the gun we give you."

But that gun was a dud. Hearing the empty click of the firing pin, Buster looked down at the shotgun in disgust. Jackie, ad-libbing, pulled his knife and lunged. Charlie had stepped back and yanked a Colt .38 Special from his waistband. The up-close explosion was deafening. Jackie's head jerked back.

Jackie was Buster's childhood friend. They grew up in the Italian neighborhoods east of 22nd Street, where the yards had room for vegetable gardens and chicken coops. They grew up stealing cars and slashing tires, teen-age rites of passage for kids like them. At 18, with no diplomas and no marketable skills, they had signed on as muscle guys, ready to do any job Santo Senior, and later Santo Junior, gave them.

A jiggling mass of bones and blubber, Jackie was nicknamed "Mangia" because of his love of yellow rice and pasta. He and Buster had planned to hit the Seabreeze after finishing the job for a late-night dinner of trout *"a la Rusa"* and yellow rice. It didn't matter that Mangia had enjoyed a big dinner an hour earlier. Killing someone always made Jackie hungry.

A second gunshot echoed distantly in Buster's stunned ears. Mangia's head rocked back again. Buster smelled the acrid stench of gunpowder. Mangia plopped into a sitting position, then tipped back. A swelling circle of blood oozed across the porch. Bits of Mangia's brain floated atop the goo like kernels of unpopped corn.

Acting on instinct, Buster pitched the worthless weapon at Charlie's head, and leapt from the porch, his stubby legs carrying him toward the empty street. Bullets whizzed past. His ears rang, but he could hear Charlie yelling from the porch—"Run you dirty dago! Run and tell your boss—you can't kill Charlie Wall!"

Was it thirty years ago? Thirty-five? That failed hit was his last job for the Trafficantes. Nineteen fifty-five was just about the end of an era for the Tampa mob. The tough guy trade continued for another decade or so, but for Buster it all vanished that night. The first-generation of Sicilian mob bosses had died, a few younger ones, like Santo Junior, held on, but most of the children and grandchildren became accountants and lawyers. Ignacio Antinori's grandson became the State Attorney. Booze was legal. Cops and politicians stopped accepting envelopes. South Americans hijacked the drug trade. Bolita, the numbers racket that made the mob, became "The Florida Lottery."

Buster adjusted. He became a bouncer at "beer-and-a-bump" bars on the fringes of Ybor City, dismal places run by old hoods trying to keep their economic inner tubes afloat. He got $5 an hour and a room above the bar, with a smelly bathroom down the hall. Buster could live with that and all the indignities of old age—his muscles loosening, his bladder always demanding relief, his feet achy and sore. But a newspaper story? The bastard who killed his best friend smiling for the camera on the front porch of a house where he was supposed to die? Outside of a house much nicer than anyplace Buster had ever lived? To make it worse, the smug bastard called Buster a "coward." That was too much to bear. No, he had one last job to do. And to do it, he needed to get out of Our Lady.

"Hello? Anybody home?" It was Angie. "You okay? I think you kind of floated away there for a minute."

Angie walked toward him holding the black violin case Buster kept under his bed. "You didn't tell me you were a musician."

Buster yanked the case from her grip. "That's private!"

"Sorry. I didn't realize…"

Buster hobbled over to the bed and slid the case back underneath. When he stood, spasms shot up his back. He held back a curse. Angie didn't mention the case again.

"So, the movie? Whad'da ya' think?"

"What movie?"

"*Casablanca*! Tampa Theatre? Have you even been listening to me?"

"No movie. I gotta do some thinking." Buster plodded slowly across the room. He opened the door. Angie got the message. Planting the silver cane with care, she slow-walked toward him.

"You're just like my Ferdie."

Her face was a few inches from his. Her lips parted. He was shocked by the whiteness of her teeth. She smelled like a flower he remembered from his Nana's garden. Buster wanted to bend close to her neck and get lost in that smell, but he didn't.

"Just like Ferdie!" She whispered into his ear. "Both of you as stubborn as the day is long. I guess I like that in a man." She brushed his hand with hers before she walked away. Buster listened to the fading tap of her cane on the terrazzo.

He returned to the recliner, determined to round up all the stray thoughts he'd corralled earlier. It would have helped if he'd written down the plan while it was fresh in his head, but Nick had another important rule:

Never write anything down. A written plan, that the cops can find, is just asking for trouble.

Not that Buster could have written out a plan. When required, he signed his name with a shaky X. He had dropped out of St. Joseph's in the ninth grade because the words in his books refused to hold still.

Buster pulled the handle of the La-Z-Boy and sank back into his thoughts. Slowly, the strands of his plan wove themselves together again. He'd broken out of tougher places than this. Hell, the doors at Our Lady were only locked at night. This escape would be a cinch. In a few days, if all went well, he'd get a second shot at Charlie Wall. He'd make this one count.

CHAPTER 18

While I was working, I could chase Ava from my thoughts, but back in my narrow room, she was always in my head. In our one night together, we didn't talk about the future. Like my family, Ava and her parents lived in a world cushioned by wealth and prestige. If I wanted a life with her, I needed to acquire my own wealth and status. I could have gone home and fallen in line, but that wasn't my path.

And that's when I had the vision.

It was a frigid February morning in 1919. I awoke shivering but too tired to get up and find a blanket. Instead, I watched stalks of sunlight shoot through pinholes in my window shade. Floating dust motes ignited, turning my squalid room into a celestial cathedral. I stared at that kaleidoscope and saw the glittering face of something divine. God-like.

My God isn't some pious old man with a long beard. He's a sharp-dressed guy with a sense of humor; he's a gambler, or better yet, he's a croupier, who sets a lot of games in motion and enjoys seeing who hits and who misses. When you see life as a game of chance, it makes a lot more sense.

After a few magical moments, the sunlight shifted, and my room was again a narrow box above a bar. It didn't matter. I'd seen a vision of my future. I knew what to do and exactly how to do it.

In Tampa, just after the war, Bolita was a mom-and-pop business, catering mostly to the city's Latin immigrants, though lots of white and colored residents wagered their nickels and dimes too. What I knew for certain that morning was that a smart guy could bring all the small games together into a big one. All those penny-ante bets would add up to some real money. Sure, the odds were higher, but so were the payoffs, and all the bettors really cared about were the jackpots. That smart guy could turn some of the profit back to the small-timers who'd give up their throws, and he'd share another sliver with the white guys who ran the city and the county, so they left the smart guy's games in peace.

That afternoon, I bought a paisley satchel with leather handles. I opened an account at a menswear store on Franklin Street run by Jewish tailors, who worked in suit pants, suspenders, and shirtsleeves, their tape measures dangling around their chalky necks. I still worked nights at Joe's, but during the day, dressed in a custom-made seersucker suit, a straw boater on my head, I went from game to game, at bars and corner grocery shops.

In those days, most Tampa bars and gaming parlors had a guy on the payroll with muscles in their arms and in their head. Always Sicilian or Cuban, they were paid to stand near the bar or just outside the front door, guns holstered beneath their jackets, blades strapped to their leg, ugly expressions pasted on their faces. A muscle guy was like a sign in the window—"Mess with this place, and you're messing with me."

Gambling and booze operations were all-cash businesses, and you needed some muscle to make sure nobody messed with you. It was as simple as that.

Before Prohibition turned everybody into criminals, the muscle jobs didn't pay much. Certainly not enough to buy a big man's loyalty. It didn't take a lot of cash to gather a lot of muscle. I had saved all my earnings from Dirty Joe's and, despite the best attempts by Aunt Katherine's lawyers, I had five thousand dollars in an account at the Bank of Tampa, an inheritance from my father, who fell dead from a heart attack at age 55, a few months after I left home. It was enough.

I needed muscle to protect my games and all the cash, but my vision was bigger than that. There would eventually be bars, nightclubs, brothels, and other businesses that needed physical protection.

My growing business also required another type of protection. Gambling, including Bolita, was illegal. The white crackers who ran the city saw Ybor City as a place to be tolerated, as long as the *spics, wops, and Cuban coloreds and their vices stayed on their side of the invisible line. I was the perfect guy to cross that line. The police chief, the mayor, the sheriff, and the county commissioner who oversaw the district that included Ybor City were all friends of my father. I was one of them.*

I made appointments with those powerful men and after some pleasantries about mutual acquaintances, I set fine linen envelopes embossed with my initials on their desks and followed it with a polite request. The men in the suits smiled and gently slid the envelopes into desk drawers before standing and shaking my hand. And why not? We weren't talking about real crime. Bolita was just a lottery. A friendly game of chance. People loved spending a few spare pennies on a dream. Why should the cops, the sheriff, the mayor, or even the governor, stand in their way?

CHAPTER 19

"Shit and double shit!"

The coffee stain oozed across the front pocket of Sammy Albano's starched shirt like some kind of golden amoeba. He had slurped his *café con leche* too quickly, and some of the milky brew dribbled from his chin onto his tan shirt, barely missing the matching tie. The tie fell just north of the black utility belt, that circled Sammy's black-beans-and-rice belly. The belt held a baton flashlight, a billy club, a clinking jumble of silver and gold keys, and two holsters currently stuffed with his favorite candy bars—Snickers and Almond Joy.

Sammy lived by the Boy Scout motto: Be Prepared. He opened the drawer of his narrow desk, in his equally tiny office off the lobby of the OLPH Senior Community and pulled out a fresh shirt.

Sammy's dad, Jimmy Albano, had been a Tampa cop and Sammy had loved to see him dressed in the navy slacks and white shirt as much as he loved hearing his father's war stories about life on the beat. In Jimmy Albano's day Tampa cops were more amateur than professional. It was like being in a city softball league. And as in those week-night leagues, there was a lot of drinking involved.

For Tampa cops during the first 60 or 65 years of the 20th century, the rules of the game were simple: You played hardball in the colored districts and softball in the white districts. In the Latin enclaves you were a fielder, snagging envelopes of cash from mobsters and bookies. Jimmy Albano liked to joke that all those envelopes gave him a sore neck, because he spent so much time looking the other way.

Cops didn't make much in those days and the envelopes helped Jimmy keep his wife at home, cooking and cleaning for a family of five. Jimmy mostly ate out—a cop in uniform never paid for food. Eventually all the complimentary calories took their toll. As Jimmy was about to blow out the 52 candles atop his birthday cake, his heart exploded. A week later, a hundred uniformed cops stood stiffly on the grass at Myrtle Hill. There was a color guard, and a cop played the bagpipes.

All these years later, Sammy still hated the nasally whine of a bagpipe. He joined the force the year after the funeral, anxious to wear the uniform, and enjoy the free food and the contents of all the envelopes. But his timing was bad. He found himself in a 1970s department that was all about reform and professional policing.

Never a guy who liked to exercise, Sammy managed to survive the academy and get the uniform, but he didn't make it beyond his six-month probation. After hearing reports of his "old-school-policing," Sammy's sergeant confronted him at the end of a shift. Sammy's pockets were stuffed with envelopes.

A week later his Captain told him there was no room on the modern TPD for someone like Sammy. "The bad old days are over." The Captain held out his hand. Giving up his badge and gun was hard enough, but Sammy also had to return the uniform.

In private security, Sammy bought his own uniforms. His mother starched and pressed them. He spent his days loitering outside bank branches and savings and loans. But day jobs didn't match his lifestyle. Sammy liked to sleep late and hit the dog track and the jai alai fronton in the evening, so a job at Our Lady was ideal. The midnight to eight shift was easy as long as you could stay awake. During the small hours, the old folks' home was quiet as a graveyard, except on the night Buster Maniscalco tried to make his getaway.

Sammy heard the footsteps as he buttoned up the clean shirt he'd pulled from his desk. Crime was not an issue at Our Lady, nobody willingly broke in, so Sammy wasn't worried, just curious. He stuffed a half-empty pack of Marlboros into his shirt pocket and stepped into the lobby.

The lobby lights stayed on all night, illuminating fading murals of shapely milkmaids holding water vases and shepherds leading their flocks across rocky hills. Whoever had remodeled the hospital into an old folk's home, had left the lobby alone, except for the addition of a steel and glass front door wide enough for wheelchairs. Sammy heard the door click shut, like someone had eased it back into place.

Despite his protests, Sammy's job at Our Lady didn't come with a gun. Fingering the hard rubber handle of the billy club, he stepped outside. He recognized the old man on the sidewalk, lumbering toward the street, his big body rocking a bit with each step, a black violin case in his right hand.

"Buster? Is that you?"

The hulking figure stopped.

"Buster?" Sammy repeated and Buster turned, like an oil tanker coming about.

He wore a dark, pin-striped suit at least 30-years out of date, with a white shirt, thin black tie, and heavy black brogans. With the violin case in his paw, he looked like what he was—an old mobster headed to a hit on a full-moon night.

"What are you doing out here?" Sammy let the door swing shut behind him. "Out for a smoke?"

The old man looked confused. "Yeah. A smoke. Yeah."

From day one Sammy had pegged Buster for a low-level mobster and called in a favor at the cop shop. Buster Maniscalco's rap sheet—armed robbery, assault, disorderly conduct—contained all the usual muscle guy stuff. But even tough guys got old. And Buster didn't look like he had too much fight left in him. Still, he seemed intent on something less than legal and Sammy was certain there was something more lethal than a violin in the case.

"So, what you smoking? A ciggie? A stogie?"

Buster looked stumped. His free hand patted his coat pockets.

"Guess I forgot."

"I got a cigarette here." Sammy held out the pack of Marlboros.

The old man didn't reach out for one. Instead, he rubbed the top of his fire hydrant head.

"Buster, you got a lady around here somewhere?" Sammy offered a sly smile. "You sneakin' out for a little after-midnight delight?"

Buster pawed his head again, like a guy rubbing a lamp, hoping maybe a genie would pop out with the right answer.

"Why don't you come back inside with me." Sammy took Buster's arm. "I only got one job and that's to make sure all the folks who were at dinner show up for breakfast. Or if they don't show up, we find them in their rooms and call the ambulance or the funeral home. You know what I mean?"

Buster looked over his shoulder at the sidewalk leading away from Our Lady.

"A walk," Buster muttered. "Taking a walk."

Sammy looked down at the violin case. He knew better than to make a big deal of it. "Need any help with that case?"

"I got it." Buster pulled it closer to his body.

"It's a little late for a walk. I suggest you wait until tomorrow morning. Come on, let's get back inside."

Sammy held open the glass door. Buster limped inside.

* * *

"It drives me crazy!" Katrina's face was coral in the neon glow of the Ritz marquee. "Tomas loves Tereza but he can't stop cheating on her."

Katrina had insisted that Trip read *The Unbearable Lightness of Being*, with its love triangle and unhappy ending, even though the book upset her. It was the topic for their midnight walk from Rough Riders to Katrina's Seventh Avenue apartment. They passed Valenti Dry Cleaners, West of the Moon glass studio, and a few boarded-up storefronts. The air was clear and crisp.

A few pin-prick stars pierced the wash of the Ybor streetlights.

On nights like this, Trip and Katrina shared the hex-block sidewalks with an occasional clutch of young artists, or a gaggle of frizzy-haired club-goers, headed to El Goya, and the lingering ghosts of three generations of immigrants.

Trip thought a lot about what it would feel like to kiss Katrina but he never acted on the thought. Whatever this was between them, he was content to let her take the lead. There would be no arrows and no hired Cupids. He could feel the wall she kept around her heart coming down brick by brick. She expected him at the bar for the end of her shift, and he no longer had to ask to walk her home.

"What drives me crazy is that he clearly should be with Sabrina." she said. "They're perfect for each other, but he marries Tereza instead. He doesn't really love her. And things don't turn out well for any of them."

Trip had fallen hard for the sexy, uninhibited artist in Kundera's book. "But he can't be with Sabrina," Trip said. "They are exactly alike. It would never work."

Katrina ignored his remark. She wanted Tomas and Sabrina together. She stopped and looked off at the street. "It's so frustrating. Why do men always make the wrong choices?"

Trip was struggling to come up with a response, when Katrina jumped from Kundera to the gaggle of American authors she called "The Terrible White Men"—Updike, Cheever, Styron. She loved their writing but hated their *milieu.*

"And those smug bastards telling the same story over and over. Nothing but country-club white men drinking too much and cheating on their wives, who needs to read another one of those? But last night I read *The Witches of Eastwick*, and now I'm forgiving Updike for all his sins."

Katrina started walking again. Trip followed.

"Witches?"

"Proto-feminist witches, discovering their power. Of course, they all fall for the wrong man. But maybe that's life."

"You don't think a witch, or even a normal woman, might

sometime meet the right man?"

They arrived outside the double-doors of Katrina's building.

"You mean, like a happy ending?"

"Something like that."

Katrina curled her hand inside his, offering Trip a crooked smile. In that moment, he saw the child Katrina had been—cautious but open, quick to laugh, ready for life to find her. She had kept that little girl behind a brick wall.

Katrina took a small step toward him, her face inches from his. She rose on tiptoes and kissed him. It wasn't passionate. More like a hello. Trip savored the moment, the touch of her lips on his, her soft ivory-soap scent.

"You never know." Katrina unlocked the door. "Maybe there can be a happy ending."

She turned back. The light from the staircase haloed her. She was the most beautiful woman he had ever seen.

"So, you believe happy endings are possible?" Trip asked.

"Maybe," she whispered.

CHAPTER 20

One week after his failed attempt, Buster escaped from Our Lady. He was dressed in his black hit-man suit, with two hundred dollars in small bills folded into an ankle wallet and the violin case in his left hand.

Around the complex, he wore the soft slippers issued to all residents, but for his escape, he wore his leather brogans, which delivered a fresh spike of pain with each step. He'd never known anyone who'd had their feet sunk in cement and pushed off a dock—in Tampa they just filled you with buckshot—but concrete overshoes couldn't be any more uncomfortable than his own footwear.

Waiting a week had given him time to devise a better escape plan. He had also enjoyed more lunches and dinners with the tall woman named Angie. He liked how she smiled when he set his tray next to hers. And how she touched his hand when she talked. But Buster was a single-minded man. This new friendship would not distract him. He was determined to get out of Our Lady and put a bullet or two in Charlie Wall.

At 3 a.m. on the appointed night, he watched from a doorway as Sammy headed out for his hourly security check. The guard strolled through the lobby and into the hallway that led to the dining room, whistling a tune Buster didn't recognize. When Sammy was around the corner, Buster crossed the dark lobby, as swiftly as his stiff legs and achy feet would allow.

The April night was cool, without a trace of humidity. A pale blotch of moon, pushing through a sheet of flat clouds, lit the brick battlements and carved stone filigrees of Our Lady's second story rooftop. Years before, Our Lady had been a hospital for Ybor's immigrants. Buster's mother had dragged him here to visit some relative who was losing an appendix or giving birth to twins. Kids weren't allowed upstairs, so Buster had spent what seemed like a lifetime squirming in the hard leather chairs of the first floor waiting room. Almost eighty years later, Our Lady looked like what it had become, a prison for people like him, aging, arthritic, used-up humans, sentenced to eventual death inside these pale brick walls.

Buster shook that morbid thought from his head. He was out. He was on the streets of Ybor City, where he'd spent his entire life. Sure, all the people he'd known growing up were dead or had moved away, but it still felt like home. He breathed in the late-night aromas of his childhood—Cuban bread baking in the ovens of the La Segunda bakery, coffee roasting in the Naviera mill, carbon monoxide wafting off the warm brick streets.

The park, the baseball field, the bodegas, and laundromats around Our Lady were buttoned up for the night. A lone sedan cruised north up 15th. Buster's eyes followed the fading tail-lights. The hex-block sidewalk bulged up in places, and every time Buster stubbed a toe, he cursed the extra spike of pain. His destination was the mob safe house he had shared with Nick. He hoped it was still there and still empty, some forty years later. That part of his plan was a leap of faith. He needed a few days to learn Charlie's routine and do this job the right way.

He walked for almost 20 minutes. The house was farther away than Buster remembered or maybe it just seemed farther because every step was painful. He got turned around a few times, which was crazy, since he had once run these streets, but his eyes weren't so good at night and some of his old land-marks were gone.

The safe house sat in the middle of a block alongside other narrow boxes built seventy years earlier to hold immigrant cigar makers and their families in relative comfort—if all the kids slept in the same room. The house was set six feet from identical ones on each side, all of them fifteen paces back from the street and crowned by A-frame roofs. Long ago someone had screened in the front porch of the safe house, but the screen had torn and long sheets of it drooped like unzipped mosquito netting.

Still, to Buster, this old house, bathed in a milky wash of moonlight, was a welcoming oasis.

He struggled up the steps. Why didn't they ever put handrails on these houses? He gently twisted the front doorknob. It was locked. Bending forward, he pressed his face to the front window, a move that sent icicles of pain slicing down his legs. Through the cloudy glass, Buster made out a bare room but no light or movement. It's still empty, Buster thought, and after corralling that happy thought he had one more—I'll wait until dawn to break in. There could be rats, or maybe a rabid raccoon inside. Better to deal with all of that in the first light of day, before any of the neighbors wake up.

A folding chair sat open on the porch. In the moonglow, Buster could see the sagging plastic straps. The chair screeched and tilted as it took his weight, but it didn't collapse.

Buster felt good about his plans so far. Tomorrow he'd need coffee and some food, but he had found the safe house, he was in a neighborhood he knew as well as any in the world, and the spring night held not even a hint of winter. He'd be fine as soon as he got himself out of these goddam shoes. He pried one, then the other off his aching feet. He promised himself he would stay awake until sunrise.

* * *

Buster wasn't sure how long he'd been asleep when he sensed a presence close to him. If this was death come to fetch him, he wasn't scared. He'd seen that black-cloaked figure up close plenty of times.

Buster parted his eyelids, snake-like, into narrow slits. A glint of moonlight flashed off something metal. Some kind of weapon, Buster was sure of that much. Even with his bad ears, he could hear shallow, raspy breathing. Someone was close! He drew his own silent breath, then struck like a viper. He snagged a forearm and twisted it with such force his attacker gasped and toppled onto the concrete floor. The weapon clattered as it landed.

Buster came out of the chair and dropped to his knees. His prey writhed beside him, like a fish on land. Buster's hand pressed hard on the squirming, babbling creature.

"Se-se-sorry! Sorry! Yeah, sorry! Nothing to worry about here. Ouch! You're hu-hu-hurting..." The voice was high and whiny, like a child's.

Buster's senses weren't what they used to be, but even his battered nose could tell this thing he had caught reeked like a public toilet in a bus station. He ignored the flares of pain in his back and knees.

"...You're hu-hu-hurting me! But that's okay. I deserve it. All of it. So-so-sorry!"

What he had caught was a man. A tiny writhing man. Keeping one arm pressed on his chest, Buster raised a fist. His captive struggled to breathe, spurts of words escaping between gasps.

"Don't hu-hu-hurt me! I'm harmless. A fly. Wouldn't hurt one. A fly, I mean. No. Not me. Scared. I mean...You. Scared. Me. Okay?"

Buster unclenched his fist and snatched up the weapon that lay beside the quivering body—a rusting 12-inch-long screwdriver, Phillips head. Buster tossed it over his shoulder. It clattered off the hex-block sidewalk.

"You bite me, and I die of rabies, I WILL come back and kill you."

Buster wasn't sure why he'd chosen those particular words, but they worked. The writhing stilled, but the creature's feral eyes kept up a herky-jerky dance.

"No biting. Not me. Can't really ba-ba-bite." He opened his mouth. Buster could see dark gums and a smattering of actual teeth.

"I let you go, you behave? Got it?"

"Ga-ga-ga-ga..." The man struggled for the words to do his bidding. "...Ga-ga-got it! I definitely got it!"

Buster clambered to his feet. Below him, the man was on his back, his arms and legs flailing like a flipped bug. Buster had raised dogs, including some meant for the dogfighting pits in the woods east of Ybor. He knew a sign of submission when he saw one.

"Peace," the man said. "I come. In peace."

"With a screwdriver at my neck?" Buster used the mean voice he reserved for deadbeat gamblers who owed his boss some money.

"Just a precaution. Just a...I was sleeping inside. And you. You. Scared. Me."

"You live here?"

"Me? Oh, just visiting. Really. This you're house? I can go. Now. If you want."

"Anyone else living here?"

"No. Nada. Just me. A few rats, but they don't bite, mostly."

Buster's eyes were adjusting. He saw the man's rodent face a little clearer—unshaven, whiskers jutting like weeds from sunken cheeks. The tip of his beaked nose was bent, a break that hadn't been fixed. A mottled mass of greasy hair splayed out on the porch.

"Get up!" Buster wished he could make his voice quieter, but he wasn't sure how.

"Yes. Getting up. Got it. Check!"

The man rolled to his side. He pushed himself first to his knees, and then onto his feet. He shook himself, a process that started with his head and descended, like a choppy wave, down to his bare feet. When he finished, he stood straighter. Buster wasn't tall, but he towered over this creature.

"Again, I'm sorry for...uh...the thing...the...ah...incident earlier. So sorry. Really." The man's voice had lowered a notch.

"We're going inside. You're going to show me around. And not cause trouble. Right?"

"Absolutely. No trouble at all. *Mi casa, su casa*, as they say in Ybor City. Which means, you know, my house is your..."

Buster raised his fist in the man's face. "Not so much talking.

Got it? Don't like a lot of talking."

The man pressed his index finger against his lips.

"Shhhhhhhh! Less talking. Absolutely. As you wish. Silencio!"

A narrow band of pale blue light glimmered at the far edges of the night. The first hint of sunrise.

"When we get inside, you're not going to talk unless I ask you a question. Right?"

The man coughed and the phlegmy spasm doubled him over. Buster looked over his shoulder. A light went on in a nearby window. "We gotta get inside. Now."

The man wiped some viscous goo from his chin.

"Come ... in," he whispered, his voice still choked. "I'll ... show you ...around...my little grass shack."

CHAPTER 21

Katrina awoke remembering the softness of his lips. It had been a year since she had kissed a man. She had forgotten all of it—the subtle mint of his toothpaste, the stubble against her cheek, the way her heart seemed to stop when their lips met.

Easing out of bed, she slipped on her silk robe. Her hand-sewn curtains, hung from large gold hoops, parted easily, letting in a wash of crisp morning sun. A soft breeze drifted through a wide window held up with a stick. On Seventh Avenue, one flight down, a bread truck idled outside the Trolley Stop Cafe. Rick Melby, blond hair cascading around his shoulders, walked toward his glass studio, his morning coffee in a glazed ceramic mug.

Turning back, Katrina straightened the covers on her narrow double bed. Her kitchen was a single pine counter, with a two-burner stove, a small oven, and a dorm-sized refrigerator.

Tonight, she decided, I'll invite him up for a late dinner.

She pictured the two of them at her small table, the meal eaten, the room lit by candles and the glow of the streetlights. She'd leave her hand on the table. He'd bring his down on top of hers.

She was glad her first impression of Trip had been wrong. All the stoned cockiness she had seen on that open mic night had disappeared. He had cleaned up his life. Given up drugs. And in all their night's together, he hadn't made any demands, except that she talk to him about writing and books.

Up until now, she had liked it that way. She had read enough literature and penned enough sad poems to know the truth:

Love always broke your heart. Her mother, Katrina's favorite human in all the world, had been crushed inside her car when Katrina was 12. Zach, the high school boyfriend who had taken Katina's virginity after months of flirting, had never called after that drunken Saturday night. Brian, the college fiancé, a man she thought would be a life-long partner, had left her stranded in Ybor City, hundreds of miles from home, with just his one-sentence apology and a stack of twenty-dollar bills on the bedside table.

But last night's kiss had shifted something inside her.

She checked the antique alarm clock beside her bed. It was 8 a.m. She rushed to her dresser and pulled out some clothes. She had a lot to do before starting her shift at five.

* * *

"I've made dinner. If you're hungry."

"You're inviting me up?"

"I mean, yes. There's dinner."

So far, the night had gone according to Katrina's plan. Trip had been at the bar. They'd walked home as usual. And now, for the first time, she'd asked him to come up. Suddenly, she was nervous. Would he turn her down?

"Dinner sounds great," he said. "I'm starving."

Upstairs, Katrina slipped behind a folding Japanese screen, adorned with images of egrets spreading feathered wings. She emerged in a thrift-store cotton sundress, her feet bare, her hair held behind her head by a chopstick.

Trip asked for a second helping of the steaming yellow rice and chicken. He had written a lot in the past few days and was excited, between bites, to tell her about it. Again, she offered to read his draft. Trip shook his head.

"I want it to be, you know, more polished before I share it with you. But you'll be the first reader, I promise."

Katrina cleared the dishes and put on a Sergio Mendes record that her mother had loved. The album was one of the few possessions she had packed when she'd left Ann Arbor with Brian. She turned off the overhead light and lit the candle on her bedside table.

Katrina and Trip danced in the buttery glow of candlelight to a samba version of the Beatles' "Fool On The Hill." After the song ended, they continued to sway, their bodies close. Katrina was almost five-eight. Trip was easily four inches taller. He pulled the chopstick, and her hair fell to her shoulders. He lifted her chin and kissed her. The next song played and then the rest of the record, but by then, Trip and Katrina were joined in a more intimate dance.

The next morning, over mugs of café con leche, they sat at her tiny table, bare knees touching, his hand resting on hers. Neither of them needed to say anything.

CHAPTER 22

Once I had the muscle guys, the police, and the politicians on my payroll, it was time to talk with the Dirty Joes and Dirty Jills who ran small-time Bolita throws. First, I'd share the bad news that their muscle now worked for me. Then I'd deliver the good news—I wasn't putting them out of business. My organization would do all the hard work. We'd run the games, pay off the winners, make sure the city cops and the county deputies didn't raid their joints, and I'd cut them in for a bigger taste than their single game provided.

Like a good retailer, I added door-to-door salesmen—vegetable peddlers with horse drawn wagons, and the Piruli men, who sold hard candy on a stick from rolling carts. I gave them another product to sell—a chance, a number, a dream you bought with a penny or a nickel.

I struck deals with a well-connected downtown attorney and a cagey bail bondsman. No matter how many people you paid off, Bolita was still illegal and occasionally somebody was going to get locked up. Finally, I took part ownership of a brick box on the fringes of Ybor City called The Yellow House. Like Dirty Joe's, the Yellow House, was a speakeasy in front, with a lavish gaming room in back, where we did our daily and weekly throws.

And somehow, the whole thing worked. From 1918 to 1920 my income doubled, then tripled. Prohibition only made it bigger. The cops focused on booze and bootlegging and left gamblers and Bolita alone.

In Tampa, the name Charlie Wall started to mean something. People often nodded politely when they passed me on the street. Beat cops waved. Street kids called out, "Hey Charlie!" and I'd flip *a quarter or, if I was feeling flush, a silver dollar in their direction.*

The only downside was that the Volstead Act had activated the Sicilian families, who moved into bootlegging and rum running. As my Bolita operation grew, and they saw how much I was making, they wanted what I had. I thought there was plenty for everyone. The Sicilians didn't agree.

Tampa's Sicilians came from four tiny villages in the dusty hills above Agrigento—Santo Stefano, Alessandria Della Rocca, Bivona, and Cianciana—and they were all related. La Cosa Nostra, the Black Hand, the Mafia, call them what you will, criminal clans were deeply rooted in the culture of that island, and they followed the immigrants to Tampa. The biggest crews were the Trafficantes and the Diecidues, both led by powerful patriarchs, and built on networks of sons, nephews, cousins, and a few trusted friends. The clan I was most worried about in those days was led by a first-generation immigrant named Ignacio Antinori.

Sicilians had always made wine, and when booze was outlawed, many of them, including Antinori, started distilling their own liquor for speakeasys around the city. Antinori was making good money, and I couldn't buy his muscle, because they were his two plus-sized sons, Paolo and Francesco. Antinori ran a speak behind a laundry on 12th Avenue. He didn't have gaming tables, but his customers played poker and dominoes in the pine-paneled back room, and he ran a mid-sized Bolita throw.

I wanted to propose a working relationship, but I'd been warned that Ignacio was a hard case, so I sent my lawyer on the first visit. On a signal from their dad, Antinori's bruiser sons flung him through the laundry's front door. Fortunately, the door was open.

I knew that tossing out a lawyer was just phase one of a negotiation. I needed to visit this obstinate SOB myself. I should have been scared, but that's not in my nature. I love life and, like anyone else, I try to avoid pain, but deep down, I've always felt like nobody could really hurt me. After all, Brother Abernathy had promised me everlasting life!

On a fine summer morning in 1922, dressed in my best

seer-sucker suit, I walked confidently through the laundry, setting off the little bell at the front door. I tipped my straw boater to the hawk-faced woman folding clothes on a long table and stepped through the double doors to the back room. As if by magic, Paulo and Francesco appeared. They stood behind me with their arms folded, quiet but menacing, two bulldogs awaiting their owner's order to attack.

Ignacio, the patriarch was on the other side of the scarred pine bar. He tended a steaming silver coffee pot and a saucepan on a small stove against the wall. Unlike his massive sons, he was small and solid, his silver hair combed back and held firm by pomade, his short-sleeved white shirt crisply pressed. A white bar rag, fresh from the laundry, hung over one shoulder.

"Mr. Antinori, I'm–"

Without turning around, he cut me off with a wave of his arm. "I know who you are." His voice was rich and low, and carried no anger or concern. "I am making coffee. Would you like a cup?"

"Yes, thank you," I said.

He poured the boiling brew from the pot with his left hand and added the steaming milk from the saucepan in his right. Ignacio was only a few inches over five feet. All those inches were straight and regal, making him seem taller. He was clearly a king in this castle. I kept my eyes on him to make sure he didn't add any of his own spit to my coffee cup, though that didn't seem to be in his nature. Like me, he had other people do his dirty work.

He slid the ceramic cup and saucer across the bar. On his pale, hairless forearm was a black tattoo of an open hand, the symbol of old-world Sicilian gangs. His dark eyes were somehow gentle and menacing.

"You are either very brave or very foolish to walk into my business alone. Which is it?"

"You could say I'm a practical man." I took a slow sip. "Yes, I walked in here alone, and without a weapon. But there are six men smoking cigars on the sidewalk outside. If I come out the front door on anything other than my own two feet, they'll kill everyone in here."

Ignacio burst into laughter, showing off some very white teeth. Ybor's immigrants weren't rich, but through their social clubs, they had access to doctors and dentists. It was a town of very good teeth. Antinori slapped the bar with his hand, like I had delivered a hilarious joke. His laughter stopped abruptly, and he looked up at his sons.

"He's funny, right?"

The boys didn't laugh.

"You're funny. I like that." Ignacio's accent was thick, but I knew it was a mask he wore so his opponents would underestimate his intelligence and cunning. I took a deep breath, our eyes locked.

"I know who you are," he said. "And I know you have only two men outside with guns. I have two men inside with guns. I believe that is called a standoff."

I took another sip before speaking.

"Look, I'm a man of business, not violence. I'm here to make you a legitimate offer for your Bolita operation and to tell you I have no plans to get into the liquor business. In fact, I'd be happy to have a second conversation about offering some of your products at The Yellow House and in a place I'm opening soon called The El Dorado. Should be done in few months. I'll invite you to the grand opening. Drinks, dinner, a floor show—it's on me."

He showed me a placid poker face. There was no anger in his eyes. No fear either. Looking down, he added four spoons of sugar to his milky brew, stirring it in with a tiny silver spoon. He drank his coffee like a gentleman, his index finger curled through the cup handle, each sip quiet and precise.

"I will listen to your offer."

That was progress. I gave him my best sales pitch—protection from the cops, a bigger slice of the profits, higher jackpots that would draw more customers, the whole megillah. When I finally ran out of gas, he remained silent. I felt like an ugly guy asking a beautiful girl out on a date.

"No."

"Excuse me?"

"No."

"That's your answer?"

Suddenly, his voice was harsher. His eyes darker. "That is my answer. No cracker bambino is going tell me how to run my game or my bar. You got that?"

That wasn't exactly what he said, since a lot of it was in Ybor's gumbo dialect, a mix of English, Spanish and Italian, but that's the gist of it. I pushed my half-empty cup of coffee toward him and stepped back. "I had hoped you'd be a reasonable man."

He smiled again, showing off those fine teeth, only now they seemed sharper, like he might come across the bar and sink them into my neck. He picked up my cup and saucer. Turning, he dropped them with a clatter into the sink. He spoke without looking back.

"I am a reasonable man. You are leaving my business with your head still attached to your body. That seems very reasonable to me."

His sons moved closer. I could feel their canine breath on my neck. Despite my cockiness, a mortal chill shot though me. I struggled to keep my voice calm.

"I'll be going then. Thank you for your time and your fine coffee."

I picked up my hat. The two hulks parted just enough to let me slip through the double doors.

* * *

My muscle guys, Joe Diaz and Johnny Rivera, had waited for me on the sidewalk. They wore loose-fitting dark suits—good for hiding shoulder holsters and sawed-off shotguns. I had not lied when I told Antinori I had six men outside—Joe and Johnny were the equal of six men. Joe had scrub-brush hair and deep dimples in his fleshy face. His nickname was "Baby Joe." Johnny's swarthy face was pockmarked by his teenage acne, so everybody called him "Scarface."

Joe was quiet, his violence lying deep in his barrel chest. Johnny was nervous, dangerous, his eyes always in motion, his fists scabbed from brawls, his nose bent and swollen from the street fights he always won.

Johnny stepped up to look me over. I pulled out my handkerchief and wiped sweat from my forehead.

"You okay?" Johnny asked.

Nodding, I strode away. I wanted to put several blocks between me and Ignacio Antinori.

"He go for it?" It was Johnny again.

I shook my head. We turned the corner onto Seventh Avenue, stepping into the weekday crowd—women with kids, men in jeans and work shirts, peddlers pushing carts, bent widows in black. I felt safer in the bustle of an Ybor sidewalk.

"What now?" Johnny asked.

I stopped. I knew what I needed to do. I didn't like it, but in my business your reputation was your calling card. You had to protect it at all costs. Ignacio Antinori was pissing on my reputation. He had left me no choice.

"I'm afraid we're gonna have to hurt somebody."

CHAPTER 23

A shaft of sunlight woke Buster. He snorted and his head snapped forward. His hands gripped the arms of the folding chair. He had slept in the chair, next to an east-facing window he'd managed to pry open. He had told himself to stay awake, but sleep had crept in like a slow-moving tide.

Thanks to the open window, the skunk smell had shifted from horrible to merely funky. He scanned the living room. The ragged creature he'd encountered the night before was curled in a far corner under a thin blanket. Rising slowly on achy feet, Buster set off on a tour of a house he'd once known very well.

Some things hadn't changed. The front door opened into a box of a living room, with two windows looking out onto the porch and one on each of the side walls. A hallway sliced along the east side, opening onto two tiny bedrooms, and ending at a kitchen and bathroom in back. The plaster walls were bare, the paint yellowed.

The kitchen had no appliances. There was a hole in the bathroom floor, and the tub and part of the sink were missing. But when Buster turned the spigot, water flowed. The city had never turned off the water.

Stepping carefully around the holes in the floor, Buster faced the pull-chain toilet, unzipped and opened his own spigot and felt relief as his water flowed—a little slower than it used to, and not as steady, but still, it flowed. Back in the hallway, he felt the spell coming on. He was dizzy and darkness rimmed the borders of his vision. These sudden spells had been happening more lately. He had to wait them out.

Closing his eyes, he saw his long-dead mother. Angelica Maniscalco was a cigar roller who also had managed a house, four kids and a drunken husband. She had taken a long bath every night before bed—filling the family claw-foot with Epsom salts and lavender—her one indulgence in a life of hard labor.

In his vision, it was early morning and Buster's mother, barely five-feet-tall and gaunt as a scarecrow, stood beside his bed. She tickled his ear. "Up and on them, bambino." She whispered in her broken English. "Up and on them." Jolting awake, the adolescent Buster corrected her sternly—"It's at 'em, Ma! Not on them! Jeezus!"

Did I really say that to my mother? In a smelly hallway almost 70 years later, Buster's emotions overcame him. He gasped for breath and bent forward, and for almost a full minute, he sobbed. Sudden tears were another part of these mysterious spells.

Eventually, the image of his mother faded, and his vison cleared. He was back in the stinky safe house, in a hallway clotted with trash and debris. He kicked a battered cardboard box, and a battalion of winged roaches took flight. Buster stepped back to avoid the airborne assault.

* * *

Back in the living room, daggers of light lanced through the cloudy windows. Buster stood a few feet away from the sleeping figure in the corner. His nose wouldn't let him get any closer.

"OK! Who are you?"

The little man's head jerked up. He raised his arm in front of his face, as if trying to deflect a blow.

"Is that a question?"

"Yeah. That's a question. Who the hell are you?"

The man's eyes fluttered, then opened wide. "You told me to only answer when you asked a question. I wanted to be absolutely sure you were asking–"

Buster raised a fist. "I am asking a question. Now give me an answer. Who are you?"

He took a long, rasping breath and stared up at Buster. "I would give you a simple answer, but life is so complicated. You know? Hard to boil down a question like that. I mean, 'Who are you?' Think about that for a minute. It's a question with so many possibilities. Not easy to answer at all."

"Try."

"Can you repeat the question?"

Buster shook his fist.

"WAIT! I remember. I'm Se-Se-Seymour. Seymour Grassley...I'm Dr. Se-Se-Seymour Grassley, Ph.D. Religious studies, Princeton, 1961. A bit down on my luck at the moment."

The man's words came out pinched and squeaky, like air seeping from a balloon.

Buster snorted at the thought of this dissipated bum, squatting in a filthy, abandoned house, bragging about his education. "You're a doctor? And I'm a fuckin' astronaut. Princetown? Is that a place?"

"Ton. Prince-ton!" Seymour said earnestly, his hand returning to his side. "And it's very much a place. A place of refinement and high ideals." He stared at the ceiling, apparently savoring a memory. "The site of my matriculation."

"Your what? I don't like how you talk."

"Sorry. So sorry. It's just...how I talk...can't help myself."

"Talk simpler."

"I'll try."

It was full-on morning now and the room had brightened. Buster could clearly see the corner where Seymour had slept. His bed was a mat of old newspapers with an overturned orange crate for a bedside table. Two red candle stubs atop the crate poked from thick cascades of wax.

"You live here? Like this?"

"It's a temporary situation. Extremely temporary. Awaiting instructions. Top secret stuff. But there's money involved and intrigue. Yes, both. So, right now, I'm waiting. Or awaiting."

"How long?"

"I'm sorry?" What?"

"How long you been here?"

"Hard to say. Very hard to say. I mean – "

Buster raised his clenched fist.

"Arrived via Greyhound. What? A year ago? Two? Invited to teach biblical studies at the University of Tampa. But needless to say, th-things didn't work out. Found my feet engulfed in quicksand, so to speak. This domicile was available and, well... does that answer your question?"

"You mean you broke in?"

"In a manner of speaking, yes, but no one has complained. There was a for-sale sign out front, but I took it down. Nobody ever came to put it back. So I...ah...assumed we had a deal."

"You had a deal? Never mind. But nobody has come around? No owners. Nobody?"

"Just you. Last night."

Seymour sprang to his feet. Buster raised his arms to deflect an attack, but the little man only bent his head, his palms coming together in front of his chest, like he was about to pray.

"Is this your house? If so, I sincerely apologize. I will take my leave." He bowed from the waist.

"Just tell me how long you've been here."

Seymour rose from the bow. "I really can't say."

"You won't say, or you don't know? Never mind! The neighbors haven't called the cops on you?"

"Only a few neighbors. And no cops."

"You planning to stay much longer?"

"You seem particularly obsessed with time."

"What?"

Seymour smiled. "No offense meant, but time is the fabric we use to stich our own straightjackets. It's a tick-tock trap. A self-imposed prison."

Buster wasn't sure what to do with this crooked gargoyle of a man. Hitting him did not seem like the right solution. Seymour continued to talk.

"The Master taught me you have to kill time. Smash it on the rocks. Crush it under your boot. Do that and what do you get?"

He looked up at Buster. Buster glared back.

"You get freedom! Incredible freedom! Kill time and the stop-watch of life stops spinning!" Seymour started to spin, a move apparently designed to illustrate his point.

"Kill time and BOOM! The dates in your date book disappear like they were written in invisible ink. BOOM! You're not early. BOOM! You're not late. BOOM! You're just a molecule floating free inside a vast infinite moment."

"An infant moment?"

"Infinite, my new friend, in-fin-ite!"

At the end of one spin, Buster dropped his hands on the man's shoulders. Seymour stopped turning, but his eyes kept up a corkscrew dance. His voice dropped to a whisper.

"Yes, you're floating in an infinite moment. As vast as the Milky Way. As deep as the ocean. As silent as the moon."

Seymour's arms dangled. His index finger ticked back and forth, like a metronome. "You freeze that moment. Lock time in amber and you...you are...dare I say it? A FREE MAN!"

Buster let go and Seymour sagged against the wall. He slid down, his lips moving, but he whispered, as if he was speaking to someone inside his own head. Buster rubbed his face with open palms. This accidental roommate confused him.

"No more talking!"

Sharing the safe house with a smelly madman had not been part of Buster's plan. He was only certain of a few things at this point. He wanted this creature to stop talking. He wanted to spray him down with a hose. And he really wanted a strong cup of *café con leche.*

Buster took a long slow breath....in....out. And just like that, the fog lifted, his mind cleared, and words poured out. "I have to figure out what to do with you. But for now, don't sneak up on me with a fuckin' screwdriver or anything else. And no more talk about time. Got me? I need to stay here a few days. And I need some coffee and food and maybe a few other things."

The little man bounced again to his feet, as if some unseen puppet master had yanked his strings. "Say no more. You are most welcome to stay. And things—not a problem. Finding things is what I do. I mean—you need something, just say the word. I'll find it for you."

"New shoes." Buster said. "Size 9-and-a-half. Extra wide. And a broom. I gotta sweep this place out if I'm staying here."

"Shoes. Broom. On it!"

The little man stood taller, carefully smoothing out his filthy clothes with his hands. A crooked, gap-toothed smile clung to his face. Staring at Buster, he snapped off a military salute.

CHAPTER 24

A ngie Castellano banged on Buster's door with the curved handle of her metal cane. She delivered a couple of hard, staccato smacks, then added "shave and a haircut, two bits." She was sure he wasn't inside. That morning she had found a scrap of paper he had slid under her door. The note was written in child-like block letters with no commas or periods: OLD JOB MUST DO BACK SOON I HOPE B.

Buster had been her meal companion the past two weeks, but he'd taken it no further. He'd not invited her to his apartment. Or accepted her invitation to watch one of the classic Hollywood movies shown nightly in the card room. The gruff hulk of a man was playing hard to get, but Angie wasn't worried about that. When it came to men, she was like a big game hunter, patient and persistent. Once she got her prey framed in the scope, they didn't stand a chance. Buster's note was evidence that he was moving in her direction. They always did.

When she was a teenager, so many years ago, the boys hadn't pursued Angie. They wanted curvy, Latin girls with oval faces framed by cascades of black curls. Tall and thin, an A-student at the all-girl Academy of Holy Names, Angelina Giglio was more Katherine Hepburn than Dorothy Lamour. But getting male attention was easy once she realized that teenage boys were a lot like puppies—they had large appetites and were easily trainable. She learned how to French kiss, and her girlfriend, Sylvia, showed her the secret of implanting a blue-black sucker bite on the muscled neck of a willing football player. A little makeup. A sigh. The seductive snap of her mascaraed eyelashes. That was all it took.

It didn't hurt that she was quick with a wisecrack and stood her ground when the Jesuit or the Jefferson High boys teased her. She'd let her tongue slide over her lips and give them a wide-eyed stare. Not that Angie was in danger of losing her virginity. Like a football player from a small school, she learned to play offense and defense, pushing the boy's passion buttons, but making it clear that things would only go so far. Most boys seemed fine with hours of deep kissing in the bucket seats of roadsters or the plush banquettes of sprawling sedans borrowed from dad. If they were especially promising, she let their fingers brush across the budding breasts she kept safely locked behind a rigid wall of Playtex.

She knew what boys wanted but Angie wasn't sure she understood her own longings. Why did making out with handsome honor students and wise-cracking class wits leave her cold and indifferent?

She was behind the stands after a Jefferson High game, going tongue-to-tongue with Tony Capitano, a lumbering defensive lineman out for the season due to acute indifference, when his hand brushed across her well-protected chest. Electric charges sizzled down her spine and a string of firecrackers snapped in her groin.

What the hell? she thought. Why this guy?

It took her entire senior year and a few more bone-headed boyfriends before Angie realized that the men she really liked were large and not too bright. When a small-time hood named Ferdinand Castellano cornered her at a *Centro Espanol* tea dance, his rock-hard body so large it seemed to block out the light, she felt a rush of excitement.

Ferdie Castellano was perfect: taller than Angie and roughly handsome, despite his broken nose, a quivering pair of inner-tube lips and the Neanderthal ridge across his forehead. His smile was wide, his tannin-tinted skin unmarked by acne. A couple of well-oiled "Clark Kent' curls fell over his forehead. He raced around Ybor City in a cherry red Packard roadster, a roll of cash in his pocket. He got the cash and the car doing what he said were odd jobs—jobs that Angie was sure were misdemeanors, maybe worse.

Angie was more than smitten. Six months after picking up her Academy diploma, she endured a full wedding mass, in front of a menagerie of in-laws and outlaws, at Christ The King. On the wedding day, Ferdie, who she had kept at bay for months, was drooling with desire. He rushed through the vows and the reception in the church hall and drove like a madman to the tiny vacation cabin on St. Petersburg Beach, where the wedding night excitement lasted about 10 seconds.

"There, there," Angie said, after he grunted and rolled onto his back, apparently poleaxed by the suddenness and the magnitude of his ejaculation.

She had studied for this night and knew that 10 seconds of joy was not how it was supposed to go. Had she been grading, Ferdie would have gotten an F. But Angie was a patient teacher. After four days at the beach her pupil was scoring all "As" on his love report card.

During their months of courting, she had figured out that her fiancée made his money beating up deadbeats for some Sicilian capos. Now that he was a husband, that had to change. Angie was excited to explore her new-found sex life, and that couldn't happen if her husband was in jail. Time for more training, she decided. Her program of request and reward—Ferdie loved the reward part—took a few months, but soon her husband was running a one-man tobacco, espresso and candy stand in a narrow, Ybor City alcove. It wasn't a lot of money, but the job was simple and legal, and Ferdie was home for dinner every night, and in their bed later, as eager as a teenager. Angie earned a nursing certificate, and between them there was enough money to live in relative comfort in a small casita next to a cigar factory in West Tampa. It was what she wanted from life. Maybe she had wanted kids, but when they didn't come—despite all the trying—that was fine too.

Eventually, Ferdie's muscles softened, his belly expanded, and his hair thinned, but one part of him continued to work perfectly right up until the night he went face down in the MacDonald's parking lot, two happy meals scattered on the asphalt around his prone body.

Angie had moped around the empty house for a year or so, before deciding to sell it and move into Our Lady, where at 68, she was one of the youngest residents. In the dining room on her very first night, she met Raul Vega, a brawny widower who wore tailored suits to dinner and liked to finish his evening meals with a Cigarillo and a snifter of Grand Marnier. Several of his meaty fingers sported gold bands set with semi-precious stones. His moustache was oiled, his hair neatly trimmed and dyed shoe-polish black. He limited his reading to the Tampa Downs racing form.

All the widows at Our Lady had their eyes on Raul, but he quickly focused on Angie. They started as dinner companions, then progressed to heavy petting in the shadowy outdoor courtyard after dinner. A month later, they skipped the courtyard and went straight to his apartment. Raul was quiet and generous, but he was a man of his generation. Jealousy was baked into his macho psyche. He kept close tabs on his new lover, snapping at her if she looked at, or God forbid, spoke to another man. But given Raul's talents in the bedroom, Angie was willing to overlook that one character flaw.

After a simple marriage in the county clerk's office, Angie and Raul lived like newlyweds for two years, until his heart gave out during a particularly strenuous evening. Extricating herself took almost two hours. Angie vowed to give up the missionary position forever.

After Raul's funeral, she returned to the widow's table with the Katies, Lenas, Carmens, and Marias. She went back to gin rummy and hearts in the afternoon. To a glass of Chardonnay before dinner. And a book or magazine in her empty bed at 9 p.m.

A few months after the funeral, a retired Tampa cop named Tony Alfonso appeared in the dining room. Tony had spent 25 years on the night beat, retiring as a sergeant. Angie moved from the widow's table to a two-top with Tony. He liked to schedule their sexual encounters, writing them down in a small notebook he kept in his back pocket. He wasn't jealous or possessive. More than anything, he was punctual.

On Monday, Wednesday and Saturday, they shared dinner in the cafeteria at 6, sex in his apartment at 7 and Wheel of Fortune at 7:30. The routine suited Angie just fine, though after a few months on Tony's "night shift" she realized he had fallen hard for her. She wasn't in love but like other women of her generation, she believed sex was better when there was a license involved. She accepted his proposal and showed the widows the flashy, European mine-cut diamond Tony's mother had once worn.

On a June afternoon, they exchanged vows in the tiny chapel at Our Lady. The widows tossed rice at the newlyweds as they strolled to the elevator that would whisk them to their honeymoon retreat—Tony's two-bedroom apartment on the top floor, with views of Ybor City and the Port of Tampa.

They stayed for three days, making love while watching the banana boats enter the port of Tampa. A waiter from Our Lady brought up meals on trays. On the fourth night, they arrived at dinner like aging royalty. The widows and the dining room staff gave them a standing ovation. The marriage was three months old when Tony choked on a trout bone at the Friday night fish fry. He turned a purplish blue, then expired on Our Lady's dining room parquet, as the paramedics arrived.

The widows offered comfort and for two months Angie, now 76, kept a linen handkerchief and a box of Kleenex handy. But her tears were more joyful than sad. Tony's lawyer called her two weeks after his passing to say he had left her $250,000, a widow's portion of his pension, and possession of his apartment for life.

A month later, she noticed Buster in the cafeteria. He was built like a Mack truck and the light in his eyes was maybe twenty watts. She liked that in a man.

Despite Buster's appeal, she ignored him for another month. It wasn't easy. Losing a spouse always made Angie horny but there were rules. At Our Lady, a widow who didn't observe the proper mourning period would find herself with no friends. Angie wanted Buster, but she also wanted to keep the support of the widows—they always outlived the men.

Four months after Tony's funeral, Angie started hanging around the dining room after the other widows had left. Buster was always the last man down for dinner. It took a few weeks, and a lot of wasted smiles before he noticed her and another week or so before he realized she wanted him to sit with her. Soon, they shared a table at every meal. Buster even attempted to make conversation.

But just as things were warming up, something changed. Buster became preoccupied and prone to silence. Then came the note slipped under her door. She showed it to Sammy, the security guard.

"I got this odd note. I think it's from Buster."

"He broke out. It was his second try. I caught him sneaking out a couple of nights ago and brought him back."

Buster's disappearance caught Angie off guard. Normally, she could read her empty-headed men like a book. But she hadn't known this one long enough. She didn't know much about his life before Our Lady. They hadn't even kissed.

When he didn't answer his door, she went inside. His bed was unmade. She fingered the change and crumpled slips of paper on the top of his dresser. They were unfilled prescriptions. Men, she thought, why didn't they take care of their health?

Two notebooks lay on his recliner, the pages filled with hand-written lines of numbers and a cluster of tickets. Buster had been playing the lottery. Leaning down, using her cane for support, she lifted the bedspread. The black violin case was gone.

Inside his trash can, she found a single sheet of crumpled newsprint. She spread it out on the bed. A profile of Charlie Wall, the retired mobster, described a failed mob hit in 1955. One hit man was killed, another got away. Buster had circled the old mobster's face in black ink. Charlie Wall's face seemed to float inside a bullseye.

Angie Castellano knew exactly what Buster was up to. Her simple-minded men may not have accomplished much in the grand scheme of things, but when they started a job, they finished it. For Buster, Charlie Wall was clearly unfinished business.

She slipped the folded clipping into the pocket of her cardigan. He's my kind of man, she thought, large, determined, and not too smart. She remembered how she had turned Ferdie away from his criminal life. She would straighten Buster out before he did something foolish. Men who fit her profile were in short supply at Our Lady. Angie was determined to hang on to this one.

* * *

A woman's voice purred in Larry Pardo's ears: "You go to my head like a sip of sparkling burgundy brew/And I find the very mention of you/Like a kicker in a julep or two..."

Physically, Larry was in the parking lot of Our Lady, polishing a Dodge minivan with a soft rag. Mentally, he was floating in a black and white film-noir Oz of gumshoes and guns, with a soundtrack by Rosemary Clooney.

A metallic tap on his shoulder sent Larry plummeting back to full-color reality. He spun around, holding the cream-soaked rag in front of his chest, like a shield.

"Wh-what?"

"Oops, sorry Larry."

It was that woman, the loud one, who liked to shout from the back seat, telling him where to turn—"Hey, idiot! You're going the long way!"

When he was driving, Larry could drown her out by turning up the volume on the Walkman. He preferred his human interactions to be framed, well-lit and viewed on a movie or TV screen. He was never sure what to do or say around actual living humans. But here was a female human, rapping on his shoulder with her cane. Larry pressed the pause button on the Walkman.

"Angie? Mrs. Castellano, I mean. What? Are you? I mean, do you need something? I'm about to head home."

Larry voice was high and breathy. He sounded like a refugee from a boys' choir. Angie Castellano smiled; her tongue slid across lips freshly painted a crisp coral.

"Larry, we need to talk."

"We do?" Larry tried to take a step back, but he was pressed against the van, the quivering rag raised. His hands tended to shake when he was nervous.

"Relax, sweetie. I don't bite," Angie said. "I've got a business proposition to discuss."

"Can it wait until tomorrow? I really need to get home. Mother will have dinner waiting."

"You mean Grace? I called her. She said you'd be happy to help. After dinner, of course."

"She did?"

"Your Mom and I were at the Academy back in the day."

"The Academy?" Larry was clueless.

"Holy Names? We were school mates in plaid skirts and knee socks. She never mentioned it?"

Larry wasn't sure what his mother might have mentioned. She did a lot of talking but he didn't always pay attention. Larry only needed to give her an occasional "hmmm…" or a wide-eyed nod and she was happy to keep talking. She never seemed to notice the tiny speakers covering his ears.

"I don't think she mentioned it. I'm kind of busy now."

"I thought it was quitting time?"

"Well, that too. I'm busy and it's quitting time." He tried to sound stern. "Both!"

Larry slid away from the van, putting a few feet between him and Angie Castellano. Hoping to look decisive, he put his hands on his hips. Something felt wrong. Looking down, he saw then rag was pressed to his side. He it let go. It plopped atop one of his Hush Puppies.

Small and round, Larry resembled a well-fed Koala. A fuzz of dark hair retreated from his temples and above his wide, pale forehead. He kept his gray-green eyes, and long, dark lashes—by far his best features—hidden behind black-framed bifocals. In high school, a teacher had written in his yearbook: "Larry has a lovely smile. I wish he'd use it more." But Larry had spent his 50 years on earth trying not to be noticed.

He had worked predictable, low-stress jobs. He'd been an assistant at his aunt's florist shop, office clerk at his uncle's one-man tax preparation office, and for the past 10 years, the van driver at Our Lady, taking residents to doctor's appointments, the Blue Ribbon grocery, or the mall near the football stadium. The mindless work left his imagination free to disappear into the songs on his Walkman or become a character in the black and white movies he watched each night. Movies that always swept him into the middle of the action. Last night, while his mother slept at his side on the couch, Larry had become a wild-eyed Bogie, hiding atop a rocky ridge. Ida Lupino, the femme fatale, was with the cops at the bottom of the hill. She had led them to him, but still, Bogie loved her. Pistol in hand, he rose from his hiding place. The cops put two slugs in his chest as Ida screamed. That, Larry knew, was how a man should die.

In his reveries, Larry never kissed the femme fatales or the sassy secretaries. During his senior year at Jesuit, behind a cluster of trees in Al Lopez Park, Larry had spent ten passionate minutes kissing Jesuit's star running back before the boy ran away. He had ignored Larry the rest of the year. That was the extent of Larry's sexual life.

He could feel Angie's breath on his cheek. Smell her flowered perfume. He grimaced, like her words were weapons.

"Larry, listen to me now. I know you drive the van home at night. So tonight, after dinner, I need you to pick me up at eight. Not in front. Out back here." She pointed down the driveway to the street. "I'll be waiting on the sidewalk just around the corner."

"I can't do that. It's against the rules." Larry wasn't sure if there was a rule, but he had another Bogart video in the queue for tonight after dinner.

Angie unsnapped the hook on her boxy purse, decoupaged with spring flowers. Slipping her hand inside, she came out with a twenty-dollar bill. When Larry made no move to take it, she stuffed it into the pocket of his blue polo shirt, right under the lettering that spelled out "Larry." She tapped his shoulder with her cane.

"Your mom said you'd love to help me. So, we're all set? Right? See you tonight at eight."

One thing I learned from the Sicilians—don't handle your business like it's personal. Ignacio Antinori was going to pay a price for defying me, but I wasn't in a rush. That would have been personal. I filed Antinori away under unfinished business and got back to building my empire.

In just five years, my business was a cash register that brimmed with bills when the slotted drawer snapped out. I couldn't keep a set of books that the cops or the tax man could find. I'd always had a head for figures, and that's where I kept the books. If I needed to see the big picture, I wrote it on a freestanding chalkboard in a spare room at the house I had built on the corner of 17th Avenue and 12th Street. After my morning coffee, which I drank at noon, I'd stand at that board and put down all the numbers from my head, double-checking my math. And when I knew what-was-what, I'd pick up the soft black eraser and sweep away all those incriminating numbers, leaving just a light dusting of snow on the floor.

It all seemed to come naturally to me. When you think about it, the gambling business is a big equation. Addition here. Subtraction there. Knowing the percentages. Figuring the odds. Calculating your risk. Essentially it was a lot of small numbers adding up to some very big ones. Everybody in Tampa loved Bolita. Some spent a little, some spent a lot, and by the late 1920s, most of that money was coming my way.

Another way people in my business got into trouble was forgetting they needed a little income for the tax man. Since Volstead, bar income wasn't legit, but people still needed places to go and spend money. Places that served food. Places with musicians blowing behind matching music stands, and floor shows with sexy dancers in skimpy outfits. What I needed was a high-class nightclub.

I had the name for the place even before I hired an architect to design it. The El Dorado. The name conjured images of a gilded city of great wealth. A secret place the elders whispered about, and adventurers risked death to find. A place where all life's pleasures were on the menu. Or some malarky like that. Truth was, I just wanted to open the best joint in town. Politicians and preachers could put a pretty frame around it, but what's life but a long chase for food, booze, sex, and money? Why not open a place where a man could find all of the above?

For a decade or so, Bernie Saul had owned a three-story brick building on the corner of Eighth Avenue and Fourteenth Street. His store catered to cigar-rolling immigrants newly settled into shotgun houses. He sold them couches, chairs, dining tables, cups, glasses and silverware. He rented rooms on the two upstairs floors, sometimes monthly, but mostly week-to-week, to new arrivals from Cuba, Spain, Sicily, running from poverty, and Jews, from Russia and Romania, who had fled for their lives. In 1925, Saul left dry goods for the garment business. He opened a factory in West Tampa where land was cheaper. We struck a deal for the building.

I hired the best builders and craftsmen in town, bringing specialists in from Savannah and Saint Augustine. Downstairs became a gilded nightclub, with a marble and zinc bar, tables for two and four under black cloths, lit by tapered candles. The ceilings were pressed tin. The floors were Italian marble, except for a hard pine dance floor in front of a stage big enough for a 14-piece dance band, singers, and a dozen showgirls doing high kicks—at 8, 10 and midnight. Drinks were served in ceramic mugs. After they repealed Prohibition, we served drinks in fine crystal. I decided not to do Spanish or Cuban fare—the Columbia already had that business. My kitchen churned out steaks and chops, and an occasional Florida lobster.

I hid the marble staircase to the gaming floor behind double *doors and a wall of maroon velvet curtains. Two of my best muscle guys stood guard, stepping aside only when my club manager gave them a nod. The El Dorado had poker tables mostly, but like the big Cuban casinos, there were tables for blackjack, craps, and a roulette wheel. The floor was carpeted, the walls hung with more velvet curtains that absorbed sound. Over the low buzz of conversation, a man could hear the tinkle of the dice, the snap of a fresh card hitting the table and the whispered encouragement of a languid lady in a long, beaded dress. We drew Tampa's elite and even some visiting celebrities. During spring training, when he wasn't downing Café Diablos in an upstairs room at the Columbia, Babe Ruth watched the floorshow or leaned over the gaming tables.*

Since this was Ybor City, I added a room for dominos. Working men would have dinner with their families, then cluster around my tables, sipping coffee laced with whiskey and smoking fat cigars. They were keeping up an immigrant tradition—men were kings and kings went out at night and played dominos with other kings.

Bernie Saul had rented some third-floor rooms to immigrants. I envisioned a different type of business. One that catered to the gambling trade and the sailors who walked over from the Port of Tampa looking for rent-by-the-hour companionship. My third-floor customers also included many of Tampa's wealthy Episcopalians, Methodists, and Baptists, who loved God and country by day, but preferred to worship other things after dark. I enclosed the wooden staircase on the back of the building, so that men didn't need to pass through the restaurant or the casino to get to the third floor. A red door at the top of the stairs opened into a small bar with gilded mirrors, oil paintings of old-world aristocrats in gilded frames, and leather club chairs. I brought a Creole piano player down from New Orleans. On fainting couches, under slow-turning ceiling fans, reclined the most beautiful women north of Havana.

I learned fast that an operation that included food, booze, performers, bouncers, floor managers, dealers, madams and whores required a lot of attention to detail. I could do it, but I'm a big picture guy. I needed a partner.

Later, after I'd found him, I discovered that I was really looking for a brother. Ever since I'd fled the Tampa Heights house, my brother and sisters had pretended I didn't exist. My mother and father were dead. And you know how I felt about my stepmother. Don't get me wrong, I didn't want my father's straight lifestyle. I loved being Charlie Wall. Someday soon, I told myself, I'd pull up to Ava Corral's Boston address in a black limo and bring her back to enjoy the world I'd created. But before I could do that, I needed a business partner. And just when I needed him, in walked Tito.

Tito Rubio reminded me of William Powell, The Thin Man. He was a classy guy who felt at home around street characters, hustlers and gamblers. There was plenty of money in the city, but at its heart, Tampa was a working-class town where men wore overalls or cheap suits. Not Tito. His brother owned Tampa's best men's shop, complete with an Italian tailor who cut custom suits and shirts to Tito's measurements. He owned half-a-dozen tuxedos, two white dinner jackets, and knew how to tie his own black satin bowtie. You could comb your hair in the reflection off his spit-polished patent leather shoes.

Tito always arrived with a small circle of businessmen, and most nights he was joined by a tall, raven-haired woman in black high heels and a dress slit up the side, exposing legs that went on for days. Tito flashed a fat wad of cash in a silver clasp. His hair was pomaded and parted down the middle. On the street, he wore a black homburg. In a town full of pinky ring thugs, Tito wore a college ring, and a wedding band set with small diamonds, and an art deco Rolex Oyster, secured with a leather band. His fingernails were freshly manicured.

I hired an ex-cop to find out everything about Tito Rubio, but I think I already knew he was the right guy. What sealed the deal was his profession. Tito had worked his way through the University of Florida and come home an accountant. His clients were the cream of Tampa's Hispanic society—including Ava's parents, the Corrals. He had a wife and four children at home, but that didn't slow down his late-night lifestyle. Tito never seemed to sleep.

I had a private table, set two steps above the rest of the bar, wrapped with silver stanchions and purple velvet ropes, so I could see and be seen. The night Tito and I officially met, my maitre'd parted the ropes to let Tito step through. Up close, he was handsome, with deep-set gray eyes and a nose never bent by a fist. He was clean-shaven, smelled of menthol and hair gel. His suit was gray with dark pinstripes. A white rose bud bloomed on his lapel.

"I can't keep it all going," Tito told me, after we'd gotten through the small talk. "People want their accountants up at dawn and available all day. I don't even want to get up before noon."

A tall, skinny Cuban named Raul, the only waiter allowed at my table, appeared with a bottle of champagne and two glasses on a tray. From our raised perch, Tito and I looked out at the crowd clustered around cocktail tables, strands of smoke rising from silver ash trays. Onstage, an eight-piece Cuban band, with a conga pounding frontman, beat out Caribbean rhythms for a kick line of twelve showgirls in ruffles and sarongs. They gyrated so hard that their fake fruit hats jiggled along with their almost bare breasts.

"What you need is a night job," I told him. "I got a good business going here. And it all happens after dark."

Tito pulled a cigarette from a silver case. He took his time, snapping a lighter, exhaling a first puff. "Only if that night job comes with an income that supports my...habits..." Tito lifted his champagne glass. His cufflinks were crusted with tiny diamonds, his fingernails coated in clear polish.

I was wearing my usual—a rumpled seer-sucker suit, white shirt, paisley bow tie, my straw boater upturned on the table. I didn't need to be a sharp-dressed man. My look was more the easy-going southern gentleman who kept forgetting to get his hair cut. It went over well when I dropped off my envelopes at government offices and police stations.

I pulled a note card and a fountain pen from my inside pocket. I wrote a number on the card and beneath it two words: "Times Twelve."

I slid the card across the table. Tito read it with solemn formality, then he tore it into tiny pieces and dropped the detritus into the ashtray where my cigar sat smoldering. I knew he wasn't dismissing my offer. He was destroying the evidence. Tito took another draw on his cigarette, his words flowing out with the circle of smoke.

"When do I start?"

"You've already started."

CHAPTER 26

After Seymour left in search of brooms and shoes, Buster fell back asleep in the folding chair, his rock of a head nodding forward. In his dream a drummer slid brushes across a snare, but he awoke to find it wasn't a drummer, it was Seymour. The little man waltzed around the house, holding a broom like Fred held Ginger. He pushed debris down the hallway and into the open floor of the bathroom. There was plenty of room for trash under the house.

"Sorry for the mess!" Seymour tap-danced through his chores. The broom swung in wide arcs. Trash flew. Roaches took flight. "I wasn't expecting company. You know? I would have cleaned up."

It was late morning and Buster was hungry now, wishing he was back at Our Lady, walking down the long hallway to the cafeteria, where there were eggs and pancakes, and buttered Cuban toast, and mugs full of café con leche, and a seat at a round table next to Angie Castellano. What else could a man ask for? He wondered if she had noticed when he didn't show up for breakfast.

"Hungry," Buster said, as much to himself as to Seymour. "Need food."

Seymour stopped sweeping and turned around. A single chocolate-colored roach perched, like a winged epaulet, on his left shoulder.

"Food? Cuisine? Sustenance? Of course, how rude! I've lived here alone too long. Forgotten my manners. Totally forgotten. You are my guest and what I have I am happy to share."

Moments later, in the shell of a kitchen, Seymour produced

a can of Vienna sausages.

Seymour peeled back the tin lid. Two smudged fingers pushed into the goo, coming out with a wiggly minnow of meat, coated in salmon-colored phlegm. Buster felt his stomach flip as his new roommate gummed the sausage.

"There's four more. Help yourself!" Wet nuggets of pink meat clung to Seymour's lips.

"Not hungry now, but later, maybe. Is there someplace around here that sells food? And coffee? Coffee would be good."

Seymour pinioned another wiener, waving it at Buster like a snot-covered worm.

"There is what the locals call a bodega two blocks away. With a sandwich counter and a coffee pot. Filthy place. Run by this fat troll who sits on her stool all day dipping snuff. Disgusting. There was an unfortunate incident. Not my fault, but I've been banned. You. You could go. Just watch out for flying tobacco. And please don't mention my name."

Buster backed out of the kitchen. He needed to get away from this strange little man. He also wanted to brush his teeth and wash his face. Why hadn't he thought to bring a toothbrush or his razor? The plan that had seemed so good when he was on the recliner at Our Lady, now seemed to be unraveling.

Back in the living room, Buster pulled on his heavy shoes, wincing as he tied the laces. Seymour appeared at the end of the hallway, holding the sausage tin. "And I'm sorry about the shoes. They're coming. Just takes a little more searching."

The sickly-sweet smell of the Vienna sausages, mixed with the skunk smell of Seymour's bedding was making Buster dizzy. He was outside quickly. The street was quiet. Only a ragged dog asleep on a front porch across the street. Buster felt his stomach calming. Maybe he could handle this crazy house and this crazy roommate for a couple of days, while he figured out the right time and place to kill Charlie Wall.

* * *

"You don't have to live there. You know that, right?"

Katrina's lips were at his ear. It was almost 2 a.m. and Trip was drifting off after a half-hour of naked gymnastics, his eyes closed, his head on the lacy pillowcase, his tree-trunk body—sheened with sweat—swaddled in Katrina's butter-soft sheets.

"Hmmm?" He hoped a non-answer might give her the message—I'm falling asleep here. Now a regular guest in Katrina's airy apartment in Upstairs South, a cluster of spacious rooms above an Ybor City jewelry store, Trip knew his ploy would fail. When Katrina had something on her mind, she was a dog with a bone. In a moment of after-glow, he had told her about the arrow and Charlie's wet trousers. He'd hoped for a laugh. He was wrong.

"Did you hear me?" She had rolled out of bed and looked back at Trip. She wasn't whispering anymore.

Trip reached for a pillow that had fallen to the floor. Sitting up, he nestled the pillow behind his head. "I heard you."

Katrina was naked, her body honey-gold in the flickering light of the bedside candle. Looking at her, Trip felt himself stirring. He loved how Katrina's black hair tumbled thick to her shoulders, framing a face that was all sharp angles—nose, cheekbones, chin—softened by long lashes and arched, bristling eyebrows. He loved how her skin stretched taut over a grid-work of bones he could trace with his fingers or his tongue—the two narrow rods at the base of her neck, a cascade of ribs leading down to the angled ledges of her hipbones.

After their first night together, Trip had called his younger brother, another refugee from the Armstrong clan, who currently shared a Mission District warehouse with dozens of San Francisco artists, his bed a fireman's catch net hanging 10 feet off the floor. Trip told Doug to imagine a combination of Chrissie Hynde and Patti Smith.

"And this Chrissie-Patti girl likes you? Sounds like the kind of artsy type who'd go for a Ramone or that guy from The Cars. But you? A cross between Meat Loaf and Ozzie?"

"I consider myself more of a plus-sized David Byrne, but whatever, she likes me. At least she acts like she does."

"And you like her? That's a first."

"I'm starting to like liking someone."

And lately, *like* had developed into something that might be love, a feeling that lingered even when Katrina had him on the defensive.

"What's wrong with Charlie?" he asked her.

"What's right with Charlie? Come on, Trip! This is getting bizarre. An arrow? Are you kidding me?"

Trip shook his head. He wished he could take back the arrow story.

"It was kind of your idea." Like an infantryman who hears the metallic click of the land mine under his boot, Trip knew an explosion was coming.

"Oh no you don't! Don't put this on me!" She backed away from the bed, her eyes wide. "I said to cheer him up, not stage some Grand Guignol performance piece with a fucking arrow. A few inches either way, and you're dead or he's dead. Jesus, Trip!"

"Look, it made him happy. It got him out of his funk. Anyway, it's important to him."

"It's important to him to think someone is trying to kill him?"

"It's important to him to think he's still important."

Katrina put her hands on her hips but said nothing. She's so clever, Trip thought, knowing the right moments to stay silent, letting his words dangle, like week-old bananas on a hook, ripening into absurdity.

He had gotten straight for Katrina, as much as for himself. But conversations like this made Trip question that decision. Wasn't it better to glide through life in a drugged-up haze than to face the reality that what you were saying or doing didn't make a lot of sense?

Katrina settled on the edge of the bed. Her voice was softer. "And you're in a bar with the guy every night? I worry about that. I mean, you know..."

Trip hadn't come close to falling back into his old habits, so

Katrina's concern was more annoying than helpful. "Drinking was never my weakness, you know that." He tried to figure out how to get back to that sweet after-glow moment. "If I'm not working for Charlie, what am I gonna do for money? I can't go back to my old business."

Katrina cocked her head to give him "the look." Trip knew what she wasn't saying. She was a poet, but she was also a practical, Midwestern girl, from Dayton. Family mattered. And in a pinch, family helped. Trip could apologize to his father and stepmother, promise to restart college, or get a straight job, and he'd have access to plenty of money. But Trip wasn't ready to apologize to anyone or to restart his privileged life. Like his new boss, he'd never felt at home in that world, his future laid out in narrow, well-tended rows.

Katrina leaned toward him, her hand settling on his cheek. "I love you, but what you're doing with the old man doesn't make a lot of sense."

Trip raised his hand and covered hers. "There's a book there. With him. You told me to write about something real. There's nobody more real than Charlie."

"He's so real you have to find somebody to pretend to kill him?"

There she was again, he thought, delivering one of those jabs he couldn't parry. "I'm on to something here, Kat. Really."

Katrina kept her back to him as she slipped on a silk robe, covered in pale roses. When she turned, Trip could see her mind working, as she chose her words.

"Look, I went to the library. Did some research. This guy is dangerous. He's killed people or had them killed. People tried to murder him four times and that's just the ones we know about. And my boyfriend is this guy's bodyguard!"

"Nobody wants to kill him now," Trip offered meekly.

"Nobody you know of. But you're at his side every night. If somebody wanted to shoot him, you'd be in the line of fire."

"It's not like that. Charlie's a relic. He's harmless. And what else do I have to write about? My life? A decade or more floating atop a psychedelic inner tube? All that gave me was some bad poems."

"I can't argue with that last bit." Katrina came back to the bedside. "Look, I've lost enough people I love. I don't want to lose you too."

"I can handle this. And when I'm done, I'll have a book. A real goddam book."

"And when are you going to let me see it?"

They had talked a lot about the book, but Trip hadn't shared any of it with Katrina, afraid some well-meaning criticism might dim his enthusiasm. He wanted to finish first. Charlie was a novel, he knew that much. Hell, Charlie might be a bestseller. And more than that, Charlie was a fellow traveler—a prodigal son from a wealthy Tampa family. Another refugee from the straight world. He had to finish telling Charlie's story.

"You'll be the first reader, when it's ready."

Katrina walked to the far side of the wide studio, to her simple kitchen. Trip saw that the storm had passed.

"You want something to eat?" She pulled open the tiny refrigerator. "I'm suddenly starving."

CHAPTER 27

I t had been seven years since Ava had slipped out of my room above Dirty Joe's. Now, with the El Dorado open, and my Bolita business booming—the mountains of cash overflowing my safety deposit boxes, my Cuban bank accounts and my private hiding places—it was finally time to reach out. I could take care of her now. I could give her anything she wanted.

One of the cops on my payroll got me an address in Boston. On a cool morning in May, I wrote Ava a love letter. I planned to mail it at the downtown post office, after I finished the Sunday Tribune.

"Mr. and Mrs. Enrique Corral, owner of Corral Tobacco International, are proud to announce the wedding of their daughter, Ava Corral, to Mr. Henry Dalton Merrill, of Cambridge, Massachusetts. The couple were wed on May 1, 1925, at Most Holy Redeemer Church in Boston, and honeymooned in Cuba. Henry and Ava Merrill live in Cambridge, where Henry is completing his surgical residency."

I couldn't read any more. I wadded up the paper and the letter and threw them across the room. I had made my fortune for Ava. She had never said she'd give up her life to be with me, but knowing I didn't get a chance to make her an offer was a gut punch.

That's the first time I remember falling into a well so deep I couldn't see a trace of light above me. I let Tito run the business and I retreated to the bedroom of my Ybor house. Tito assigned armed guards to protect me day and night. Waiters from the El Dorado brought food and coffee, but I couldn't eat or drink. For a month I sat in an old rocking chair, staring out though the iron bars of my bedroom window.

It was Tito who got me out of my chair. He arrived late one Friday afternoon with a bottle of Tennessee whiskey and a folding map of Florida. He insisted that I join him on the back porch. He wore a pin-striped suit. I was still in my terry-cloth robe and house slippers.

We sat side by side, across a wicker table. I had spent a month looking east from my bedroom window. The porch looked west. The sun was setting behind the pitched roofs. I traced intricate patterns in the criss-crossing telephone and electric lines as the sky turned the color of ripe peaches.

Tito tapped the map to draw my eyes there. With one of his kid's crayons, he had colored in my Bolita empire. The large red circle took in both sides of Tampa Bay. It spread east to Orlando, north to Brooksville and south to Sarasota.

"You like this?" Tito said. "It's what you did. And if you don't get your ass out of that room, you're going to lose it."

Tito was right. I had built this thing. Now, there were lots of guys ready to take it away. That's the problem with being on top—there's always jerks who think they should be savoring that incredible view and not you. And when those jerks are Sicilian mobsters, they'll do whatever it takes to knock you off your perch.

Tito filled our glasses and threw back his shot of whiskey. I picked up the crystal glass. I held it an inch from my mouth, letting the warm, spicy smell reach my nose.

"Go ahead, Boss. Drink up."

I winced as it hit my throat, but then it rushed through me, sending an electric current down to the fingers and toes. I stood up and brushed my hair down. I patted Tito on his shoulder and returned to my bedroom. Back in the rocker, I allowed myself to savor the pain for one more hour. Then, I filed it away.

I called the club and asked for Tito.

"Yeah boss?"

"Stick around, will ya. I'll be there in an hour."

I took a hot shower, staying under the stinging water until it turned tepid. During my weeks in my room, I had grown a sparse, salt-and-pepper beard. I lathered up and shaved it off. I *would see a barber the next day, but that night, I doubled-up on the pomade, combing my long hair back like Tito's, before hiding it under the straw boater.*

A bodyguard drove me across Ybor to the El Dorado. It was 10 p.m. A black jazz band from New Orleans was blowing, the dance floor was full, the bar and the tables crammed with Friday night revelers. The doorman, in his military style red suit, with gold buttons and epaulets, smiled when I approached. "Welcome back, Mr. Wall," he said.

* * *

Once I was back among the living, I pushed Ava from my thoughts. I'd missed that opportunity. But I hadn't missed any others. When the country fell into a depression, my revenues increased. Everybody needed a jackpot.

With all that money jingling in my pockets, and others with nothing or less than nothing, I felt guilty. About once a week, Johnny drove me to the children's home or the soup kitchen downtown. I stuffed the pockets of my white linen suit with silver half-dollars and passed them out to the orphans or the shuffling men and women waiting in line for a bowl of watery soup and some day-old bread. Everybody knew what I did for a living, but to people who were hungry, out of work, and losing their homes to the banks, I was a folk hero, like Dillinger or Bonnie and Clyde. And I wasn't robbing banks! All I was doing was giving the people some fun and a chance to win some much-needed cash. And I didn't mind sharing my good fortune. To the members of my highfalutin' family, I was still the black sheep, but on the streets of Tampa, working-class folks called me "The White Shadow."

The only people who didn't appreciate the world Charlie Wall had built were the damn Sicilians. In 1931, Ignacio Antinori's distillery mysteriously burned to the ground. Cops called it arson. I called it a business decision. A decision made, not in haste or anger, but with cool calculation. Losing the distillery hurt Antinori, and naturally, the cagey Sicilian retaliated. I had covered all the angles, and I never saw his revenge coming.

One night, after closing time, a smoky fire broke out in Dirty Joe's gaming room. Joe was stretched out upstairs with a needle in his arm. They found his body the next day. I called Boza's and ordered up the works: the best mahogany box, the full funeral service, and a plot under a granite headstone at Oaklawn. Only a few people showed up for the funeral mass, but I figured I owed that much to Dirty Joe. Meanwhile, I plotted my next move.

I'm not a violent man. I don't want to hurt anyone. But I've got to protect what's mine. I can't stand by and let the jerks kill my friends and attack my businesses.

A few months later, one of Antinori's bag men died in the alley behind the family speakeasy, a splatter of buckshot in his belly. By this time, Ignacio had partnered with Santo Trafficante Sr., and they had grown a Bolita operation almost as big as mine. They were also making money on bootlegging and whores, and they peddled heroin in the dark parts of town.

Personally, I thought there was enough business for everybody. I had opened my own distillery during Prohibition and kept it going after liquor was legal again. A few of my colored Bolita bookies were selling dope and cutting me in for a piece of the action. Everyone can prosper on the west coast of Florida; that was my motto. But the Sicilians never saw it that way. I was making money and they wanted it—at any cost.

Things got bloodier.

First, Sicilian thugs blew a hole in the head of one of my Boliteros. They fled with a few thousand of my dollars. We took out one of Antinori's bag men when his big maroon Buick was stopped for a light. It was a tit for tat war, aimed at the lower-level guys. But then, Antinori raised the stakes. I was on my front porch, reading the newspaper, when someone fired at me, sniper-style.

After that, somebody shot at one of Ignacio's beefy sons while he stuffed his greasy puss with a deviled crab from a cart on 15th Street. Paulo Antinori was a very big target, but somehow, the buckshot missed.

A few months later, in my front yard, a man with a shotgun stepped out of the shadows. Johnny Rivera pushed me to the ground. His quick reaction saved my life. I escaped with just a little buckshot in my forearm and Johnny took some pellets in his side. He managed to unload his revolver at the shooter. Later, we found splatters of blood on the sidewalk, but the gunman had disappeared. We didn't waste time looking for him. When you needed to hit somebody in Tampa you brought in a guy from New York, Chicago, or Boston. When the job was done, they dropped the weapon in the river or the bay and left town.

The next night, I was back at the El Dorado, my arm wrapped in bandages. I joked about the shootout using a term I'd heard from one of my colored bag men, who had also escaped a shooting with only a flesh wound. "The slugs didn't hit me—they just glimpsed me."

Truth was, I wasn't worried about getting whacked. Somewhere in the back of my mind, I was still that little boy, freshly baptized, who had God's assurance he would live forever. But God helps those who help themselves. I took precautions to prevent another "glimpse."

I spent more time in my secure apartment on the top floor of the El Dorado. When I was at home, Johnny and Joe took turns sleeping in the back bedroom, with a small arsenal stacked by the front door.

Knowing they couldn't hit me at home, the Sicilians came after me on the road. It was around dusk on a Wednesday in the summer of 1934. Johnny was driving me to a rendezvous with a U.S. Senator when a black Packard sedan pulled up behind us on Palm Avenue. A shotgun blast shattered my back windows, bathing Johnny and me in shards of safety glass, but somehow none of the buckshot hit us.

The sedan raced up alongside. There were two men inside, both in dark suits and black fedoras. The passenger pointed a shotgun through the open window. Johnny slammed on the brakes and threw the Cadillac into reverse. We heard the shotgun blast, but we weren't hit. The Packard spun around and came at us head on. Johnny set his shotgun up on the dashboard and fired, first shattering our windshield, then the Packard's.

I mean, picture this, our car has no front or rear windows, and Johnny is firing a shotgun, driving in reverse at 50 miles per hour, dodging cars coming from behind, and still smoking his Camel. Johnny ultimately betrayed me, but I will always give him credit—he was a hell of a driver. I carry a .38 Special in my waistband. I got off six shots from the passenger's seat, though I'm not sure I hit anything. I'm a terrible shot, even when I'm not going backward in a speeding car.

Johnny and I ran out of bullets. Cars were clustered behind the Cadillac. Johnny slammed on the brakes. The big black sedan barreled straight for us. Just when I could read the letters on the hood the Packard spun out of control and bounced up over the high sidewalk in front of the Church of the Holy Redeemer, flattening two tires.

One of us must have hit somebody. The chase was over. Johnny and I sat in the middle of Palm Avenue for a long beat, the world suddenly silent. Even the cars waiting behind us knew not to blow their horns. My hand was shaking, and I couldn't make it to stop. My empty Colt dropped to the floorboard. I looked over at Johnny. His prize-fighter face was framed in black curls. He took a final drag on his cigarette, then flashed me a sly grin.

We aren't going to die, that grin said. Not today.

Johnny blew out a cloud of gray smoke and popped the Cadillac into first gear. He blasted the horn and eased around the smoking Packard.

Ten minutes later, I sat with a United States Senator in a private dining room at the Floridan Hotel.

But that's a story for another day.

CHAPTER 28

"There's this thing and I need some help."

It was morning. Buster had returned from the bodega and awakened Seymour, who slouched against the living room wall.

"My help?" Seymour's voice was choked and gravely.

"That's what I said already. I need your help. With a thing."

Seymour leaned his head back and gargled, without water. He spit a wet wad of something into his hand and wiped it on his pants. And just like that, Seymour was his normal, over-stimulated self.

"A thing? Like a big thing? A little thing?" Seymour rocked on his heels. "I mean, is it your thing? My thing?"

"Stop!" Buster summoned his best tough-guy baritone.

"Sorry. Stopping. Now." Seymour's arms hung limply at his sides, his fingers rising and falling, like a pianist running scales.

"It's a money thing. This guy named Charlie owes me. He welched. I need to get close to him. Get my money back."

Seymour offered a mostly toothless smile. "A confrontation? A financial transaction? A bad debt made good? I like all of that. What can I do? I'm rested. I'm ready. Just name it."

"I need a scout. Best he don't see me until I'm ready to get up in his face. So, you scout things out. Can you do that?"

"Not a problem. You can see me right now, but when I concentrate, I can become completely invisible. It's a talent. Served me well tracking the Viet Cong through the rice paddies. They'd hear my footsteps, but I was just a mist. A cloud." Seymour snapped his fingers. "I'm the invisible man!"

Buster had decided to indulge his roommate's flights of fantasy.

"Invisible is good."

The little man rocked back and forth on his heels. Seymour's head nodded eagerly, his sunken eyes darting left and right.

"Listen now," Buster said. "I gotta know when he leaves the house and when he comes home. I gotta know who is with him? Driver? Bodyguard? That kind a thing."

"So, the time he leaves? The time he returns? Ah, well, the thing is, ah...you know how I feel about time?"

"Remind me." Buster said.

"It's a myth. A tick-tock trap. A construct we create to build our own prison cells. A hallucination—"

"ENOUGH!" Buster shouted. "If you want to be part of this, you need to deal with time. Just for a few days. Can you do that?"

"Right. Check. Can do. Give me a ...well, you know...a moment."

Scrambling to his corner of the room, Seymour lifted the orange crate. He kept a menagerie of junk underneath—screwdrivers, a ball of twine, fingernail clippers, a small glass heart, and other items that Buster couldn't make out. Turning back, he held out a small wristwatch, on a gold, flexible band.

Seymour was frantically winding the watch, muttering to himself: "Time waits for no man. No time like the present. Time is on my side. The best of times, the worst of times...."

He lifted the watch to his ear to make sure it was ticking. Bringing the watch face up close to his own, Seymour yanked the tiny rotor, which snapped out a fraction of an inch. Clasping the knob with two dirty digits, he gave Buster a cock-eyed stare.

"Do you happen to know what time it is—right now?"

* * *

"So where are we going? Is it close?" Larry was not happy driving Our Lady's van after hours. "I really shouldn't be out here, you know. The rules about use of this van are very specific."

Next to Larry in the passenger seat, Angie grimaced. As a young woman without her own children, she'd never had patience for other people's obnoxious kids. Now, well into her '70s, she had even less patience for this babbling man-child.

"This isn't my van, you understand. It's the company van. I just drive it home and back. It's a perk. I mean, they called it a perk. See when I started–"

Angie decided it was time to use her "outside" voice.

"JUST DRIVE!"

Larry was quiet for five seconds. "See when I started…"

Angie slapped her hands together. With the windows up, the clap was like a gunshot, echoing through the van. Larry jumped; his teddy bear belly pushed against his lap belt. "What I mean is…"

Angie clapped again, silencing Larry. This time, her voice was a snarl.

"I said drive…"

Despite Larry's babbling, Angie was excited to be outside of Our Lady, and not on her way to a doctor or a movie theater. Before leaving she had made up her face—the base, the eye shadow and liner, and her favorite coral lipstick—a little, but not too much. She had wrapped her hair in a pink silk scarf and let a few strands push out at her forehead and around her neck. Now, out at night in the van, she felt young and free. Like a girl on a first date.

She wasn't sure where Buster might be hiding but like most people who'd grown up in Ybor City, Angie knew where to find Charlie Wall's house. Before they drove there, she wanted to cruise the ten city blocks that had been the heart of Tampa's Latin Quarter, where she had gone to movies and restaurants and shops and nightclubs; where she had jostled along sidewalks thick with Spaniards, Cubans, Sicilians and Eastern European Jews, their voices harmonizing in the scrambled polyglot that passed for a common language in the immigrant enclave. She missed the smell of the car exhaust, the jangling bell of the streetcar and the shouts of the vendors, selling hard candy on a stick or deviled crabs from a hot box on wheels. But the reality didn't match her memories. The department stores, the hat shops, the hardware stores, the laundries, the street vendors were gone.

A low-lying fog had seeped in from the port a few blocks to the south. It cocooned the old globe streetlights in glistening webs, their muted glow promising a night of mystery or romance. Angie knew the fog was a mask, hiding missing bricks, cracked stucco, and broken glass. She closed her eyes, and she was with Ferdie, her new boyfriend, walking arm-in-arm to the Sunday afternoon tea dance at *La Union Italiano*.

Larry's high tenor yanked her from her reverie.

"Where are we going? Seems like we're just cruising here."

Angie started to yell but she couldn't manage it. A sob caught in her throat. She reached into her purse for the silk handkerchief. She had not planned to cry tonight but she couldn't stop the tears.

* * *

Looking over, Larry cringed. The strange woman was crying. He didn't mind when actors cried after a sad or tragic scene in a movie, but real-life tears frightened him.

He gripped the wheel and squinted at the road ahead. Larry never drove at night. The glare of the headlights left him scared and confused. Barely 50 years old, Larry considered himself an old man.

The woman dabbed at her tears and told him to drive north, under the highway overpass. In the neighborhoods, she gave him block by block instructions, until she shouted: "That's it!"

The van stopped in front of a big frame house that took up most of a corner lot. The lot was wrapped by a low, carved-block fence, topped with iron spikes. A roof-top security light flashed on, reminding Larry of the guard tower searchlights in a prison-break movie.

"Oh, for God's sake," Angie said, "don't stop in front. Pull around the corner."

Larry followed orders.

"Now turn it around, and park under that tree, so we can see the front of the house, but he can't see us."

Larry eased into an alley, then backed out. He parked the van with its nose pointing east, in the shadow thrown by a massive oak. From here, they had a clear view of the house, stark in the glow of the security light. They sat in silence for a while until Larry summoned the courage to speak again.

"My mother says she didn't really know you that well at Holy Names."

Angie's voice was gentle now. "Your mother was always nice to me. I wasn't that popular with the other Academy girls. But the Jesuit boys liked me."

Larry didn't like thinking about his days at Jesuit, where he was ridiculed for his doughboy body, his girlish voice, and his complete lack of skill in any sport. He had been enamored with a couple of the Jesuit boys but, except for one brief encounter, he was always too shy and scared to do anything about it.

"Can you tell me what we're doing out here?"

"You don't know who lives in that house?"

Larry shook his head.

"Your mother never mentioned Charlie Wall to you?"

"Wasn't he some kind of mobster? But he's dead, right?"

"He's not dead. And keeping him alive is kind of the reason we're here."

Larry's eyes widened. Angie turned to face him.

"Your mother says you like mysteries."

"Sure. Gumshoes. Film noir. Hitchcock. All that."

Angie slid close to him on the wide bench seat. Larry could smell her crisp, gardenia scent.

"I'll tell you a mystery story, but you need to promise it stays between us. Can you promise me that?"

Larry nodded. "Uh...okay."

"Not even your mother..."

"Not even my mother.".

Angie leaned closer, her voice a whisper. "It's an old Tampa mystery. In 1955, two men tried to kill Charlie Wall. He didn't die, but one of the shooters did. And one got away. It was a long time ago. A real-life who-almost-dun-it that the cops never solved. And now, the one that got away has gone missing. I think he might be planning to finish what he started 30 years ago."

"Finish how exactly?" Larry felt a twinge of excitement deep in his gut.

"I'm not sure. But it could be bad."

"You mean gunfire?"

Angie nodded solemnly.

"And this time Charlie Wall might die?

Angie nodded again.

"Wait. I don't understand. What's our role in all this? Are we the detectives?"

"You could say that. We're trying to keep the incident, the bad thing, from happening. Trying to keep someone from doing something he shouldn't. And to do that, we need to stake out this house."

"It's going to happen here?"

"I think so. Anyway, that's my hunch."

Larry swallowed hard. The story grabbed him. This wasn't a movie. He was part of an actual plot. Larry's first response to any out-of-the-ordinary situation was fear, but this was different. He'd watched plenty of detectives tuck fear into their back pockets and stride directly into harm's way. All in black and white on his home TV. Maybe, he could do the same thing in the actual, living-color world.

Larry?" Angie asked. "Are you with me?"

"Larry?"

Larry took a long breath. He realized he had been furiously tapping his foot on the floorboard. He willed it to stop. He wanted to do this.

"Can I ask another question?"

Angie nodded.

Larry looked over. Angie's face was lit by the glow from Charlie's house. He liked her coral lipstick. He liked how the scarf wrapped her hair, a few gray strands falling across her forehead. The tears had smudged her make-up, but Angie looked like what she was—an aging femme fatale.

"Do you really think there will be gunplay?"

"Maybe. But nobody will be shooting at us. At least, I hope not."

The security light on Charlie's rooftop snapped off. Angie's face disappeared. He felt her pat his arm. "Larry, are you with me?"

A Latin bandleader was pounding on a conga drum in Larry's chest.

He started his breathing exercises; a technique he'd used in the past to halt sudden panic attacks. In. Out. Repeat. In. Out. Repeat. After a few moments, the conga player took a break. Through the open van window Larry listened to the hum of traffic from the nearby highway.

"Okay then." He looked over at Angie. He hoped he sounded like Bogie. "I'm in!"

"Then we're partners," Angie said. "I like that."

CHAPTER 29

The Cadillac eased to a stop in the driveway. The security light snapped on. Angie watched as the young driver emerged, his plaid shirt stretched over a wide chest, his head low on his shoulders. He could have been a lineman for Jesuit, Angie thought. The driver turned in a slow circle, staring hard at the dark houses along 12th Street, then glancing toward 17th Avenue, where the van sat in the shadows. He stepped around the car and opened the passenger door. A lanky scarecrow emerged.

"That's Charlie Wall!" Angie whispered.

The old man wore a seersucker suit and a straw hat that hadn't been in style for decades. His features were whited out by the light, but he walked with the clutching, hesitant steps of an old man.

The driver said something to him, and both looked in the direction of the van.

Angie raised her index finger to her lips. "Shhhhhhh…"

Charlie shook his head and continued toward the house, the driver beside him, shielding him from the van with his body. They were inside for less than a minute when the young man emerged, holding a golf club and a flashlight.

"I think he's coming to check us out," Larry whispered.

The wide silver beam swept left and right, as the driver opened the front gate. He was soon on the sidewalk, his pace quickening. Angie reached over and unhooked Larry's seat belt. She pulled him across the bench seat, and into a tight embrace. When the inside of the van filled with light, Angie's lips were mashed against Larry's. Her tongue probed his mouth. Her fingernails dug into his back.

"Oh, gosh. Excuse me!"

The young man was at the passenger window. Angie lifted her mouth from Larry's and looked over.

"Please, don't tell my husband!"

The flashlight snapped off.

"Sorry. Very sorry." He backed away from the window. "Please, uh, you know, ah, carry on."

Angie yanked Larry back into an embrace. When she glanced over her shoulder, the young man was back on Charlie's front porch. When he was inside the house, she pushed Larry away with both hands. He slipped off the seat and onto the floor, the steering wheel pressing against the back of his head.

"What?" Larry stammered.

"You were liking that a little too much." Angie reached up to straighten her scarf. "Get us out of here. Now."

Larry squirmed off the floor, his belly just fitting under the steering wheel. Angie stared into the lighted mirror on the back of the visor, wiping off her smeared lipstick with a handkerchief. Larry pulled down his visor, but there was no mirror or light.

"Trust me, you're a mess." Angie flipped her visor back into place. "And you're not that good a kisser either. You need practice, but not with me."

Larry ran a palm over his mouth. He pulled the rear-view mirror around so he could see his face. Angie yanked the mirror back into place.

"Enough with that! We're leaving. But not too fast. Just start the van and ease us away from here."

* * *

Trip lifted one of the venetian blinds on the window facing 17th Street. He had left the living room lights off. Charlie was already in bed.

The van slowly pulled away, the lights off. When the van was two blocks away the headlights snapped on. Why would that kissing couple do that? It didn't make sense.

"Anything?" Trip jumped at his master's voice. He'd thought the old man was down for the night.

Charlie had been in fine form earlier, finishing off four old fashioneds, telling Trip a half dozen dirty jokes on the way home—"Okay, three guys walk into a whorehouse, a rabbi, a priest and Herbert Hoover..."—jokes as stale as the air in Charlie's old Cadillac. When Charlie got this drunk, he always disappeared quickly down the hall. Trip didn't see him again until at least noon the next day. But here he was, his face ashen, his paisley silk robe, drawn tight about his lanky frame, his bony calves bare, his feet stuffed into soft slippers. Trip was so surprised to see him, he forgot Charlie had asked a question.

"So? Was it anything? Wake up son!"

Charlie flipped the light switch, and the room went daylight bright. Trip covered his eyes.

"I don't know," Trip parted his fingers slowly, adjusting to the glare. "It was a couple, a mousy guy with an older woman, making out in the front seat. She asked me not to tell her husband."

"You know her husband?"

"Hell no. I think maybe that's just what came out of her mouth when she saw my flashlight. Or maybe it was an act. I don't know. Something's not right."

"Well, we know that much already, don't we? Freakin' phone calls. That arrow just above my head. It's heating up again." Charlie rubbed his hands together, a crooked, toothy smile rearranging the wrinkles on his skeletal face. "Just like the old days."

As the guy who hired the archer and made the threatening phone calls, Trip knew nothing was really going on. Or was it?

"I don't know," Trip said. "They looked harmless."

But something was troubling him. While he was doing his bodyguard charade, before opening Charlie's door, he had seen something in his peripheral vision—a small man, scampering away down the dark street, hunched over, arms rising and falling like paddles, or like the flapping wings of a bird.

Trip decided he was being paranoid. A condition he remembered well from his drug days. It was all easily explained. Bums squatted in some of the empty houses. And if someone wanted a dark block for an illicit make-out session, Charlie's was a good choice.

Of course, Trip didn't want to tell Charlie it was nothing. Better to use these odd incidents to keep his innocent game going.

Moments later, he faced Charlie in the living room.

"So, was it something?" The old man asked. "Or nothing?"

"Maybe something. Maybe not. Hard to say. I don't know why that couple would pick our street for a romantic rendezvous, and I'm pretty sure somebody was hiding behind an old oak tree on 12th. When I spotted him, he ran off. I mean, I think it was a him—what I saw was some kind of small, strange-looking humanoid."

"Humanoid?" Charlie cleared his throat with a guttural "harumph." "But this humanoid creature is gone?"

Trip nodded.

"And the van is gone."

"Yeah. Really, I wouldn't worry about it." He didn't want to overplay his hand. "It all seemed pretty harmless."

"Easy for you to say," Charlie snapped. "They're not trying to kill you."

Trip almost wanted to tell him—it's a hoax. I made it up. You're on nobody's hit list. Instead, he walked to the front door and picked up his 8-iron, waving it in Charlie's direction.

"Don't worry boss," Trip smiled. "I'm on it."

Charlie gave him a tight smile. With both hands, he brushed strands of hair away from his face. "Just when you think it's all behind you and nobody gives a hoot, it comes racing back. Charlie Wall may not be such a relic after all."

The old man released a guttural burb, then padded down the hall. Trip felt his paranoia rising again. He was no bodyguard, he knew that. He refused to wield any weapon except his 8-iron. If somebody did want to kill Charlie, could he do anything to stop it? Was he willing to throw himself in front of a bullet for his boss?

Trip wished someone had given him a handbook for bodyguards. He was making it up as he went along.

* * *

Buster was in his lawn chair in the living room when he heard Seymour's footfalls on the creaky porch, back from his first night as a scout. Buster closed his eyes, feigning sleep. The door groaned, as Seymour slipped in. There was more creaking, this time on the wood floor of the living room, and the reek that said Seymour was close by. The little man cleared his throat, which sounded like someone gargling over a bathroom sink.

Buster opened his eyes. Seymour needed no further encouragement. He barked out a full report—the Cadillac appeared at 9:33. The bodyguard scanned the neighborhood, then helped the old man into the house.

"...and then bodyguard guy came out with a flashlight and a golf club. I was expecting violence, but he looked in the van window and backed away."

"Wait, there was a van?"

"On the side street. Yes. Definitely a van."

"With people inside?"

"Two, I think. It was dark."

"And then what happened?"

"The big bodyguard went back to the house, and the van drove off."

Standing at attention in front of Buster, Seymour could have been a soldier, fresh from battle, reporting to his superior officer.

"And nobody saw you?"

"I told you. I was invisible."

CHAPTER 30

When a sitting United States Senator reaches out, you don't cancel just because some thugs tried to gun you down on the way.

Barely ten minutes after the car chase and gunfight on Palm Avenue, Johnny and I pushed through the revolving doors of the Floridan Hotel, in the heart of Tampa's downtown. We stopped in the hotel bar, where I tossed back two fingers of rye. I felt my heart slowing down. The highball glass was steady in my hand. That didn't surprise me. I was so damn exhilarated after the shootout that I needed a drink to manage a normal conversation.

Park Trammel met me upstairs, in a plush private room, with carved wainscoting, long jade-colored curtains and a carpet as soft as a Florida beach. You could get to the meeting room without passing the main dining room and bar. People loved me in Tampa, but it still wasn't smart for a U.S. Senator to be seen with a gangster, even a cracker one like me.

Trammel stood as I approached. He was stout and rosy cheeked, with a fine headful of hair, slicked back in the current style and parted down the middle. His wool suits came from Savile Row in London. His cufflinks were diamond studs. It was no wonder he needed to supplement his official income.

During his first term as governor, Trammel had been a reliable friend. After that, he was Florida's attorney general, the state's top law enforcement official. That just meant his price went up. He won a seat in the U.S. Senate, but his re-election in 1934 was not assured. A New Deal upstart named Claude Pepper was challenging him in the Democratic primary. (In those days everybody was a Democrat, so the winner of the primary won the race.) Pepper was a reformer, who gave a heck of a stump speech. I kind of liked Claude Pepper, but he wasn't on my payroll. Trammel was.

That night, Scarface Johnny stood guard in the hall outside the private room, along with two young Senate aides in matching tan suits. Inside, the senator and I ate rare steak and lobster tails. He ordered a bottle of French wine. We never talked money or elections. That would have been rude.

"Washington is a hell hole," Trammel said after we sat down. "I liked Tallahassee much better. The governor's job came with a mansion a few steps from the capitol. You have any idea how much it costs to live in D.C?"

I said I did. I didn't tell him I was supplementing the income of two other members of Congress. I asked about his wife and children. He inquired about my health.

"I'm just peachy." I didn't mention the incident on Palm Avenue. "There are certain people in Tampa who would like to see my name on a headstone in Oaklawn Cemetery, but I refuse to comply. You could say the devil takes care of his own."

Trammel laughed and waved his arm for the waiter to bring the cigars and brandy. He was putting on the dog for me, knowing at the end of the night, I'd be the one picking up the bill.

Trammel never asked me for anything at our meetings. I knew what he wanted, and I was happy to comply. It wasn't money he was after, even though Johnny had already slipped an envelope into the pocket of one of his aides. Trammel needed votes. And I had them.

Buying politicians was good, but a big part of my job was to make sure guys on my payroll not only got elected—but got re-elected. I controlled seven precincts around Ybor and West Tampa. In a tight race, those precincts could give a candidate the edge.

As we sipped the last of the brandy, Trammell smiled and leaned across the table, about to say something. I waved him off. He didn't need to ask.

"You worry about the rest of the state," I told him. "You'll do okay in Tampa."

On a November evening a few months later, my precincts went

heavily for Trammel. I had one West Tampa precinct captain add 300 Trammel votes to a box they had emptied of the actual paper ballots. The tally in precinct 34 was going to be 341 for Trammel and zero for Pepper. But the precinct captain objected.

"I know for a fact that Pepper's local campaign manager and his wife voted here this afternoon. And they didn't vote for Trammel."

We saw the logic in his argument.

When the votes were tallied West Tampa's precinct 34 went to Trammel 341 to 2. Trammel beat Pepper statewide by just two percent, his margin of victory coming largely from a few select precincts in Tampa. Not that I was there when the votes were tallied. I had people for that.

Johnny and I spent the early hours on election night at the El Dorado. The place was packed, the heavy heels of the chorus girls rat-tat-tatted against the wooden stage. A half-empty bottle of bourbon sat on my table. Tito leaned over to light my cigar with his gold Zippo, the kind with a circle of flame, made especially for cigars.

I savored the moment. On that November night in 1934 I was the big boss, the undisputed heavyweight champion, the gal-darned king of the entire gal-darned world.

But deep down I knew that nobody wore the crown forever. Not even Charlie Wall.

CHAPTER 31

Larry settled on the edge of his single bed, in the narrow room where he'd slept almost every night for the past 50 years. His mom's homemade Caldo Gallego was warm in his belly, his fuzzy tabby, Tallulah, asleep at his side. He could hear his mother in the kitchen, whistling a show tune while she washed the dishes. It was almost 7 p.m. Angie would be waiting for him outside Our Lady in an hour.

Like Larry, the bedroom never changed. Original posters for *The Maltese Falcon*, *The Big Sleep* and *Farewell My Lovely*, purchased thirty years earlier, were push-pinned to the walls. There was the same tall wooden dresser, a few pull handles missing, the top drawer brimming with the flotsam of Larry's life—movie ticket stubs, chewed pencils, coin collections in blue booklets, keys that hadn't turned a lock in years, and receipts from drug stores and grocery stores that were no longer in business.

Tonight, though, the room felt different. Larry felt different. Staking out Charlie Wall's house with Angie, like some film-noir gumshoe, had flipped a switch in him. Maybe it was the kiss in the van. Or what he heard the next morning when he asked his mom and Aunt Frances what they remembered about Charlie Wall.

That morning, Grace Pardo had made her son's usual breakfast—scrambled eggs, cheese grits, extra crispy bacon, and rye toast. Aunt Frances, who lived two blocks away and drove over daily in a pristine Buick, had settled her considerable girth at the kitchen table. Her head reminded Larry of a house that rested atop a sagging foundation, with a slash of red at the front door, and an arching, hair-roller roof.

"Wait. Charlie Wall...isn't he dead?" Aunt Frances set down a coffee mug rimmed in cherry red lipstick.

"Still alive," Larry said. "So far."

His mom joined them at the table, and the sisters told their Charlie Wall stories. During their childhood he had been a one-man-galaxy in the Ybor firmament. Everybody knew him. Or knew of him. He was a gambler, and a dangerous mobster, but he was also the tall white guy in the seersucker suits and straw boater strolling along Seventh Avenue handing out silver coins to children and old ladies.

"He would leave bags of cash on the steps of the Children's Home," Larry's mom said.

Like other Ybor girls, Grace and Frances Congelio had been sheltered by a blockade of doting parents, grandparents, and battalions of relatives, but you couldn't live in Tampa in those days without at least glimpsing the wilder side of the city. Grace recalled the night that they stared through the El Dorado's swinging front door, catching a view of the stage, where long-legged women in glittering costumes and headdresses, shimmied to a Cuban beat, moves they later tried to replicate in the safety of their bedrooms.

"I'll never forget my first dead guy!" Aunt Frances announced.

Out for a Sunday stroll with their father, she had heard an explosion of some kind, then watched a black sedan veer out of control, slamming grill-first into a light pole. The windshield shattered. The passenger door sprang open. Aunt Frances broke away from her father and rushed up to the open door. Inside a man in a black suit was slumped against the steering wheel, half his face blown off, his blood pooling onto the floorboards. She had stared until her father led her away.

"Did the accident do that to him?"

Vincente Congelio stared straight ahead. "Somebody shot him."

"Who?"

"Don't worry about who." He stopped walking and looked

down at his daughter. "Just know this—it's not smart to mess with Charlie Wall."

Back at the kitchen table, Larry's mother sat straighter in the tall wooden chair. "You're not chasing Charlie Wall, are you?"

There was real fear in her voice. She'd been so careful with Larry, keeping him close, safe from neighborhood kids, who liked to push him down and make fun of him.

Larry had promised Angie he wouldn't talk about their search for Buster, but he couldn't help himself.

"We're just trying to stop something bad from happening. It's a job. Don't worry, Precious. I got it handled."

Larry hoped he sounded Bogie-like. Cool. Unafraid. As if staking out the houses of famous mobsters was something people did all the time. His mother wasn't so sure.

"When did you start calling me 'Precious?' Maybe driving Angie Castellano around Ybor at night isn't such a good idea. You want me to speak to her?"

"Look Ma, I got this. We're not getting anywhere near Charlie Wall. It's more of a stake-out kind of thing."

His mother turned to her sister. "I knew I shouldn't have let him take that job at the old folk's home."

In his room an hour before he was to meet Angie, Larry was fretting. Not about his mother's concerns or getting shot or beat up. It was his wardrobe. It wasn't working.

He'd worn his normal work clothes for the first night with Angie—khaki pants, black polo shirt and shiny white Reeboks, scrubbed clean weekly by his mother using moist baking soda and an old toothbrush. The work uniform was the same thing he wore around the house.

Larry didn't like change. Until now. Mom's big TV, the VCR attached by multiple cords, and the girl singers who once lived in his head, all the things that used to make him happy, didn't seem to matter so much. He was on a case. People's lives depended on him. And if he was doing the work of a real detective, he clearly needed a better outfit. There was something in his closet that might be right, but he'd have to go look for it. Well, somebody would have to go look for it.

"Ma!" He hollered from his perch on the single bed as Tallulah raised a fuzzy head. "Ma!"

His mother toddled into the room. As a young woman, Grace Congelio had been slim and petite, but 71-year-old Grace Pardo was pudgy, with pink cheeks and a head of swirled up auburn curls, tinted weekly at Katie's Hair-um in West Tampa. She was in her pale blue, plus-sized housedress, with short sleeves and a band of lace at the collar, her fireplug ankles rising from a pair of black orthopedics, her face flushed after rushing from the kitchen to answer her son's call.

"That suit," Larry asked her. "The one you got me for Angelica's christening. What did you do with it?"

"I thought you hated that suit?"

"Then, I hated it. Now, I like it. Can you find it for me?"

Larry knew what clothes were in his closet, but he liked to pretend he didn't. Better to have Mom pull them out, something she'd been doing since he was six. Back then she had helped him into his clothes, buttoning his shirts and yanking up his zipper. When he turned 21, Grace continued to pull out his clothes, but made Larry do his own buttoning and zipping.

She rooted about inside the closet for a few seconds, hangers screeching across the metal rod.

"You mean this one?" She held up a steel-gray suit, wrapped around a wooden hanger.

"That's it!" Larry shouted.

Grace hung the suit on the hook Larry's father had screwed into the closet door 30 years ago just before the big heart attack sent him to Myrtle Hill years before his time.

Larry stood, causing the cat to scamper. He waved his mother from his room and lifted the suit from the hook.

Sharkskin, narrow lapels, tight pants. It was the right suit for his nightly excursions. Now he just needed a white shirt and a skinny black tie. And maybe his dad's hat.

* * *

"What's up with the suit?" Angie asked, as she settled herself into the passenger seat.

Larry was buttoned into a shiny suit, at least two sizes too small for him, a narrow tongue of a tie dangling atop a white dress shirt. A black fedora, too big for his head, rested just above his glasses.

"I thought I needed to wear something more in line with this job."

Angie stifled a laugh. Larry was now her partner in her hunt for Buster. Laughing at him was not the right move.

"Don't tell me. Wilderman's? Right?"

"How did you know?"

Wilderman's was a legendary downtown store, where a stocky Jewish tailor, a canary-colored measuring tape draped around his neck, fitted Easter suits on boys as their young mothers looked on. It was also where older mothers bought suits for grown sons who were still the size of children.

"Just a guess. Nice suit. And the black hat, it's something."

"I thought so. Sam Spade had a hat like this. I thought the suit needed a hat."

"I totally agree." Angie stifled a snicker.

Larry pushed the brim up from his glasses. "It was my dad's."

A wicker basket rested on the bench seat between them. Angie saw a thermos, with the kind of top that doubled as a coffee cup. Two sandwiches were wrapped in waxed paper. They sat in the basket beside two shiny apples.

"Are we going on a picnic?"

Larry smiled. "Mom thought we might get hungry on the stake-out, so…"

Moving aside some napkins, Angie saw a pint of Canadian Club. "What's this?" She held up the bottle.

"Detectives drink. It's required."

Angie swallowed another snicker. "Well, I guess we're all set then."

Larry gunned the van's V-6. The motor didn't roar. The sound was more like a hand blender spinning in a mixing bowl. Angie watched her partner check his image in the rear-view. He adjusted his hat and practiced a tough guy sneer.

"You look fine. Let's get going."

"Better put your seatbelt on Precious, it could be a wild ride."

Larry had shifted his boyish voice into a lower gear. He dropped the van into DRIVE.

CHAPTER 32

Waking up on his third morning in the safe house, Buster was startled to see Seymour standing above him with two blocks of white fabric and ridged rubber, the sides adorned with a single bold swooshing black stripe.

"Running shoes!" Seymour announced. "For you!"

"I don't run." He remembered the night he had run from the bloody scene on Charlie's front porch. "At least not anymore."

"You don't have to run to wear running shoes. They're a thing!" Seymour pointed down at his own feet. Below the grease-stained pants, Seymour's shoes were now bright red and ankle-high, with fat laces and thick rubber soles.

"Come on, try 'em on! You'll never wear a pair of those grand-pappy brogans again. Did I tell you I was a pioneer in the running shoe business? Should have made a fortune. My roommate at Princeton had family in the footwear trade. We hatched this idea to take tennis shoes to a whole new level. He wanted to call the shoes Nicky's after his dead uncle. I told him nobody wanted to own a Nicky. Drop the C, drop the Y. Call 'em Nike's."

Buster had given up trying to parse Seymour's impossible tales. He had never heard a word like Nike.

"What's wrong with Nicky," Buster snapped. "I like that name."

"You, my friend, are not really anybody's target market," Seymour set the shoes in front of Buster's empty chair. "You're too old and grumpy. But I'm telling you, you're going to love these shoes."

Buster rolled over and pushed his plus-sized body off the foam sleeping pad Seymour had brought home the day before.

Once on his feet, the room spun, and a swarm of what looked like tiny black insects blocked his vision. He grabbed the arm of the folding chair and plopped down. The spinning slowed. His vision cleared.

Seymour produced a white wad of fabric tipped in gold. With some huffing and puffing, Buster managed to get the gym socks on his wide, hairy feet as Seymour continued his running shoe saga.

"So, the slimy snake takes my idea for his brand name, and he forgets me, and my phone number. I never heard from him again. So here I am."

Buster got his feet inside the shoes and tied the wide laces. It felt like he had just laced a pair of pillows to his feet. Taking a few tentative steps, Buster was suddenly optimistic about the plan. Seymour was nuts, but as a scout, he was reliable. He was also a surprisingly competent scavenger. As far as Buster could tell, Seymour had no money, but he kept coming back to the house, a place he now called "headquarters," with lots of stuff. By the second night, Buster was sleeping on the foam pad, under an actual wool blanket. He had silk pajamas and a terry cloth robe, plus toothpaste, a brush, a razor, and shaving cream. All "retrieved" by Seymour on his excursions. And it turned out Seymour also had housekeeping skills. The safe house was almost clean. Something else Buster never expected.

Buster walked around the living room, getting a feel for the new shoes.

"What'd you see last night?'

"The guy and his bodyguard got home just after 10. Normal. That van was there again last night. A block away. The same man at the wheel. Same woman in the passenger seat."

"Hmmm." Buster wasn't sure how to handle that information. He liked his plans simple. The van and its passengers were a complication.

"I need to know more. I want to do this thing tomorrow night."

"Let me complete last night's report and stake out the house tonight," Seymour said. "Then you should be good to go."

"What do you mean by 'good to go'?"

Seymour waved him off and went back to his side of the living room. A ring binder sat on the orange crate table, next to a sharpened No. 2 pencil. Seymour sat cross-legged, like a man in a yoga class. He opened the ring binder and touched the tip of his pencil to his tongue.

"Relax. Go get some food. Everything you need to know will be in my report."

* * *

After the Trammel election in 1936, I owned a U.S. Senator, the governor, the mayor, the police chief, the sheriff, and lots of uniformed cops. My gambling operation was the biggest in the state. I was on top of the world, but I could feel the foundation crumbling beneath my hand-stitched leather shoes.

In the '20s, I bought up other people's muscle. By the late '30s, enriched by bootlegging and rum running during Prohibition, the Sicilians were luring away my muscle guys and killing the ones they couldn't buy. While my envelopes kept the cops from going after my operation, they were also collecting from the Sicilians, so despite my requests, they didn't harass them or shut them down.

And it wasn't just money. I couldn't compete with their blood ties. Tampa's Sicilians were all cousins! I was a white outsider who would never be part of the family. Even men I considered brothers like Scarface Johnny would eventually choose the Sicilians over me, but I was not ready to give up without a fight.

Ignacio Antinori was convinced he was untouchable, thanks to his partnerships with the Trafficantes and the Diecidues. We knew he had breakfast each morning at the Palm Garden Inn. Just before Halloween in 1937, he was sipping a café con leche when somebody stepped up behind him and blew off the back of his head. People thought I ordered the hit. Truth was, Antinori had been skimming from some Chicago wise guys and they got to him before I did.

But the death of Ignacio Antinori didn't change anything. Or maybe it did. For years, Santo Trafficante Sr. had let it be known that he didn't think whacking Charlie Wall was good for business. But the old man was handing more power over to Santo Jr., who let word get around that I'd make an excellent dead man. The pressure on me and my operation got worse, and I didn't have the manpower to stop it.

To get to me, they came after Tito.

At that point, we were more than business partners; Tito Rubio was my surrogate younger brother and second in command. Like me, he was a classy guy from a good family, a charmer of the ladies, everybody's friend. Also like me, he had a head for numbers—he never needed a notepad or a pencil to make his calculations. Along with his other qualities, he was loyal—I knew he had turned down three offers from the Sicilians to switch sides. It didn't hurt that he was a high-class Cuban, not a hick from Italy's deep south. I paid him well for his loyalty.

While I focused on the protection side of the business, Tito ran the day-to-day operation out of the El Dorado. At this point, the El Dorado was a clubhouse for me. I had a private room off the main floor, where I could draw the curtains for meetings and pull them back when the floor show was in full swing, the girls high-kicking in sequined bras, with headpieces made of fake fruit, as a Cuban bandleader pounding the congas.

Tito was the host. He wore a wide smile and a tux. He could produce a front table for special guests at the snap of a manicured finger. If he hadn't been such a masculine guy, you could have called him a dandy. He smelled of the popular new fragrance—Old Spice. He combed his black hair straight back and oiled his moustache to fine points. His suits were sewn by his brother's Italian tailor.

Everybody loved Tito, including his wife and children, and a regular cadre of dancing girls, divorcees, and the prettiest Cuban whores working on the third floor. It didn't hurt that he was charming and generous. He didn't mind sending one of the muscle guys to put the squeeze on a gambler who owed us money, but he *was a soft touch for any family or friends who had unexpected hospital bills or needed extra cash for Christmas.*

Tito and I kept the same schedule—work all night, sleep most of the day, start over. Like other Latin men, he loved his freedom AND his family. Some nights he'd bring me home with him at 3 a.m. Tito would rush around the house turning on all the lights. He'd stand in the middle of the living room and holler "Papa's Home!" His wife and kids would stumble out of their beds for a couple of hours of hugs and games and a full meal around the long dining room table.

"A man needs to see his children." Tito told me more than once. And in Tito's world, it didn't matter if family time happened in the early hours before dawn. As the sun was coming up, I'd leave and everybody would go back to bed, Tito giving me the sly wink that said he was going off to the master bedroom to make another kid. That fit with another thing he told me—a man can't have too much family. He knew I didn't have one, and he was happy to share his with me.

World War II had been good for our business. Soldiers and airmen stationed in Tampa needed food, floor shows and women you could rent by the hour. The war had also put a pause on the Bolita battles.

Still the Sicilians kept quietly turning the screw. They lured away the last of our Sicilian muscle guys. Tito and I took to hiring Cubans and Jews as our bodyguards and enforcers. Lew Feldman was a former boxer, with broad shoulders and a lantern jaw, who looked as tough as any Italian mobster. I never felt completely comfortable with Lew, but Tito trusted him. Then, just as the European war was ending, I was proven right.

It was almost dawn on a December morning in 1944 when Lew drove Tito from the El Dorado to his house in Robles Park, just north of Ybor City. Sitting in the driveway that cold morning, his headlights aimed at the front porch, Lew assured Tito the coast was clear, but why didn't Lew get out to check behind the white bed sheet draped over the rail of Tito's front porch? No. The rat stayed in the car, leaving Tito to climb his porch steps alone. The

Sicilians had bought him off.

As Tito reached his front door, two men in black suits stood up from behind the sheet, the silver plating of their shotguns glistening in the car's headlights. Tito struggled to get his key into the lock. He wasn't quick enough. One shot blew a hole in his right side. Two more shots ripped his hips.

When the shooting started, Lew—the traitorous coward—ducked down behind the wheel of the car. He rose in time to see Tito stagger and fall as the gunmen sprinted into the shadows. Lew never got off a shot.

Tito's wife came out, screaming his name. She threw herself across her husband, now sprawled out, his life oozing away. His kids stumbled out soon after, crying. The older ones ran inside for towels they pressed to their father's bleeding body. Tito was dead when the ambulance arrived. I was just an hour or so into my daytime sleep when a phone call awakened me. It was Johnny Rivera.

"They got Tito." It was all he needed to say.

Everybody came to Tito's funeral—there were eight trucks filled with flowers and the convoy of cars heading to Oak Lawn Cemetery stretched back for more than a mile. Motorcycle cops led the funeral parade, and the mayor sent me a personal note of sympathy. But none of that mattered. The detectives assigned to solve Tito's murder came up empty. Nobody was surprised. In Tampa, mob murders were investigated but never solved.

I put up a $5,000 reward for information on Tito's killers. I wasn't expecting to lose that money. We all knew it was the Sicilians—most likely the Trafficantes—who ordered the hit, and they didn't rat.

In his weekly column, Victoriano Manteiga, the editor of La Gaceta, described Tito as "a good man in a bad business."

But Tito knew the business he was in. So did I. I'm guessing Lew Feldman knew it too. A month after Tito's murder, a farmer found Lew's battered body in a shallow grave in a cypress swamp near Riverview, which is what he deserved for being such a rotten bodyguard.

By the fall of 1945, the Allies were celebrating victory in Berlin and Tokyo. But in Tampa, I was losing a war of attrition and there were no reinforcements coming to help. No celestial vision was required for me to see the future.

The Sicilians had never given me a list of demands, but I figured if I gave up my Bolita operation, I could continue to run the El Dorado. I had given away a lot of money over the past 25 years or so, but there was still plenty of it stashed in Tampa and Cuba. Enough for me to live comfortably for a very long time.

I wasn't afraid of dying but I was a realist. My time at the top of the Tampa rackets was almost over. I managed to hang on a little longer, hoping for a lucky break of some kind, but it never happened. Just as President Truman was announcing an airlift to keep Berlin from being swallowed up by the Reds, I dialed a phone number I had been keeping on a sheet of yellowed paper in the top drawer of my dresser.

CHAPTER 33

It was almost midnight, and Seymour was late returning from his final scouting mission. Buster paced the safe house in his new shoes. Nike, he thought. A weird name, but they made a very comfortable product. The running shoes reminded him of the night he had run from Charlie's porch, bullets whizzing around him. He found himself reliving that night again.

When he and Mangia were hired to whack Charlie in 1955, there was no time to bring in a pro from Miami or Newark. Rush jobs, Buster knew, always went wrong.

"It has to happen tonight." The call was from Buster's boss, a mid-level player in the Trafficante organization.

Buster should have turned it down but whacking someone paid the most of all his jobs. He and Mangia could use the money. And you didn't survive in the mob saying no to your boss.

"How much time do we have?" Buster checked his old Timex.

"You got an hour to get there."

"And who is the target?"

"Charlie Wall."

Buster had to stop and breathe.

"You want me to hit Charlie Wall? In an hour? You sure?"

"No. I don't want it. The boss wants it. He told me to call you."

"What about his guards?"

"He's alone and he'll open the door when you knock. That I guarantee."

Buster couldn't say no.

He was told to knock twice on the back door of the Broadway Bar. He expected to be handed a well-oiled Lupara, the shotgun of choice for Sicilian hitters. But instead, he was given a cheap,

Stevens .12 gauge.

"Looks like something a redneck would sell out of the back of his pickup." Mangia said from the driver's seat as they left the bar.

Going into a job with a gun he didn't know was a bad idea, especially when the target was Charlie Wall, but Buster had no choice. And, sure enough, it all went to hell after the Stevens failed to fire.

For his second shot at Charlie Wall, Buster would use his own gun. He'd taken three days to figure out exactly when and where it would happen. He felt good about the weapon and the plan, but this house, his crazy roommate, they were too much. His stomach was in knots from living off Cuban sandwiches and coffee. His body ached from sleeping on a mat on the floor.

Buster stopped pacing. He felt the ball rising in his throat. His hand went to his face and came back wet. Some old guys couldn't control their bladder. For the past few years, Buster couldn't control his tears. He didn't always need a reason. He was easily overcome with emotion and tears spilled out without warning.

I'm only doing this last one, he told himself. It will be over tomorrow night. If I don't die, I'm going back to Our Lady to live out the rest of my days.

When he was sure the tears had stopped, Buster stepped out onto the front porch. He hadn't spent much time outside. He didn't want to be spotted by a curious neighbor, but at midnight the street was dead quiet, the air sticky and thick. Summer was officially a month away, but in Florida nature's thermostat rose early. One more reason to finish the job and get back to the air-conditioned comfort of Our Lady.

In the tepid glow of a streetlight, he could see a few cars hunkered along the sidewalk, many of them permanent residents, knots of weeds spouting around the tires. A dog barked somewhere. Once. Twice. Even with his bad ears, he could hear the semi-trucks gearing down as the interstate highway curved toward downtown Tampa. A siren pulled Buster's eyes to the far end of the block. A patrol car flashed by with chase lights spinning.

As the siren faded, he watched Seymour skitter around the corner. He raced from one oak tree to the next, pressing up against their thick trunks. His jutting, rodent face swiveled, checking his surroundings. He only had to travel a half a block, but the way he was doing it, like some insane cat burglar, it could take a while. Buster decided to wait inside.

Ten minutes later, the screen door squeaked. Seymour was home. Buster stood in the center of the living room, his arms folded across his chest. Seymour, sweaty and disheveled, stopped two feet away and drew himself up into "attention," his body quivering a bit as he snapped a salute. A thicket of pencils sprouted from his front pocket. Buster stifled a laugh. If Seymour saw himself as a soldier in a two-man-army, Buster would humor him.

"So, what do you know?" Buster asked.

"If you'll give me just five minutes, I'll give you a complete report!"

Buster nodded. Seymour raced to the orange crate and picked up the white ring binder. He hunkered beside the crate and speared a sharpened pencil. After licking the tip, Seymour wrote furiously in the binder, bending close and turning pages.

Buster went down the hall to the ruined bathroom, where he relieved himself and splashed some water on his face. The bathroom was still a disaster, with a hole in the floor and a broken sink, but the water flowed, the toilet flushed and now a pop-up air freshener, the size of a shotgun shell, was open on the edge of the sink, throwing off a minty bouquet.

He returned to find Seymour standing at attention in the middle of the living room. He held the ring binder at his side.

"Whad'da ya got?" Buster grunted.

"Here's my report." Seymour handed Buster the notebook. "Fully illustrated. Cross-checked. Complete."

Buster pulled a crooked pair of reading glasses from his pocket. The house had no electricity, but Seymour had brought home a kerosene lamp after Buster had complained about how dark the place was. Buster moved into the circle of light.

Seymour's report was as incomprehensible as Buster's junior high geometry textbook—page after page of lines, graphs, triangles, rectangles, dots and dashes, that tracked Charlie's comings and goings. There were pie charts, including one that resembled the face of a clock, with lots of intersecting arrows. Three full pages were devoted to rough charcoal drawings of what appeared to be a large black car, a burly young man holding a golf club, and a skinny old man wearing a straw hat. On each page were notes, in Seymour's tiny, precise lettering, often with Roman numeral headings and subheadings with the letters A, B, and C.

Buster closed the notebook.

"Just tell me when I can get to him. Day? Night? Where and when? That's all I'm asking."

Seymour snatched back his report. Pulling his own bent, smudged reading glasses from his pants pocket, he leafed carefully through the pages, holding them close to his face. Finally, he tossed the entire report over his shoulder. He removed the glasses and smiled up at Buster.

"At his house. Every night sometime between 9 and 10 he gets out of his car and walks to his front door."

'And the bodyguard?"

"He's there. Every night."

"Is he armed?"

"I've never seen a gun."

Seymour snapped back to "attention," but Buster was deep in his head, eyes closed, drawing together the final strands of his plan. Something needed to be done tonight.

Sighing as he bent down, Buster eased the violin case out from under the lawn chair. He rested it on the chair and flipped the clasps.

"A concert. A little night music!" Seymour danced in place. "I was waiting for you to pull out the fiddle."

Buster raised the lid, and from a bed of red velvet, lifted out an antique Holland and Holland birding gun. The gray Damascus steel barrel had been sawed off by a previous owner. Like a master carpenter who kept his tools clean and oiled, Buster treated the gun with love. He'd prepped the weapon while Seymour was out scouting, using a brass bore brush on the barrels, wiping down the works and the engraved steel stock with Hoppes No. 9, polishing the carved walnut stock with linseed oil. He pulled a white cloth from the case and wiped the weapon, from stock to barrel.

Seymour stared at the shotgun.

"What I need is for you to distract that bodyguard." Buster did not look up from his polishing. "Draw him away. Out to the street. I'll do the rest."

"That's not a violin!" Seymour squealed, his voice breaking on a high note. "That's a gun!"

Buster looked up. "Yeah. It's a gun."

"You're not going to shoot this guy, are you? I'm a registered pacifist. Live and let live, that's my motto. Roaches, rats, people. I believe in peaceful coexistence with all creatures great and small. You didn't say anything about a gun!"

Buster leaned into Seymour's face; his voice low but not menacing.

"Guys like Charlie and his bodyguard, they got guns. It's how they operate. So, if I want him to give me the money he owes, I gotta have a gun. It's how my business works. You understand?"

"For leverage?" Seymour's eyes blinked furiously.

"I don't know that word," Buster said. "What I know is, you don't just ask somebody for money they owe you. They'd laugh in your face. You gotta scare 'em. That's why I got a gun."

Buster raised it and pressed the stock into his shoulder. He pointed the business end at Seymour's face. The little man jumped back a foot and threw up his hands, his body going into a head-to-toe shimmy.

"Don't shoot!"

Buster settled the shotgun back into the violin case. He rested his hand on Seymour's shoulder.

"Scary, right?" His tone was gentle now. "That's how it works. You show the gun, but you don't shoot it."

"So, you show the gun, but it never goes off?"

"That's the idea. No shooting."

Buster lifted his hand off Seymour's shoulder and the little man straightened into his military pose. "You mean it?"

Buster nodded solemnly.

"Yeah."

Seymour snapped off a brisk salute.

"Alright. I'm in. Tomorrow night?"

"Tomorrow night."

Seymour was calm now. As calm as Seymour could be.

"Just tell me what to do."

Buster closed the case and flipped the silver clips. He didn't look back at Seymour. This job was almost over. He pictured himself in the dining room at Our Lady, a hot meal on the table in front of him, and that tall Angie woman smiling at his side.

CHAPTER 34

For the first time in a while, Trip woke up in his single bed at Charlie's. Katrina had caught a cold the day before. After she called in sick at Rough Riders, she told Trip to stay away in case she was contagious. Trip used the night to write. The words flowed easily. He looked back at his early chapters and thought they weren't bad. They needed revision but they weren't bad.

He had been straight now for almost six months. And he was sure the writing was better for it. Putting down the pot and the 'schrooms had given him a burst of energy that he'd poured into the writing. The previous night's session had lasted until almost 3 a.m.

Waking late the next morning he pulled on a pair of gym shorts and a "Don't Fear The Reaper" T-shirt he'd picked up at a Blue Oyster Cult show in Lakeland. In Charlie's kitchen, he grabbed the quart bottle of milk from the refrigerator.

Trip moved through his morning routine—rinsing out the squat metal coffee pot, pressing the dark granules of freshly ground Colombian beans into the basket, and firing up the stove, one burner to heat the coffee pot, and another to warm the milk. Once they were ready, he poured them simultaneously into a large mug, the steam rising from the creamy brew. It was only when he sat down that Trip saw the large jelly jar open on the kitchen table.

He had kept one jar of black, motor-oil-thick mushroom juice stashed in the back of Charlie's refrigerator, marked with the hand-lettered sign: "NOT FOR HUMAN CONSUMPTION." He thought of it as an insurance policy. If he needed quick money, he could sell the juice for a couple of hundred bucks.

But here it was, open on the kitchen table, next to a white mug with a sheen of dark juice at the bottom. Trip looked around the kitchen.

"Charlie?" he called out softly.

His boss wasn't in the living room. The hallway door leading to Charlie's lair was open. Trip pressed himself against the wall beside the open door. Now that Charlie was over his depression, Trip figured his rule about shooting first and asking questions later was back in effect.

"Charlie?"

He heard footsteps. Trip threw a quick look around the doorframe and there was his boss, in silk bathrobe and slippers, his hair spiked from his pillow. He waved the Colt .38.

"They're out there!" Charlie shouted at Trip, his eyes wide and wild. "Outside my window!"

Trip shouted at Charlie: "Who's outside?"

"Gotta be Trafficante Junior, the slimy wop. Or one of his goons."

Trip snapped another fleeting look down the hall. It was empty. He heard the old man shout: "Don't think you can scare Charlie Wall!"

The shots were like thunderclaps, mixed with the sound of glass shattering. Trip edged down the hallway, his back against the wall, trying to figure out how to get the gun out of Charlie's hand. He pictured a neighbor or the postman dead on the sidewalk. With Charlie high on 'schrooms, paranoid and agitated, and firing at imaginary hit men, Trip worried that he could be next in Charlie's line of fire.

He heard a clatter as something hit the floor. Trip bobbed his head around bedroom door. Charlie sat in his chair by the window, his eyes closed, his lips moving, looking to Trip like a monk, reciting a prayer. The Colt rested by his slippered feet.

Trip eased into the room. Charlie's head rotated in his direction. The old man grew anxious again, his fingers tapping the arms of the rocking chair.

"I'm pretty sure I got him," Charlie nodded toward the shattered window. "They never give up."

Crossing the room, Trip placed his palm on Charlie's bony shoulder. With his toe, he eased the blued steel pistol across the floor and stashed it in the top drawer of Charlie's dresser.

Charlie continued to mutter. Through the shattered window, Trip scanned the yard and the sidewalk beyond it. He saw no dead bodies.

Trip gently perp-walked the old man out of his bedroom and up the hallway to the kitchen. Trip purred his own calming mantra into Charlie's ear: "Relax...breathe...relax...breathe..."

The chant, and the thick bathroom towel Trip had wrapped around his boss' shoulders had momentarily chased Charlie's paranoia. Charlie eyed the room like he'd never seen a kitchen before. A single bright bulb hung over the table. Charlie held his right hand up to the light, turning it right, then left.

"I can see every vein," he whispered. "Why have I never noticed that before?"

"Did you drink this on purpose?" Trip held up the open jar.

Charlie's gaze slowly rotated from his raised hand to Trip's face. "I've heard about magic medicine for years. I needed to see what the big deal was all about."

The jar was on the table. The lid off. The tea's dank, forest-floor smell hit Trip's nose like a lover's perfume. How long had it been? Six months since that night in Josh's hot tub? The jug was right there. Looking at it, Trip felt like a starving man at a banquet table.

He checked his boss' dilated pupils and the kitchen clock. Charlie's trip had three or four hours to go. He'd need a knowledgeable companion to get him through it and keep him away from the firearms and the car keys. In Trip's experience, the best guide for a magic mushroom novice was an experienced person taking the same ride. Plus, he felt the craving deep in his belly.

Outside the kitchen windows the day was sunny. Katrina was home sick, wanting no visitors. There was no reason not to do it. Besides, Charlie needed him.

Trip pulled a highball glass from the cabinet beside the refrigerator and poured out two fingers of the muddy liquid. Like he always did just before downing a dose, Trip crossed himself, looked to the heavens—this time the kitchen ceiling—and shouted a line he remembered from a childhood TV show: "And away we go!"

Charlie lowered his hand from the light and watched Trip empty the glass in one gulp.

"By the way," Charlie said. "That stuff tastes like shit."

"Okay, Charlie." Trip slapped the glass down on the table. "From now on we're in this together."

* * *

Katrina woke feeling fine, the body that had been achy the day before, now only ached to be near the man she loved. She told herself to wait until Trip showed up at Rough Riders at the end of her shift, but she couldn't. She had bought him a gift, a present from one writer to another, from one lover to another. *The Elements of Style*, by William Strunk and E.B. White, was the Bible of grammar and writing rules. Katrina kept a dog-eared copy among the books on her writing desk. The clerk at Three Birds Bookstore had ordered a new copy for her.

Delivering *The Elements of Style* was just a pretense to visit her boyfriend. Trip had never invited her to Charlie's house. She didn't approve of him living with a mobster, no matter how decrepit he was. But she and Trip were in love now. She was sure of that. And she needed to see where he lived, be a part of his life, even if she didn't approve.

And beyond all that, Katrina had awakened in her double bed that morning with a craving for him. Not so much for sex, but for his touch, his crooked smile, his muscled shoulders, his breath in her ear. Him.

There were no closets in her aging apartment above Seventh Avenue. A hulking thrift store armoire, scuffed and unpolished, held Katrina's simple wardrobe. A few work outfits, some peasant blouses, three long, gauzy skirts, and two soft cotton sundresses, that showed off her lanky figure. She picked the sundress with pink wildflowers, and, instead of tennis shoes, she strapped on her lone pair of white flats. She wanted to look nice for him. In her small bathroom mirror, she added a smudge of pale pink lipstick, which was 100 percent more makeup than she normally applied.

The walk across Ybor to Charlie's was no more than 15 minutes. The weather report on her radio said a storm was coming, but above her was a blue sky and cotton candy clouds that morphed into elephants, dogs, and an occasional lion. If she left Florida, she'd miss the clouds. The state was crazy and chaotic, and Tampa was an ugly, working-class town, but the clouds and the sunsets were glorious.

She crossed the vast community college parking lots, strolled up the empty street that curved under the interstate highway. A disheveled old man, hunkered in a campsite under the overpass, stared blankly at her. She flashed him a Midwestern smile. He glared back. But an angry drunk couldn't dim her mood. Her lover was waiting a few blocks away.

Charlie's house was set back from the street, behind a low wall, topped with wrought-iron spikes. It was larger than its neighbors, with a wrap-around porch and carved pillars holding up the roof. Two broken bands of concrete—what was left of Charlie's driveway—ran from a gap in the fence to the fins of a black Cadillac.

On the sidewalk, Katrina's nerves jangled a warning. She looked up and saw that the clouds, puffy and playful moments earlier, were thickening. A storm was coming. Her mind raced. What if he is upset that I'm showing up at his house uninvited? Why didn't I call first? What if he isn't alone? How do I know he's not leading some kind of double life?

She decided to leave the gift bag on the porch and wait for Trip to come to the bar that night. She opened the iron gate and walked up the hex-block walkway. Music pulsed through the open front door—cornets, trombones and saxophones bleating in harmony, the drums and bass pounding, a clarinet off on a soaring solo. Katrina dropped the bag by the door. She knew she should walk away, but she couldn't stop herself. She leaned into the open doorway.

Trip was in the living room, in shorts and a ragged T-shirt, swirling and spinning to the music, his head back, his arms swinging free above his head where a chandelier was blazing.

God, he's a terrible dancer, she thought.

Trip saw her. His smile was huge and toothy. Rushing over, he pulled Katrina into a bear hug. She had longed for the feel of his body against hers, but the black saucers of his pupils and the mad look on his face made it all wrong. He's tripping again! Probably been doing it all along. The lying bastard!

She struggled to break free. The hallway door swung open and a tall, hatchet-faced man emerged, wearing only a bathrobe, his gray hair scrambled atop his head, a pistol glistening in his hand.

"Step back, boy, I got this." Charlie was shouting but Katrina could barely make out the words over the roar of the music. "Can't believe they sent a woman this time."

Katrina struggled to break free. Charlie raised the gun. His index finger pulled the trigger. Once. Twice. Her boyfriend let her go and turned toward Charlie. Trip's face was contorted. He appeared to be shouting.

The wild-eyed old man continued to shout and pull the trigger. Katrina brought her hands to her chest, expecting to find blood oozing through the cotton sundress. But her hands came back dry.

Trip grabbed her around the waist. He lifted her off her feet and carried her onto the porch. When he set her down, she scrambled away.

"Stop!" Trip waved his arms. "It's okay! You're safe!"

Katrina ran from Charlie's house like she was the anchor leg in an Olympic relay. If she had looked back, she'd have seen Trip on the top step, holding out the cartridge he had taken from Charlie's gun hours earlier. A cartridge he'd tucked into the front pocket of his saggy shorts.

I shouldn't have been surprised when Santo Trafficante Sr. answered his own phone on a summer morning in 1948. He was old school. A rich and powerful man who didn't make elaborate shows of his wealth or influence.

"Well, well, well." His voice was amiable, but gruff. His childhood language added old world filigrees to his English. "How does a poor old Sicilian like me earn a call from the great Charlie Wall?"

"It's my honor to be talking with you." I played my role in the game of mutual respect, which was proper for crime bosses of our generation. "I was wondering if I could buy you lunch sometime? The Columbia serves a great Cuban sandwich."

"And I live for that salad," he added.

I knew the Columbia was Santo Senior's regular spot. And it was public enough for a formal sit-down. Neither of us would be in any danger. It was an unspoken rule that nothing could happen at the Columbia. The restaurant was a safe zone.

One week later, Santo and I were seated at a back table in the patio room, near an ornate fountain, the dancing water soaking the marble figure of a man, wrapped by a giant squirming fish. We both had guys at nearby tables, all looking like gangsters from central casting—dark suits, nervous eyes, scabbed knuckles, scars etched into stubbled cheeks—but one table away, Santo and I could have been two old friends, meeting for a lunch.

In my wrinkled seer-sucker suit, white shirt, plaid bowtie, fresh from a shave by my favorite Cuban barber, I looked like an old-school Tampa lawyer. Santo Sr. wore a pale blue dress shirt, a wide, out-of-fashion tie that fell to the middle button of his shirt. His ample belly was tucked into pleated wool trousers held up by gray suspenders. He could have been an amiable grandfather, retired from his dry goods business. The only nod to his real profession was the gold pinky ring, with a plus-sized diamond glittering in the center.

While I had seen Santo Sr. at funerals, weddings, and an occasional political cookout, we'd never sat down together. We acted out the required charade, smiling and chatting like longtime pals. I asked about his wife. I had heard she had been in the hospital. "She says she is fine now. Though I'm not sure she or the doctors are telling me everything. I worry about her."

"Please give her my best wishes."

"And you never married?"

"I guess I never got around to it. My hours aren't suited to domestic bliss."

A hint of a smile creased his wide, fleshy face. "Here it is not so important but back home, family was all you had. A man needed a wife, a few daughters and lots of sons."

I knew he had four boys, at least two of them taking over as the old man stepped aside. "And how are your sons?"

"They are almost men. But sadly, there's no farm for them to work. No cows. No sheep. In this country, it is easy for a young man to lose his way."

"Tell me about it. You are looking at the original prodigal son."

We both laughed. Then, he turned serious. "I was sorry to hear about your friend Tito. It was a beautiful service. I sent flowers."

I nodded and kept my poker face. Santo Sr., or one of his sons, had most likely ordered the hit. But we were gentlemen, and I was here about the future, not the past.

Lunch arrived and we chewed on crusty Cuban sandwiches, spooned up black beans, topped with raw onion, while we made small talk about the New York Yankees' disappointing 1948 season—Tampa's Italians were all Yankee fans thanks to 'Jolting' Joe DiMaggio and Phil "Scooter" Rizzuto.

"They could be bums this year," Santo said. "But still, I sit by my radio each night hoping for the best. To be a fan means one is always optimistic."

"One year you're a star. The next year you're a putz," I told him. "Baseball is like life, I think."

After lunch, an old waiter in a dark tux cleared the table and returned with cups of café con leche and two mounds of flan, a golden Spanish custard that jiggled when you sank in your spoon. As the waiter departed, Santo looked around, making sure no one could hear our conversation.

"So," he said, quietly. "I know you didn't call me to talk about baseball."

"Something a little more serious, and personal," I said.

His nod said: "Continue."

"I'd like to discuss a business arrangement."

"We are both men of business. I am willing to listen."

I wiped my mouth with the cloth napkin, stalling for time. What I was about to ask was hard for me. I had been given a sign from God, I had built something from nothing, I had built it so big, that the name Charlie Wall was known in Tampa, Orlando, Tallahassee, Havana, Miami, and Washington, D.C. I had made more money than any of my father's rich friends. I owned politicians and police. I could get candidates elected and re-elected. And when I was feeling generous, I could send bags of cash to the Children's Home and pass out silver dollars to children and widows. I was in no hurry to give it all away. Santo Sr. was wise enough to know that. He sat quietly, his hands on the table. Finally, taking a deep breath, I was ready.

"I'm thinking it's time for me to step away from my Bolita operation."

He let that sentence hang between us for a moment before responding. "A wise decision," he finally said.

I looked around the crowded room. The only people paying any attention to us were our bodyguards—two for him, two for me—with their coffee cups and smoky ashtrays. It was warm in the restaurant, but our guys wore suit jackets, to hide the holstered weapons strapped to their chests. They knew we were getting to the serious part of our lunch. When the waiter started to walk our way one of Santo's guys stood and put a hand on his chest. The waiter turned and disappeared through the swinging kitchen door. My heart told me to get up and walk out. But my head, always my most valuable possession, said no. I had started this and now I had to continue.

"Here's my proposition. I'm willing give up my bolita business. It's yours if you want it. I'd like to keep the El Dorado, for a few more years at least."

His face gave nothing away. (That was how he had become so successful.) He nodded and took another sip of coffee before responding. "And what are you asking in return?"

"That I can come and go in Tampa as I please, without any bullets or buckshot coming in my direction." I stopped there and smiled. Santo slurped from his porcelain cup, setting it down in a saucer puddled with spilled coffee. His table manners were the only sign of the old Sicilian farmer he had once been.

"There are lots of men in Tampa with guns. I don't control all of them. It is, as they say, a free country."

"But those men will listen when you speak."

I watched him spoon up a large bite of flan. A few flecks of cream clung to his lips, like gold dust. I finished my dessert and quietly drank my coffee, until there was only a muddy swirl left in the bottom of my cup.

Then, Santo smiled and gave me a wink.

He stood up, which prompted his guys, one table away, to do the same. I rose after him, and my guys stood with me.

"Thank you for lunch," he said. "Va bene." He stepped close to me and smiled. His heavy hand came down gently on my shoulder, and I knew we had a deal.

Katrina couldn't stop running. She was scared. She was angry. She was sad. She was so many things at once, the only reaction that made any sense was to run—up Charlie's sidewalk, down the side street, then under the hulking highway overpass toward Ybor's downtown and the safety of her apartment. When her flight was halted by busy traffic at Palm Avenue, Katrina ran in place, screaming at the passing cars—"COME ON! COME ON!"

The traffic parted, and she sprinted again. She ran out of steam two blocks from her apartment. Leaning against a red brick wall, she closed her eyes and tried to focus. I'm alive. I'm safe.

The sundress clung to her skin like plastic wrap. A strap on her flats had pulled loose. A jackhammer pounded in her chest. But at least she was no longer screaming. Instead, she sobbed. She wiped her tears with a shaking hand. A car horn blasted and suddenly, she was back at Charlie's house, a gun aimed at her chest, the music blaring, some survival instinct deep inside screaming—"Run!"

Katrina ran again. She took the steps to her apartment two-at-a-time. Safely inside, she turned the dead bolt. Her dad always kept a bottle of bourbon in the house, not to get drunk, but to calm his nerves in a time of crisis. He had pulled out the bottle the night of her mother's fatal car crash. Katrina had a bottle stashed away in her Ybor apartment for a moment like this one.

She poured two fingers of the honey-colored liquid and took it all in one long swallow. She winced at first, the booze molten as it descended. But soon the hot syrup turned warm. It coursed through her like motor oil, coating her throat, her stomach, her pounding heart. She could breathe again.

Her studio apartment was just as she'd left it. She fell onto her bed. She was alive, but she was not okay. The man she thought she loved was back on drugs and his roommate had tried to gun her down. She got up and refilled the shot glass. The second drink went down easier.

She collapsed back onto the bed. Should I write about this in my journal? Explore it in a poem? None of her normal coping mechanisms seemed appropriate for this occasion. She stared at the walls she and Brian had painted robin's egg blue. They had rented the apartment a year before, after a post-graduation road trip led them to Ybor. While they pushed the dripping rollers over the walls, Brian suggested they stay in Ybor for the winter. They hung some thrift-store curtains in the tall windows and splurged on new sheets. They made love on the squeaky bed, hoping that Bruce, the young photographer who lived next door, couldn't hear the commotion. She had believed her life was just about perfect. But three weeks later, Brian was gone, leaving a one-sentence note and $200 in twenties on the dresser.

She had hit bottom after Brian left. It took a year to put her life back together. Now, she was staring up from the bottom of another very deep hole.

After Brian, she knew she couldn't go back to Ann Arbor. They had met at the university. She was sure he was back in Bloomfield Hills, barely 40 minutes away from their college town. She also wasn't ready to return home to Dayton. Instead, she got a waitress job in a Seventh Avenue restaurant and showed up early to help the cook. She learned to make Ybor delicacies – *arroz con pollo, boliche, picadillo*. A month into the job, she realized she was pregnant—Brian had left a piece of himself behind—then, just as quickly, she miscarried.

She had pulled herself back from all of that. One day at a time. She wrote every morning, become a regular at poetry readings, and produced a chapbook of poems and stories. When her old restaurant closed, she landed the bartender job at Rough

Riders, in what had been the V.M. Ybor cigar factory.

She had kept men at arm's length, until Trip. She had convinced herself he was different. They were happy together. She wasn't asking for a future. She just wanted right now to be good. But all her romantic optimism had ended at Charlie's house. She saw Trip now for what he was—a drug-addled man-child, dancing in a blazing-bright living room, while an old man in a bathrobe aimed a gun at her. She wasn't sure how long she sat alone with those thoughts. Dark clouds pressed down on the old city. As her apartment darkened, so did her mood.

This is your fault, she scolded herself. You knew better. You swore you'd never do it again, and then you went right ahead and fell for another worthless, lying man.

She got up and took one more shot of brown liquor. The hurtling racecars of blame eventually ran out of gas. Her mind cleared. She knew what she needed to do.

Dropping to her knees beside the bed, she bent low, extending her arm until she felt the hard handle of her suitcase. She set it on the bed and emptied the hangers and hooks in the armoire. She didn't have a lot of possessions. The suitcase had enough room for her clothes and everything from her writing desk—the pens and pencils, the leather notebook she'd stuffed with poems and stories. She would wait until tomorrow morning before clearing out her tiny bathroom. She'd leave the pots and pans, the old bed, and the few sticks of furniture for the next tenant.

Tomorrow she'd buy a bus ticket to Dayton. It was time to go home.

* * *

By late afternoon the high had floated away as softly as it had come on. Trip dangled his legs over the edge of Charlie's back porch. He was still in gym shorts and a faded T-shirt. Time drifted. He wasn't sure how long he'd stared up at a silver dollar sun as it played hide and seek with a wall of thickening clouds.

Concentrating on the show in the sky, he could momentarily erase the image of his boss firing the empty Colt at his girlfriend.

After the shooting that wasn't technically a shooting, Charlie had disappeared into his bedroom and locked the door. Trip rattled the handle as he shouted every obscenity he knew. Getting no response, he returned to the living room, where the Benny Goodman raver *Swing, Swing, Swing* continued to blow at full volume.

Trip wanted to run to Katrina's place, tell her how sorry he was, to kiss her, to hold her, but he was in no shape for any of that. Instead, he spun in a slow circle in Charlie's living room, his eyes shut to block the prison-yard blaze of the chandelier, his index fingers in his ears, muting the roar from a record set on "repeat." He felt like a man caught in a whirlpool. Behind his eyelids, the spinning world went red, then pink, then orange. A freight train loaded with hieroglyphics clanked into view and crashed, spilling its contents.

At some point, Trip's brain switched into the 'On" position and he opened his eyes. The living room was too loud and too bright.

He lifted the arm off the record and turned off the chandelier. The house was a jumbled mess. Cleaning it up would help, he decided. He straightened the piles of newspapers, fluffed the couch cushions, and rinsed the grainy remains of espresso and 'schroom juice from that morning's cups and glasses.

Checking the front porch, he saw Katrina's gift bag on the sidewalk. He couldn't bring himself to look inside. He set it on his writing desk, next to the typewriter.

When the house was all together, Trip flopped onto the back porch. A thunderstorm was coming, shelves of slate gray clouds stacked themselves on the horizon. The dregs of the mushrooms made it all vivid and meaningful. A year ago, Trip would have enjoyed the images but today, he just wanted this trip to end.

The back door hinges creaked. The legs of a chair screeched across the porch planks. He heard the low groan Charlie always emitted as he sat down. Looking over, he could see the old man's pale ankles, his feet still stuffed into brown slippers. Trip was determined not to speak first. They sat in silence for a long time until Charlie's slow southern drawl filled the void.

"I suppose you'd like me to apologize?"

Despite all he had done to calm down, when Trip opened his mouth, his anger flared. "Charlie! What the fucking fuck! That was my girlfriend!"

"And I'm truly sorry about that. I'm not sure what came over me, but I was convinced I was protecting us both from a deadly intruder."

"From a woman? You told me women were off limits."

"I understand that it seems illogical now, but at the time, it made sense. That's really all I can say about it."

Trip had more to say but he didn't think it would do any good. They sat quietly for a few long minutes.

"Again, I'm sorry," Charlie finally said. "And thank you for removing the cartridge. That was smart. Helpful."

"And that's it. An apology and that makes it all better?"

"I'd like to point out it wasn't me who kept a jar of crazy juice in the refrigerator."

"But it was you who ignored my sign and took a dose. Right?"

"Have you heard the bible story of the forbidden fruit?"

"You're not going biblical on me, are you?"

"I was curious. Every time I opened the icebox, it was right there. In my long life, I've tried just about everything except the magic juice. I've heard a lot about it, and I was curious. And bored. And there it was, right behind the pickles."

Trip wanted to say more, to yell at the old man but he got caught up watching a cadre of inky clouds toss a blanket over the sun. Soon, there would be lightning and thunder and the usual 20-minute downpour. It was Tampa's late afternoon show, almost as predictable as the tides.

There was nothing he could do to repair things with Katrina. Charlie was Charlie. And Trip hadn't had the will power to resist the magic juice. The damage was done.

"Storm comin," Trip muttered.

"Yep."

That was it for a while. They sat silently. On the downside of the 'schrooms, Trip's thoughts were pool balls rolling in slow-motion across the green felt of his brain, sometimes striking another ball, sometimes dropping with a thunk into a pocket. With some effort, he remembered a question he'd planned to ask Charlie. It seemed so long ago now, before Charlie drank the juice, grabbed the Colt .38, and murdered Trip's love life.

Trip had finished writing the section about Charlie's meeting with Santo the Elder. In all his talk about his life and criminal career, Charlie had never mentioned the years after 1948, when he handed over his business to the Sicilians. Trip knew that Charlie had continued to run the El Dorado, but except for his testimony to the Kefauver crime commission, which was mostly a chance for Charlie to entertain the crowd gathered in the hearing room, his life story was blank from that lunch with Santo Sr. in 1948 until the April night in 1955 when two killers had knocked on his front door.

"So, what happened?" Trip's voice sounded like an echo from across a pond.

"I told you; it was an accident. I was confused."

"No, I mean, what happened after you gave up your Bolita business? You never talk about it."

"I don't remember."

"Come on. You remember everything."

"Okay, you're right, but there are things I remember I don't like talking about, especially to an amateur biographer. A biographer who never officially got permission to run my life through his typewriter."

Trip looked up at the old man. "That's why you should talk to me—because I'm an amateur. I'm worse than that. I've never written anything longer than a short story. I got no agent. No publisher. I'm 30 years old, with no college degree, no career..."

"Well, if we're listing your faults, you're a rotten bodyguard and a so-so driver."

They both laughed.

"Now you're just rubbing it in." Trip said.

"Since we're being honest, I thought I needed to mention it. But what the heck, I like you. And the writing is good."

"You read it?"

"I got to do something on those late nights when you're out chasing that poet gal."

Trip shook his head, the anger was still twisted up inside his stomach, but the conversation eased the pain. "I guess we don't have to worry about that any longer."

"Again, I'm truly sorry about that."

Thunder echoed from the east. The sky was swollen and purple, like a fresh bruise. "Look. I'm just writing to prove I can do it and because your life is so much more interesting than mine."

"Interesting is one way of putting it."

"So, what happened? I want to know. And you owe me this, after trying to kill my girlfriend."

Charlie laughed again. "Look, I'll tell you, but it's not a pretty story."

"Those are the best kind," Trip said.

Fat dollops of rain rat-tat-tatted on the concrete pad below the porch, leaving dark circles, like bullet holes. When it rained harder, the circles oozed together, covering the entire slab. The monsoon was next. It was just a matter of time.

"Doesn't look like we're going anywhere," Trip said.

"Alright, then. Why don't you make us some coffee, and I'll tell you the whole sordid story."

CHAPTER 37

Flat on my back, staring up at a pressed tin ceiling, I wasn't sure who or where I was. I could have been my 16-year-old self, recovering from the Spanish flu, in my room above Dirty Joe's. Suddenly, my guts twisted into a fist, a rush of sweat soaked my sheets, and I knew I wasn't that kid anymore. It was 1955 and I was just another junkie, albeit one who could afford a plush corner apartment high above Ybor City. A room decorated with overstuffed couches and leather club chairs, a carved wood bed frame, a full bar on a rolling cart, and a mahogany desk, home to a Tiffany lamp and a white telephone, with a cord so long I could take it to any corner of the room.

I prayed for sleep to pull me back into the candy-colored ocean, where I floated in warm salt water, a beautiful mermaid beside me, her breasts bare, her tail doing a sultry swing, as cascades of silver bubbles burst from her puckered lips. But sleep and dreams were over. I had awakened into a cold, colorless world of my own making.

The windows of my El Dorado apartment were covered by venetian blinds and maroon velvet curtains, double-lined to hold the day in abeyance, but I had forgotten to close the curtains the night before. Sharp stingers of sun found my face. In a different time, I would have risen and pulled the curtains tight and gone back to sleep, but now I was awake and aching.

I struggled out of bed, but I didn't empty my bladder, didn't brush my crusty teeth, or splash cold water in my face. That would come later. First, I picked up the zippered bag, the kind regular folks use to carry their toiletries on an overnight trip. Mine held a pill bottle with a chalky mound inside, a spoon, a vial, a box of matches, a rubber strap, a tiny bottle of alcohol, and a hypodermic.

These days the bag was always within arm's reach. This morning it beckoned from the side table it shared with an empty bottle of Grand Marnier and a cut crystal snifter. A honey-colored rivulet from my 2 a.m. drink thickened in the bottom.

I sat on the bed preparing my poison and realized I had become Dirty Joe, a bar owner whose bad habits had taken over his life. I wanted to blame the Sicilians, who had forced me to give up my throne as the King of Bolita. But it was my own fault.

The nightclub business was different in the post-war years. Husbands, even Latin ones, stayed home after work to watch Milton Berle on the small screen. Nobody wanted big bands with girl singers or boyish crooners, and a choreographed kick-line. And the cops, prodded by a new generation of good government reformers, raided gambling dens and closed whorehouses. The mayor and the police chief were still taking my envelopes, but they told me they couldn't provide the same protection I had enjoyed in the past.

My nightclub was busy only on weekends. The raids had ended my lucrative gaming and prostitution businesses, and the food and booze revenues weren't keeping up with my payroll. But I've never worried about making money. I'd figure out a way forward. Hell, I hadn't even celebrated my 50th birthday.

One weekend, to get away from my troubles, I flew to New Orleans with a couple of drinking buddies. They took me to Bourbon Street to see Blaze Starr. Performing with a four-piece band, her striptease was sexy but stayed on the good side of the law. When she finished, the stage was carpeted in crumpled dollar bills. That's when I really looked around the place. The club was clean. The small combo played in tune. Sexy sirens in sequined jump suits drifted past. Their trays held tall drinks the color of the ocean or the sunset. The tiny tables, lit by single electric candles, were surrounded by men and women in Saturday night finery.

Looking around that bar, I saw a way forward.

No amount of reform or television sets would change people's hunger for titillation. TV was squeaky clean. Burlesque clubs offered something you couldn't get at home. Once the poor step-sister of nightclubs and vaudeville, Burlesque in the '50s was mainstream. Clubs were opening in all the big cities. And if the G-strings and pasties stayed in place, it was all entirely legal.

I came back to Ybor City and fired my kick-line, replaced my big band with a small combo, built around a drummer who could pound out "Bomp-Bomp-Ba-Bomp-Ba-Bomp" on his tom-tom. I hired a foul-mouthed comic to emcee the show and added some vaudeville jugglers and novelty acts to fill out the time between strippers. To supplement the local talent, I imported performers from Havana, Mexico City and New Orleans, stocking the dressing rooms with boas and feathered fans, large enough to hide a voluptuous human body. A New York booking agent lined up a steady flow of touring stars.

And soon, young married couples, with tidy GI Bill homes in the 'burbs, were lining up around the block to see Blaze Starr, Lil St. Cyr, and Tempest Storm, the stacked siren who eventually spent a few wild nights in my bed. The El Dorado was again the hottest nightclub in Tampa and the king of Bolita was reborn as the king of burlesque.

I had Santo Sr.'s promise of protection, but just in case, I hired a contractor to build me a luxury apartment on the third floor, so I never had to leave the club. Never had to worry about the walk from the bar to my car, or from my car to my door. I still spent some Sundays and Mondays at my Ybor house, with two armed men in the guest rooms, just in case, but most nights (okay, most days) I slept upstairs above the club.

My descent into the wasteland of the white powder was slow and unintentional. Despite my newfound success, I moved through my life in a gauzy haze. I mourned Tito. I mourned my lost political clout and my lost network of games and couriers, and, my lost love, Ava Corral. Good news never seemed completely good. A single dollop of negativity could send me reeling. I had lived through these dark episodes before, eventually working my way out of them. But at some point, in the early 1950s, no amount of work and success could part the curtains and let in the light.

I needed something to change my mood, and the powder was

around and available. A few of my old bolita couriers were peddling smack. And it seemed an appropriate accessory for the ringmaster of a circus built around booze and bare bodies.

I wasn't Dirty Joe. I was Charlie Wall! I had built a thriving new business from the ashes of my old one. I was too smart to get hooked. In my luxury apartment, with one of my former bolita couriers showing me the ropes, I tried the needle.

How do I describe that feeling?

The first few times, you rise through an atmosphere that is cold and hot in equal measure, your body an airplane, your veins the runways. At some point the cotton ball clouds part to reveal a crystalline sky and you're flying solo, engines humming, propellers spinning, cabin pressurized, the cockpit seat contoured just for you. God-like as you reach cruising altitude, you take a moment to gaze down at the distant plains below, where the ruddy earth is cut into a maze of concrete corridors, choked with losers crammed inside rolling metal boxes, struggling to find their way, never seeing the celestial signposts revealed only to mythic figures like you.

It seems impossible, but you somehow rise higher into a Van Gogh night; the stars glittering diamonds, your cabin scented with lavender, your heart pumping out so much confidence and contentment you can feel it tingling at the tips of your fingers and toes. Time to flip on the autopilot, tilt back your cushioned seat, and fly. It was other people who crashed and burned. That was never going to happen to me. I was too confident, too smart, and certainly too important to plummet from such heights.

But a few years later, here I was, starting my day with my gut in a knot, my sheets soaked, trying to find a spot on my forearm that wasn't scabbed over or marked with tiny black divots.

CHAPTER 38

When Angie Castellano set her sights on a man she never wavered. Like a veteran hunter she didn't mind long hours in the blind, she was confident her prey would eventually stroll into her sights.

Buster had been missing for three days. She'd spent the past two nights staking out Charlie Wall's house, and making small talk with Larry Pardo, who had convinced himself that he was some kind of film noir private eye. Eating dinner alone in the cafeteria, beside the chair she was saving for Buster, Angie felt her confidence ebbing. I'm being delusional, she thought. Maybe my mind is going. I've seen it happen. It's old age.

After dinner, Angie slipped out the back door, onto the loading dock. It was time to meet the van, but instead she pulled a cigarette from her purse. A storm had passed through during dinner, leaving the driveway soaked, but under the overhang, the loading dock was dry. Angie eased herself down on the edge, enjoying the cool heaviness of the air and the quiet that always followed a Tampa thunderstorm.

Maybe this whole Buster thing is ridiculous, she told herself. What if I'm all wrong about him? I don't even know if he likes me. His head's so thick, what does he know anyway? And why should I think he's trying to kill someone? Maybe he just disappeared. Tough old birds like him don't fit well in clean, well-lit places like Our Lady.

Pulling out a lighter, Angie lit the cigarette, hoping she'd have a better idea of what she was doing after smoking this one and maybe one more.

* * *

For his whole life, Larry Pardo had worked hard not to stand out. He liked it that way. But Angie Castellano's invitation to skulk around after hours, trying to keep two old mobsters from killing each other, had changed him. He'd lost interest in the black and white movies on his mother's TV. He was making his own movie now in a role he was born to play. Larry thought about the "case" all the time. He called relatives he normally only spoke to on holidays, asking what they knew about Charlie Wall and the Tampa mob. He developed some "leads" and was anxious to check them out.

Standing at the end of the driveway, he saw Angie sitting in the yellow wash of the security light, smoking a cigarette, her long legs dangling below the loading dock, one shoe hanging loose from her toes. Larry ducked into the landscaping and moved silently toward the loading dock.

"Having second thoughts, sweetheart?" He spoke in his best hard-boiled, Bogey style.

Angie dropped her cigarette, her head swiveling, her eyes staring into the darkness. "Dammit, you scared me. Where are you?"

"Over here, sweetheart." His voice was a hoarse whisper.

"Well, goddammit, come out where I can see you. You can't sneak up on a person like that. And stop calling me sweetheart!"

Larry stepped out of the bushes and into the light. He had added a tan trench coat to his detective outfit.

"Let's go," Larry barked. "We got a job to do."

"I don't know if I can do this another night," Angie picked up her cigarette from the dock and puffed a few times to get it going again.

Larry pulled a pack from his coat pocket, along with the silver zippo that had been his father's. Larry had never smoked, but he knew real detectives kept a butt burning all the time. And they smoked with style. Larry had been practicing at home, after his mother had gone to bed. He was sure he had it down.

Fingering the lighter, his thumb flicked back the cover. He took his time igniting the end of a filter-less Pall Mall—his dad's brand. He exhaled slowly but couldn't hold back a gagging cough.

"Let's give it one more night." Larry said, between coughs. "Something bad is about to go down. I feel it."

"You...feel...it?" Angie's voice was mocking.

Larry spat, then stuck a finger into his mouth to root out a stray fleck of tobacco. He took another drag and exhaled—without coughing this time. He added some extra grit to his boyish tenor, "Call it an instinct. Call it a gut feeling. Yeah. Something bad is about to go down. Let's get going. One more night. What do you say?"

Angie pushed herself up off the loading dock. Staring down at Larry, she lit another cigarette.

"I like a man with an honest-to-God gut instinct, even if it's wrong." She blew smoke down at Larry. "What the hell? Let's go."

$\int$till on the back porch, Trip stared at the western sky. The storm and the psilocybin were fading. The gloomy curtain of clouds parted, making room for a hazy sun to settle behind the peaks of the shotgun houses.

Charlie, in his bathrobe, was restless, pacing.

"I got some places I want to go. And I need my driver."

Trip nodded.

"I'm going to change. I need you to clean yourself up. You're not a pretty sight."

Trip didn't need a mirror to know Charlie was right. "Give me a few minutes."

Fifteen minutes later when they met in the living room, Trip wore his suit. His hair, wet from a shower, was combed straight back and curled at the base of his neck. Charlie was in seersucker; his face shaved, his hair pomaded and parted in the middle.

"What did you do with it?" Charlie barked, back to his old self.

"What did I do with what?"

Charlie pulled out his waistband, showing Trip the butt of his .38.

"The cartridge."

"Are you sure?"

"Just tell me where it is."

"In your sock drawer. Down at the bottom. I kind of hid it."

"Right." Charlie hobbled back down the hall. He returned a moment later, clutching his straw boater.

"What've you got?" Charlie waved an open hand at the thick manila envelope Trip had pressed to his side.

"Don't ask." Trip stepped onto the porch, scanning the darkening street for trouble.

"All clear," he said, and Charlie stepped out the door.

He got Charlie settled into the passenger seat. A minute later, the Cadillac was backing toward the street.

"Where to?" Trip asked. "The Turf?"

"Not tonight. I need to make a couple stops. Here and there. I'll give you directions."

"We can do that, but I gotta make a stop first. In Ybor."

"The girl?" Charlie asked. "I think she might need a little more time to cool down."

"I'm not going to see her. I just need to leave this for her. It's three minutes away, then we'll go wherever you want."

"Well..." Charlie hesitated. He was used to getting his way.

"Look," Trip said. "You owe me this. Okay?"

Charlie grinned, his face suddenly boyish, brimming with his normal charm. "I guess you'll be holding this shooting thing over me whenever you want something? I told you I was sorry."

"I'll let you know when the debt is paid. But right now, I'm driving to her place. It won't take long."

Traffic was light on Seventh Avenue. Trip double-parked outside Katrina's building. He sprinted across the sidewalk and pushed the envelope through the mail slot.

"Alright." Trip eased back into traffic. "Where to?"

"Your little side trip wasn't out of the way. We're just going a few blocks."

Trip drove to 15th Street and Palm Avenue. Entire blocks of old Ybor had been bulldozed in the 1960s as part of a program called, "Urban Renewal." A modern community college had risen on the space. The buildings were beige bricks and sharp angles. Spindly oaks struggled for traction on the edges of vast parking lots. Modern streetlights stood in precise rows.

Trip pulled the Cadillac into a wide asphalt lot. Charlie cranked down a window and leaned his head out. "This was it."

"This....was what?"

"The El Dorado."

Trip had written a lot about Charlie's mecca of vice, his

proudest achievement. He knew the building had been demolished. Now, sitting in the empty parking lot, Trip felt the loss of the place as if it had been his own.

"I stood right there," Charlie pointed at the corner. "Watched 'em smash it with a wrecking ball and haul off the rubble in dump trucks. I came back a few days later, and it was like it never existed."

Charlie cranked up the window. "Get me the hell away from here!"

Trip headed downtown toward Charlie's regular evening haunts. When he slowed near The Turf, Charlie waved his arms.

"Not there. Not tonight."

"Where then?" Trip looked over at his passenger.

"Keep going. I'll point the way."

Tampa's downtown in 1985 was a few glass and steel high rises, vacant lots and empty storefronts. It was a daytime-only place and now it was well after the end of the workday. The sidewalks were desolate. Trip followed Charlie's bony finger to the south end of downtown, an area once known as Fort Brooke, named after a civil-war military post hunkered where the Hillsborough River met the bay. In the first half of the 20th Century, this part of downtown was all wooden docks and red-brick warehouses serving the shipping trade. Now, most of the warehouses were gone, the cleared lots choked with weeds, broken hunks of concrete, and forgotten "FOR SALE" signs. One red-brick structure had avoided the wrecking ball. Urban pioneers had converted the two-story shell into an architecture office, a men's store and a restaurant, for the lunch hour crowd.

Trip didn't know much about historic buildings, but he could see this one had not been special in its prime. Just a box of brick, with oak beams, a simple warehouse for the river trade. Instead of swinging bar doors, a glass door with sleek chrome handles led to the architecture office.

"Was this Dirty Joe's?"

Charlie nodded.

"That was my window, right up there." Charlie pointed at a

window, topped by a red brick eyebrow, on the second story overlooking Tampa Street.

There was no traffic in this part of downtown, so Trip didn't bother to pull off the street. Charlie let himself out and crossed the wide sidewalk. He stood for a moment, then placed an open palm on the bricks. Turning back, Charlie shrugged. Trip saw his boss clearly now, a sad relic adrift in his memories, shrinking inside his wrinkled suit, a straw hat clutched in a shaky, vein-covered hand. Charlie returned to the car. Trip held the door for him, looking off as his passenger struggled into his seat.

CHAPTER 40

Everyone says I opened my door that night in 1955 because I was expecting a friend, who was bringing me a bag of deviled crabs.

But that was just a story I told the cops and reporters. The truth of it is —I was strung out and searching for the evil medicine my body craved.

My regular dealer was arrested on April 17, and by April 19 I was out of powder. I woke up at noon in my El Dorado apartment, sick and craving, and turned the place upside down searching for a hidden stash. The rational part of me knew it wasn't there. I didn't wait for a driver or a bodyguard. I drove myself to The Yellow House, and the Broadway Bar. I knew some dealers hung out there, but it was daylight, and nobody who could help me was awake. Desperate, I drove downtown. I parked a few blocks from the row of dive bars on the north end of Franklin Street.

The bars had swinging doors in those days, and lots of midday customers. I pushed through several of those doors but only managed to get good and drunk. After stumbling from the last bar, I lingered on the sidewalk, wobbling and confused, trying to get my bearings. I had no idea where I'd left my car. It was after five and people were leaving downtown.

I was on the sidewalk when Johnny "Scarface" Rivera, my longtime bodyguard, pulled up in a Plymouth sedan. The Sicilians had lured him away in '49, after I gave up my operation, but Johnny and I still talked. He had called me in March with a chilling warning.

"You gotta stop talking shit about Santo Jr. and the Sicilians. The old man is dead, and your so-called protection deal died with him. You understand?"

"Screw 'em." I had told him. "I'll say what I want. They got the part of me they wanted. They don't give a hoot about what I do or say anymore."

The old Charlie Wall was cocky but smart. The drugged-up Charlie Wall was just cocky. Johnny helped me into his car. I didn't have to tell him what I needed. He could see it. Everybody in town knew Charlie Wall was on the skids.

"We gotta find my car," I muttered.

"No way you're driving home. We'll get your car tomorrow."

Johnny drove me back to my Ybor house. He still knew where I hid the key. Inside, he made me some coffee and sat me in the living room.

"You know I'm very much in need," I told him.

"I don't like it, but I can hook you up. Wait for my call."

He called an hour later, and I raced through the house to answer the phone. "What do you have for me?" I tried not to sound like a drowning man.

"Two delivery guys will be at your door at 9 p.m. A fat one and a guy who looks like a fire hydrant. They'll have what you're looking for. And don't worry about paying. I owe you. This is on me."

The old Charlie Wall would have been wary. Two guys I don't know coming to my door and me home alone. It was a recipe for disaster. But I wasn't the old Charlie Wall. When I heard the knocking, I was 18 hours from my last hit, and my stomach was cramping. I was hot and cold, grinding my teeth. I ran to the front door, yanking it open.

"What you got for me?" I asked.

The fat guy pulled out a long blade. The muscle guy lifted a shotgun. And, just like that, everything became crystal clear, like the vision I'd had in my room above Dirty Joe's almost 40 years earlier. I had turned into a hopeless junkie, like Dirty Joe, only I had a better apartment. And I saw Scarface Johnny, my former friend and bodyguard, telling his new boss, Santo Trafficante Jr., that Charlie Wall was home alone and strung out. He'd open the door to anybody who knocked.

I heard a hard click as the shotgun jammed and my instincts kicked in. I was Charlie freakin' Wall, and I wasn't going to die in my own doorway. The fat guy lunged at my belly with the knife. I stepped back and drew the Colt from my waistband. I put two rounds in the fat guy's head. Shards of bone and blood flew off him, spraying his partner. The knife fell from his dead hand and he crumbled.

I turned the Colt to the other guy, who was staring down at his useless gun. He looked up, and we locked eyes. I'll never forget that face. He wasn't scared. I wasn't scared.

"Die you dirty WOP!" I shouted, but before I could pull the trigger, he threw the shotgun at my face. As I dodged, he turned and ran, a big block of muscle in a dark suit, his stubby legs churning like pistons. I emptied the gun at him, but beyond point blank I'm a terrible shot. He sprinted up my sidewalk, turned left and disappeared into the night.

I can't explain the joy I felt at that moment. The thrill. Somehow, I was completely sober, the pain in my body gone, my brain shifting into gear for the first time in years. Charlie Wall was still important enough that somebody wanted to kill him. I had to tell myself to stop grinning. I saw the future clearly. I was going to survive this night. I was going to kick this thing.

The gunshots roused the neighbors. The cops would soon be standing over the dead man on my front porch. I ran through my house, gathering evidence of my habit, including the set of works in the overnight bag I kept under my bed. Years before, I'd had a guy bury a metal trashcan in my back yard. An old lawn chair hid the lid. I tossed the works in there, along with some unregistered handguns. I didn't toss my Colt. I had killed in self-defense. Any cop or prosecutor would agree.

The cops arrived and found me staring down at the dead man on the porch. Uniforms and detectives swarmed my house, and the newspaper assholes popped flash bulbs and lingered on the sidewalk. I held myself together. I answered everybody's questions. The street filled with neighbors and lookie-loos as word spread of a shooting at Charlie Wall's.

After detectives and forensic guys examined the dead guy and took a million pictures, two guys from the coroner's office stuffed him into a body bag and took him away. I knew all the detectives. And they knew self-defense when they saw it. They'd write up their report and if the district attorney wanted to talk to me, he'd reach out.

When everyone was gone, I took to my bed with a fifth of bourbon and a bottle of aspirin. Two of my bouncers from the El Dorado, armed with shotguns and handguns, sat on the front porch. There was no question what was going to happen next. I was about to take a guided tour of hell, but I didn't care.

I don't know how long I was in my bed. Hours? Days? A week? I screamed. I thrashed. I puked in a bucket and fell back into soaking wet sheets. Fevered and delirious, I cried out for my mother. And then one morning, I woke feeling something moist and cool brushing my forehead, the coolness along my cheeks and on my neck.

I knew this feeling. From somewhere in the distance, I heard a voice.

"Charlie? Are you in there?"

It was Ava.

CHAPTER 41

The storm had passed. The late afternoon was cool, with a soft breeze from the east. The scalloped clouds stretched above the western horizon went pink and gold in the setting sun. From the porch of the safe house, Buster thought the decrepit old houses up and down the narrow street were almost beautiful in the last blush of daylight.

He wore his dark suit. It looked strange paired with the bright white running shoes, but Buster had decided he'd never wear anything else on his feet. He wished he'd been wearing running shoes the first time he'd tried to kill Charlie Wall.

Later, Buster would pick up his violin case and walk ten blocks to Charlie Wall's house, and, if all went well, shoot him dead. But as a soft blanket of night settled over the old neighborhood, Buster felt himself tearing up again.

He had never been an emotional guy. He'd made a living with his fists and a gun. He'd done bad things but always slept well. He was an employee in a business where people knew the stakes. But now he felt wave after wave of emotion rising and cresting inside his massive chest. Was he crazy to take this on? His other hits were strictly business, but this was revenge, plain and simple. And what was Angie thinking now? Or was she even thinking about him at all?

While the evening's activities were making Buster emotional, they were making Seymour more antic than usual. He'd spent the afternoon skittering around the house, folding and unfolding his filthy bedding, straightening the treasures he kept hidden below the orange crate—the yo-yo, its white string wrapped and ready, the toy soldiers, tiny brown muskets tipped with silvern bayonets, the bottle caps stacked like poker chips. He'd spent an hour in the bathroom. Buster absolutely did not want to know what he was doing in there.

Buster returned to the living room. He found Seymour kneeling beside the orange crate, scratching notes in the ring binder.

"Do you have any empty pages in there?"

Startled, Seymour swung around, the pencil falling from his hand. He started to answer, but coughed instead, a low, phlegmy outburst, that caused his eyes to corkscrew even more than normal.

"Empty pages. I do. Yes. Of course. Yes."

"Can you write something for me?" Buster crumpled into the folding chair.

Seymour bounced to his feet, lifting the notebook, the pencils rattling in his front pocket. He stood at attention in front of Buster's chair.

"You want it in shorthand, longhand, English, Latin?"

"Just normal words, please."

Seymour flipped open the notebook, pulled a fresh pencil from his pocket, then shouted: "READY! STEADY! GO!"

"What?" Buster covered his ears with his palms.

"That's something my brother and I used to shout before we started anything. A race. A dinner. Anything." Excited, Seymour raised his pencil and shouted again: "READY! STEADY! GO!"

"Please don't yell," Buster said, lowering his hands. "I mean it."

"Sorry," Seymour whispered. "What do you need?"

"Just write this down, okay?"

"Of course. READY...uh...I mean, you know, start anytime."

Buster cleared his throat and brushed some invisible wrinkles from his old suit jacket before speaking.

"I am Buster Maniscalco. Born in Ybor City on Saturday, December 15, 1901."

Seymour looked up from the notebook. He waved his arm above his head, like a pupil with an important question. "Sorry to interrupt but what am I writing?"

"You're writing what I'm saying."

"Yes, but I'd like to put a heading on it. You know, a title."

Buster's face clinched, then relaxed. "Last will and testament." He said quietly.

"You mean like your will? Are you dying?"

Buster glared. "Just write. Don't talk. Can you do that?"

"Oh. Well. Okay." Seymour scribbled the title, then looked up at Buster.

"Where were we?" Buster asked.

"May I talk?"

"What?"

"You said don't talk."

Buster sighed and nodded. Seymour eyed the paper.

"Dec. 15, 1901..." Seymour read, his tongue darting out to dampen the tip of the pencil. He stared at Buster, ready for the next line.

"Right. In case I don't make it please consider this my last will and testament."

Seymour stopped writing.

"Excuse me. If you don't make it?"

"Things could happen." Buster said.

"I thought you said no shooting."

"I can't speak for them. Only for me. They have guns too."

Seymour saw the logic. "Right. A last will and testament. Just in case."

Buster blinked, looking off at the window, not at Seymour. He didn't want the little man to see his tears.

"Last will and testament..." Seymour said.

"What?" Buster was confused.

"The last thing you said—last will and testament."

"Right."

Buster wiped his face with a big hand, drying it on his suit jacket.

"All my possessions should go to my nephew, Dominic Maniscalco Jr., including the cigar box that is buried in his backyard underneath the teeter-totter of the swing set. He's gotta dig it up."

Buster stopped, to let Seymour finish writing. When he was

done, Seymour looked up expectantly.

"OK…"

"Where was I?"

"Dig it up." Seymour said, licking the tip of the pencil.

"Right. I wish there was more, but at least it's something. And finally, Dominic is to visit with Angie Castellano at Our Lady of Perpetual Help in Tampa, Florida, and tell her that I enjoyed our time sitting together in the dining room and I wish I could do that one more time."

Buster stopped. Seymour looked up. "Go ahead."

"That's it."

"That's it?"

"I just said that's it. So that's it. Now, hold it over here so I can sign it."

Seymour held out the open notebook and passed Buster the pencil.

Buster carefully scratched out his X on a blank line at the bottom.

"Now, tear it out and give it to me."

Seymour snapped open the ring binders and lifted out the sheet. Buster folded the paper into a tight rectangle and slipped it into the inside pocket of his coat.

"What time is it now?" Buster stared out the window into the darkness.

Seymour raised the wristwatch close to his face.

"It's almost 0-two thousand."

"What?"

"Eight. It's almost eight."

Turning quickly, Buster felt the room spinning. He stood mute until the world settled down.

"It's time." Buster said.

* * *

Angie had barely settled into the passenger seat, when Larry gunned the van toward Ybor's main drag, on the other side of the interstate.

"Where are we going?" she asked.

"I talked to my cousin. He knows things. I told him I was looking for bars owned by mobsters. Places an old hitman might hang out."

"You asked your cousin?"

"He's in the clerk's office. He knows who owns every bar in town."

Moments later, Larry parked the van in front of a two-story brick box. A red neon sign over the front door spelled out, "Broadway Bar."

"You wait here," Larry told Angie. "My cousin says this isn't a place for nice women."

"Who says I'm nice?"

"Look. It's not a place for someone like you, okay? I'm going in, ask a few questions."

Angie sighed and nodded.

Standing in the white circle thrown by a streetlight, Larry adjusted the fedora, then ran his hands down the trench coat to clear any wrinkles. He pulled a Pall Mall from his inside pocket, flicked a metal lighter, and took a slow drag. He didn't cough this time.

Larry liked how his shadow shifted from behind him to ahead of him as he walked to the bar. Pausing, he took two more puffs, the smoke circling under the brim of the fedora. He threw a meaningful glance at Angie and the van, then, tossed the cigarette aside and yanked open the bar door.

From the doorway, Larry scanned the storefront-sized joint. A pool table was garish green under a hanging plastic box adorned with hairy hoofed horses. A bald man, in dark slacks, his baggy, untucked shirt covered in paisleys, bent over the table, playing a solo game of 8-ball. Two drinkers, a gray-haired man, and a woman with a frizz of bleached blonde curls perched on stools at the far end of the bar. The pair was deep in conversation with a bald, barrel-chested bartender in a grimy undershirt. Larry memorized the scene as if he might need to give testimony later.

The bartender looked his way and laughed. "Hey, Sam Spade, come in or go the fuck away, but close the door, you're letting out the air."

A window unit chugged away somewhere. A juke box in the far corner played the '70s hit, "Feelings." The bar smelled like stale beer, poured over an ashtray. Larry heard pool balls clattering, and the soft THUNK as one dropped into an empty pocket.

Four mincing steps and Larry was at the bar. The bartender and the two drinkers stared, like they were watching a UFO landing. Over his shoulder, Larry saw the pool player eyeing him, a sour smile on his lips, the cue stick resting on his shoulder, like an emaciated baseball bat.

Larry began to question the whole detective thing. He had planned to ask around various mob-owned joints about an old hitman named Buster Maniscalco. But now, as he set his shaking hand on the bar, he felt an overwhelming urge to pee. With his eyes closed, Larry fast-forwarded through all the detective films he loved, trying to find a moment like this one. But he couldn't get any of the scenes to come into focus.

"I'm looking for a guy," Larry heard himself announce.

"You're in the wrong place, Sister," the bartender said. The two drinkers laughed. "El Goya is at the other end of the street. Lots of cute guys over there. And they're wearing costumes, too."

The blonde swung off her stool and came down the bar, tottering a bit on red high heels. She might have been thirty or fifty, it was hard to tell. Her fleshy, milk-colored body had somehow wiggled itself into a sequined, scoop-neck top and a tight black skirt that barely covered her ample thighs. Her fingernails were pink, her lips cherry red. Her front teeth were smudged with the same vivid goop.

"You sure you're not looking for a girl?" she purred, her mouth so close Larry could smell cigarettes and beer.

"I'm looking for Buster," Larry's words came out high and boyish, despite his attempts to keep them low and menacing.

"Buster Maniscalco. Anybody know him?"

"Are you a cop sweetie?" She leaned toward him. Her sequined top sagged. Her bulging breasts were like plucked birds; dark veins wormed below a scrim of goose flesh.

The woman pinched Larry's cheek, then leaned close to his ear. "Does your momma know you're here?"

"Ah...ah..." Larry couldn't get a single word to form.

She slid her hand down his back and when it reached his butt, she goosed him with a pointed finger. Larry spun out of her embrace, releasing a note that could have landed him a spot in the Vienna Boys Choir. The woman stepped back, her laughter revealing webs of wrinkles around her rheumy, mascaraed eyes.

"He's not a cop. He's a fairy!" She spun away from Larry, her hips gyrating as she returned to her barstool.

Larry looked wildly around the bar. The bartender was across from him, slapping a leather blackjack into his palm. The pool player walked toward him, both hands wrapping the wooden cue, the thick end up.

"LEAVE HIM ALONE!"

It was Angie, framed in the open front door, light pouring in around her, her metal cane raised like a weapon. She was taller than Larry remembered. Her knit cardigan, all buttoned up, could have been chain mail.

"Larry, we're leaving now!"

The bartender slipped to the other end of the bar. The pool player bent over a bank shot. Larry back-peddled until he felt Angie's hand on his shoulder. She pulled him out into the night.

Once he was safely in the van, Larry struggled to get the key out of his pocket. It wasn't easy with the trench coat wrapped around him and his hands trembling. Finally, he got the key in the ignition and the van jumped to life. He looked over at Angie, his face still ashen, his hat tilted right.

"Where now?"

"No bars, that's for sure," Angie said. "Drive to Charlie's. Park a block away. If nothing happens tonight, I'm done. You can go home and get out of that costume. My mother was right, clothes definitely do not make the man."

CHAPTER 42

Following unspoken directions from Charlie's bony index finger, Trip drove north through Tampa's downtown, passing the boarded-up retail and office towers of the 1950s, a few meandering drunks, and a restored storefront offering frozen yogurt to the office crowd. The glowing words in the window shouted: "Franklin FroYo," but the "CLOSED" sign hanging inside the glass door told the real story of Tampa's anemic downtown.

A few stoplights later, as sunset darkened into dusk, the buildings gave way to a mile of parking lots, a *Jesus Saves!* mission, three concrete block auto repair shops, garage doors pulled down for the night, rusting cars scattered across the stained concrete, and, finally, a low-slung concrete building housing Tampa Blueprint. A neighborhood filled with Victorian-style houses was visible, like a mirage, just behind this dismal street scene.

"There. That's Ross," Charlie barked. "Take a right and go slow."

If you didn't look too hard, Ross Avenue was still a majestic residential boulevard—tree-lined, with wide sidewalks behind tall concrete curbs. Hex-block walkways led to regal Victorians and Queen Annes, now the same age as the 85-year-old mobster in the front seat. Tampa Heights had been home to the first generation of the city's elite, including the Wall family.

But like Charlie, the houses had seen better days. The paint was chipped and flaking, the pitched roofs sagged, fallen tiles or lost shingles left black gaps. The houses had been cut up into apartments. Shared mailboxes hung from the walls of the wide front porches. Cars lined the curb. Trip had to brake and swerve to avoid a clutch of kids peddling tiny bikes with Harley-Davidson handlebars. Charlie leaned forward, focused on something just down the block.

"Slow down. Slow down, galdarnit! We're close. There!" He pointed. "4-0-5, that was our house, and 4-0-7 next door, that was Ava's. Sheeze, look at that. The oak tree is still standing. Pull over!"

Charlie pulled himself from the car while the Cadillac was still sputtering and shaking. A moment later, he was staring up at a massive oak, rubbing his palm along the rugged bark. The tree was leafy and sturdy, its upper branches, draped with beards of Spanish moss, arched over the rooftops. Trip stood beside Charlie and stared up.

"Look at that," Charlie pointed to two strong limbs pushing left and right toward the upstairs windows of both houses. "The path from my bedroom to hers. I called it my stairway to paradise."

A motion light flashed on, bathing them in a pale yellow.

"Look, we gotta get out of here." Trip took Charlie's arm. "This isn't your yard anymore."

Charlie's eyes moved from his window to Ava's. Trip sensed that the old man's burst of energy was spent. With Trip gripping his arm, Charlie plodded solemnly back to the car, head bent, like a man walking from a gravesite. Once Trip got him inside the car, Charlie started crying.

"I haven't been on this street since I ran away." He pushed a hand across his leaky nose, then wiped away tears with a silk handkerchief. "Too many memories."

"Where now?" Trip started the car.

"Galdangit! Take me home!"

They traveled in silence, until a stoplight on Palm Avenue. Trip turned to Charlie.

"I know there's more. After the shooting? When Ava shows up. You never finished the story."

"You're like a dog with a bone, you know that?"

"Finish the story. I know you want to."

Charlie looked out the side window.

"Jesus, Joseph and Mary! I feel like a Catholic in the box. 'Forgive me father, for I have sinned. It's been 85 years since my last confession!'"

"Tell me!" Trip demanded.

"Alright."

* * *

I don't know how many days passed like that—me sweating and delirious, squirming in my bed as Ava bathed my forehead, and then, my entire body with wet washcloths. I learned later that she was also feeding me Caldo Gallego—a soup made with greens, ham, potatoes, and white beans–when she could get me to hold still long enough to get the spoon to my mouth. I thought she was also feeding me the aspirin tablets I had brought to my bedside, but she had sent one of my El Dorado bruisers to the Trelles Clinic for sleeping pills.

"Tell Jorge Trelles that Charlie Wall needs sleeping pills. But nothing narcotic. He'll understand."

At least that's what the old doctor told me later. Word had spread about my "condition" long before the shooting. Dr. Trelles' pills knocked me out or at least left me in a limbo state that was mostly pain-free. And finally, one morning—or maybe it was afternoon, I just remember the sun shining through my window—I woke feeling calm. I still dreamed about the dark bliss of the powder, but the craving no longer lurked deep in every part of me.

Ava was standing in my doorway and I realized I hadn't been dreaming. I couldn't form words, so I just stared. She was smiling, her feet bare, her tiny body covered in soft blue jeans and one of my white dress shirts, the tail cinched into a knot at her waist.

I hadn't seen her since the morning she left me in my bed at Dirty Joes. We were maybe 20. Now at 55, she was still slim, her pale skin taut around the fine bones of her face, her always unruly curls, now salted with gray, pulled tight by a pink ribbon. A bushy ponytail fell half-way down her back. Seeing her in my doorway erased all the other women who had passed through my life. God, she was beautiful.

"Are you back among the living?"

I nodded, still unable to form words. She settled into the upholstered chair, facing my bed, her home base as I had tossed and squirmed, sweaty and delirious.

"You know they can't kill Charlie Wall," I heard myself say, in a choked voice.

"So I read. You made the Boston Globe. Nobody can resist a good mob shooting. What I didn't know was that you were also busy trying to kill yourself."

I pushed myself up in bed. Ava stood and stuffed a pillow behind my back.

"I suffer from a lack of love." I was proud of myself for being able to crack a joke.

"You suffer from being Charlie Wall." She laughed, leaning in to kiss my forehead.

"But admit it," I whispered. "You love me a little, right?"

"Not at the moment. You need a shave, a haircut, and a very long bath, then I'll be able to make a better decision about my feelings for you. All I know is every time I see you, you need a nurse, not a lover."

I thought about getting up for a shave and a bath, but the pillows were soft, a trace of her scent lingered after her kiss. Ava told me later that I slept, without pills, for the next 24 hours.

When I woke, she sat me on a chair in the bathroom and shaved away four weeks of scraggly beard and trimmed my hair. I hadn't really thought about getting older, but the clippings littering my bathroom floor were gray. After the haircut, she filled my claw-foot tub and helped me into it. I was naked but she handled me with the professional manner of a nurse, not a lover. Once I was in the tub, she slipped out, closing the door behind her.

I scrubbed away a coating of sweat and grime. I heard the creak of the door. The woman standing naked in the doorway was definitely not my nurse. I had never seen Ava naked before, though I had fantasized a lot about it. Whatever I had imagined, the real thing was better. Her pale skin was firm, her thighs gently muscled, her breasts small, the dark nipples upturned, a faded Cesarian scar sliced across her belly like a lightning bolt. Ava reached into the tub and pulled the plug, letting the dirty water flow out. When it was gone, she filled it again, smiling as the water rose around me, then she slipped in, her back settling against my chest.

We didn't leave the house for a week. It was early May, and the weather was surprisingly spring-like, dry breezes ruffling the curtains, the nights cool enough for a light blanket. The guards took turns sleeping in the back apartment, one of them on the front porch day or night, a shotgun leaning against the wall. Unless I came out to ask one of them to fetch food, or milk or coffee, the door at the end of my hall was closed and locked. Ava and I stayed behind that door, needing no one else. When we weren't exploring each other, we leaned on plump pillows and talked.

I told her my story. I didn't lie about it. She already knew who I was. I told it straight, including my descent into drugs and my arrogance that addiction could never happen to me.

When it was her turn, Ava also held nothing back. She had two girls, both grown and married. Her husband, a successful doctor from a prominent Boston family, spent most nights with a mistress he kept in a fancy apartment building in Back Bay. Like Ava, her husband was a good Catholic, so there would be no divorce. They occupied a world of private clubs and charity fundraisers, and for those they masqueraded as a happy husband and wife. He believed she was in Tampa visiting her siblings—her parents were long dead—but he wouldn't check on her. Absences like this were the good part of their long marriage—times they didn't have to keep up the charade.

"You could stay," I told her. "I can take care of you."

It was after midnight, her head rested on my shoulder, her body was pressed to my side, her leg stretched over mine.

"You know I can't do that. I never could have done that."

With another woman, I would have used all my wiles to change her mind, but Ava was right. We had started in the same world.

We'd have been a good match if I had followed my father into the insurance trade or worked at a downtown bank. But when I chose the dark side of the street, she could never join me there. Not for long anyway. And now she had children and grandchildren, and a life, of sorts, in Boston, with a summer getaway house on the Maine coast near Bar Harbor.

We shared our stories, then sat in silence, listening to the distant ticking of my old grandfather clock.

"Ava..." I whispered.

I was about to tell her I loved her, but her hand moved quickly and covered my mouth.

"Don't," she said. "Don't talk about that. Let's enjoy this."

After seven miraculous days and nights of this but not that, I woke up and reached across the wide bed. Ava was gone.

CHAPTER 43

Larry's driving was as labored as his breathing. He had drifted out of his lane a few times, forcing Angie to grab the steering wheel. When he pulled into the dark spot a block from Charlie's house, the van's front tire hit the high curb, the wheel cover scrapped the concrete.

"Oh Christ," Larry whispered. "Now I've done it."

"Goddammit, Larry!" Angie snapped. "Calm the hell down."

Larry's hands gripped the steering wheel, his eyes focused on the darkness outside the windshield.

"This is crazy," he said, as much to himself as Angie. "What am I doing playing detective? I'm not that guy. I need to go home."

Angie reached over and switched off the key.

"Put it in park, Larry."

He followed instructions.

"Larry, listen. Don't worry," Angie's voice was gentle. "You can go home soon. After tonight, I won't bother you anymore. No more driving around. And I'll buy a new hubcap for the van. Everything will be back just like it was. Okay?"

In the dashboard light, Larry looked like a boy who had just been awakened from a bad dream.

"Okay." He bowed his head, as if he was praying. "I thought I could do this. Be the tough guy. I really did."

* * *

The first time he set out to kill Charlie Wall, Buster had been driven to the job in a stolen Ford sedan. His partner, Jackie "Mangia" Aprile, had parked the black car two blocks from Charlie's house. They planned to dump it in Palmetto Beach after the hit. Mangia's rusted Ford pickup was waiting for them there.

Wearing black suits, they'd walked side-by-side down Charlie's street, the Long Tom hidden under Buster's black trench coat. Even in the darkness, anyone seeing them could guess the business the two of them were about to conduct. As usual, Jackie was jovial, gushing about the meal he'd finished an hour before at Demmi's, a storefront cafe on Seventh Avenue.

"Picadillo, with raisins and spices over yellow rice. And old man Demmi had giant tomatoes fresh from Ruskin. He came to the table and sliced 'em right there with a carving knife, poured on some olive oil, a little salt and pepper. Holy goddam! I mean, what else can I say but holy goddam!"

That's why they called him Mangia—Jackie loved his food and it showed, he was a mobile mountain of muscle and blubber, and after things went wrong it pleased Buster that Mangia had at least enjoyed his last meal. Buster had wondered what happened to the car after Mangia died on Charlie's front porch, his head opened by two slugs from Charlie's revolver, his blood and brains pooling around Buster's brogans. Buster didn't run for the car. The keys were in Mangia's pocket. Instead, he ran south, at least a dozen blocks, before stopping to catch his breath in a shadowy, brick-lined alley near Fourth Avenue.

Buster spent the next week hiding out in his single room above the Broadway Bar, waiting for someone to come for him. Someone with a gun sent to silence a hitman who had failed. But nobody came. Buster figured his bosses decided coming after him wasn't worth the trouble. Eventually, he emerged. He spent months looking over his shoulder, but no one was ever there. He never heard from the Trafficantes again. Made guys ignored him if they saw him on the street or in a bar. There were no more muscle jobs. No more train trips to mobbed-up towns. No more weeks sleeping in an aging Art Deco hotel on Miami Beach, stalking a local mobster who never saw it coming. After the Charlie fiasco, Buster kept his economic inner tube afloat with a series of bouncer jobs at fading tough-guy bars around

Ybor and West Tampa until he got too old to scare anyone, and his nephew moved him into Our Lady.

Now, as he walked toward Charlie's house on a warm, moonless evening in May, the bay breeze smelling of salt water and roasted coffee, Buster felt young again. And this time, he was prepared. He'd spent three days planning the second Charlie hit. The Holland and Holland was oiled, polished, and loaded. The gun had been a gift from Nick, handed over in what was almost a religious ritual a few weeks before his mentor was murdered by a much more basic shotgun.

"Too fuckin' frilly for my taste," Nick told Buster.

The Holland and Holland was a gentleman's hunting gun, probably stolen from a collector. Buster loved the stags and ducks carved into the walnut stock. If he'd been allowed to use the Holland the first time he went after Charlie Wall, the bastard would have died. Now, with the right weapon and the help of the strange creature skipping along beside him, Buster knew Charlie Wall would die.

If only Seymour would shut up.

"Are you nervous? I'm nervous but nerves are good, right? It means you're thinking about it. Looking at all the angles. Like when I was playing professional billiards. I had nerves, sure, but if I studied the table…"

"What?"

Deep in his own thoughts, Buster hadn't been listening to Seymour. After four days and three nights together, Buster only listened when the little man said something important, like what time Charlie Wall arrived home and what Charlie's bodyguard did before opening the car door. During Seymour's flights of fancy—his invention of the running shoe and the atomic bomb, his gigs with the CIA and Army Special Forces—Buster tuned him out.

"Not so much talking right now," Buster barked. "No distractions. Stick with the plan."

The plan was simple, the way Buster liked his plans. When Charlie arrived home, Buster would be hidden in a spot between the house and what was left of the garage. According to Seymour's journal—the entry was two pages long and included four illustrations—there was a niche the security light did not penetrate. Seymour would wait on the street, behind a wide oak tree, only revealing himself after the bodyguard opened Charlie's car door. If all went according to plan, the bodyguard would walk toward the street to check out Seymour. That's when Buster would step from the shadows. If Charlie was out of the car, all the better. If he stayed inside, Buster was fine with that. His shotgun could do the job either way.

It was 8:30 p.m. when they turned onto Charlie's Street. The Cadillac was gone. The house was dark. At the end of the side-walk, Buster turned to face Seymour.

"This is it," Buster said. "So...you know what to do and when to do it. Right?"

The little man shook himself like a dog, from his head down to his feet, then he snapped to attention.

"Sir, yes sir!" he saluted.

Buster's roommate had somehow convinced himself that they were on some type of military operation with Buster as his commanding officer. Buster had played along, even returning a salute now and then, but tonight, Buster did not salute. Instead, he placed a beefy hand on Seymour's shoulders stared into the little man's evasive eyes.

"You do your job tonight and I'll do mine. I'll give you ten percent of whatever I collect from the old bastard. But you gotta stay with the plan. Don't get distracted. Okay?"

Seymour's body twitched under Buster's hands.

"Okay?" Buster put his face close to Seymour's.

"Calm! Focused! No distractions!" Seymour shouted, like a marine grunt answering the drill sergeant. His voice causing Buster's head to snap back. "On it, Sir! You can count on me."

Seymour saluted again. Buster lifted his paw off Seymour's shoulder and brought one finger to his lips.

"Shhhhh," Buster whispered. "Let's do this."

Angie could not leave Larry alone in the van. He might panic and drive off. Reaching out, she settled her fingers around his quivering jaw, slowly turning his head toward hers. She offered a reassuring smile.

"Charlie should be home soon. We're going to get out quietly, and stand over there, behind that big tree where they can't see us. We're here an hour and then we go home. For good. You can do it."

Larry sniffed and wiped his face with a bare hand.

He whispered, "Okay."

For half an hour, they waited behind the wide trunk of a live Oak. The night was still. A few stars punctured the haze of the Ybor streetlights. They waited without speaking, listening to the distant hum of the highway.

* * *

The black Cadillac idled at a traffic light, a few blocks from Charlie's house.

"So she left?" Trip asked his passenger. "Was there a note?"

Looking over, Trip saw the old man grimace.

"Why do writers always want someone to leave a note? Why not a Hallmark card? 'Thanks for all the sex.' Heck no, there was no note. We didn't need notes. I knew where she'd gone." Charlie stared out the passenger window.

"So, what did you do?"

The light changed. Trip eased the car forward.

"You know, I'm paying you to drive and protect me, not to ask personal questions. But, what the heck, I've told you everything else. You want to know what I did after she left?"

"Yeah, I do."

Charlie turned back from the window.

"I got out of bed and went back to work. I drank but never used a needle again. I kept my bodyguards close. In 1960 the government bought the El Dorado, so they could knock it down. It was good money. I took it and never looked back."

"No more hit men at your door?"

"That whole world just melted away. Almost like it never happened. The bosses got old and died. I retired. I played the stock market. I bought a cabin in the mountains and went there when it got hot. It's boring but that's the story. Until recently, when you started your little charade."

"What?"

"Don't play coy. You think I'm an idiot? I figured it out. And I gotta give you credit, the arrow was a nice touch."

Of course, he figured it out, Trip thought. Charlie knew everything, even when he acted like he didn't.

"So how did you...when did you?"

"Don't worry about it. You did a great job. It made me feel like I was somebody again."

Trip guided the big Cadillac onto 12th Street and fell into the pattern. He slowed the car, scanning the yards and porches.

"Relax, will ya!" Charlie shouted. "There's nobody lurking. And thank Christ no one was really trying to kill me. You're a good kid but who ever heard of a muscle guy armed with an 8-iron?"

When the Cadillac rolled into the driveway the floodlight flashed on, painting the car and the front yard a steely white. When the engine quit sputtering Trip stepped out, scanning the neighborhood. He didn't expect any trouble, but as he reached for Charlie's car door, there was movement across the street.

"I saw something." He held open Charlie's door but stared toward the street.

"Relax kid," Charlie said. "There's nobody out there. They're all dead. I'm the last man standing."

Trip saw a scarecrow of a man dancing beside the barreled trunk of a live oak.

"There's somebody out there," Trip whispered. "Stay where you are."

* * *

Buster wasn't a smiler, but when the bodyguard left the car and went to check out Seymour, he couldn't hold back a smile. Charlie's car door was open. The old man's fingers curled over the top of the door.

The plan was working!

Buster had left any doubts back at the safe house. Once he was on a job, he didn't second guess himself. Still, as he waited to step into the light, the memory from the night in 1955 come back, as if it had happened yesterday, not 30 years before.

His shotgun had jammed. Mangia was dead. He and Charlie locked eyes. Charlie's revolver was pointed at Buster's chest. Flinging the shotgun was more instinct than idea. He remembered sprinting for safety, rounds buzzing around him.

Now, Buster saw his target clearly in the crystalline light. Charlie stepped away from the car, a bit unsteady on his feet. Buster liked the heft of the shotgun in his hands, his index finger curled around the triggers.

He rocked back and forth in his new running shoes. In the adrenaline high of the moment, he realized that for the first time in a long time, nothing hurt. Damn, I feel good, he told himself. Solid. Doing what I was born to do. This SOB was supposed to be dead long ago.

Buster stepped from the shadows into the light.

Angie watched the bodyguard climb from the car and check the street. In his dark suit, he looked like a chauffeur or maybe a mob enforcer. His head turned. Squinting, Angie saw what the bodyguard saw—a figure moving in the shadows across from Charlie's driveway.

"Do you see that?" It was Larry.

"I do."

The bodyguard took another step toward the moving figure. Charlie pulled himself from the car and took a couple of wobbly steps toward the house. Then Angie saw Buster, a shotgun in his grip, step into the light.

"It's happening!" She reached out, ready to put her hand on Larry's shoulder. But Larry was sprinting toward the low, spiked fence that wrapped Charlie's yard.

* * *

The security light didn't reach beyond Charlie's front sidewalk, but Trip could make out a scarecrow creature in the shadows across the street. Maybe a man, maybe a gawky boy, his clothes too big for his body.

Trip strode toward the fence. A dancing man waved his arms over his head and shouted something that sounded a lot like "Yoo Hoo!" Trip stopped at the fence. Something about this wasn't right. The dancing guy was unarmed. He was strange but didn't appear to be dangerous.

Trip spun around, looking at the house. He saw a squat figure step forward, the barrels of the shotgun silver in the security light. A fucking decoy! Trip realized. Goddammit! A real bodyguard would have seen it.

"Charlie!" Trip yelled. "Go back to the car!"

The old man did not turn. Instead, he pulled the Colt from his waistband.

* * *

Larry couldn't recall the movie it came from, but from his hiding place behind the tree, he remembered the line—"A coward dies a thousand deaths, a brave man dies but once."

His fear had killed him so many times in his life, he couldn't live with himself if it happened again. When Buster emerged from the shadows holding the shotgun, he didn't hesitate. He ran toward the scene. If he had stopped to think about it, he might have changed his mind.

The wrought iron spikes atop Charlie's fence loomed ahead of him. Larry hurdled the fence, one spike ripping his pants. He landed on one foot and then the other. Pausing to regain his balance, he saw the two men faced off, maybe thirty yards away. Larry plunged ahead. He hadn't run since he was a kid on a playground. It felt strange, his legs churning, his body hurtling forward.

* * *

Angie rushed across the street. If she had been thirty years younger, she'd have followed Larry over the fence, but now, she could only wrap her hands around the iron spikes and stare at a scene stripped of color by the glare of Charlie's spotlight.

Two armed men faced each other, like gunslingers in a TV western. Larry was in motion. The bodyguard was yelling. Angie couldn't hear his words over the clattering of leaves and branches, that ticked away in the stiffening wind.

Everything happened at once

Larry, close to Buster, took flight, his trench coat billowing behind him like Superman's cape. The running bodyguard leapt toward his boss. The shotgun and the revolver fired at the same time.

The scene shifted into slow motion. Angie saw bodies collide and falling, Larry on Buster, the bodyguard pulling Charlie to the ground, two weapons tumbling free. And who was that odd vagabond dancing nervously at the open gate? Angie wanted to rush to the crazy jumble of arms, legs, and guns, but her feet were frozen in place. Just then, the security light blinked off, and Charlie's chaotic front yard went black.

"Wow," Angie whispered into the darkness. "Wow."

The gunman stepped from the shadows. I recognized the wide, Neanderthal face, the hulking shoulders, the stubby legs. In front of me, in a stark island of light, stood the hit man from 30 years before. The one that got away.

Not ten minutes after I told the kid I knew that the threats, even the arrow, were phony baloney, here comes an actual killer out of my past. I'd laugh about it later, but right now, it wasn't funny.

Still, I gotta say, facing death on a moonless night in Ybor was exhilarating. My heart pumped blood, adrenaline sizzled through me, every cell alive and well. Just like that, I was my younger self again—no arthritis, no aching joints, my eyesight clear, my hearing crisp, my body ready for anything. And in that split second there was one thing I knew for sure—Charlie Wall was not going to die this night.

"I know you." There was no trace of fear in my voice. "I know you."

"You fucking should, you bastard. You killed my best friend."

The hit man took a lumbering step forward, and I did the same. He was old now, but wearing the same dark suit, white shirt and tie, except instead of black brogans, he padded forward in a pair of white tennis shoes.

I pulled my Colt .38. The revolver wavered a bit, not because I was afraid, but from the hand tremor that shook anything I held aloft. Okay, maybe everything about me wasn't 100 percent, but at this range, it didn't matter. The hulking guy was an easy target, I could hit him from six feet away, no matter how much my Colt was shaking.

We took another step forward. There was no fear in his eyes.

He was a pro. Weapons ready, our eyes locked, neither of us spoke for a long beat,

From somewhere behind me, I heard Trip, my worthless body-guard, yell, but I was so focused, I couldn't make out his words. I also sensed motion from the side yard, something or someone hurtling toward us, but my eyes stayed on the gunman.

"You can't kill Charlie Wall. Don't you know that, by now?"

"I can." His raspy voice carried no trace of fear. "I will."

He scrunched his face into the ugly sneer I remembered from thirty years before. It was almost funny, seeing him make that face and hearing him repeat the same stupid line—"Die you fucking bastard!"

I didn't wait to see if his gun would jam again. Before he could pull, I fired. Two slugs found his shirt, just left of his wide, out-of-style tie, two blotches of red spread on the white cotton. And then, from nowhere, a flying figure slammed into the hitman, pushing him to the ground. Both barrels exploded as they fell.

I looked down at my chest. No blood. I felt my face. My hands came back dry and clean. That's when I laughed. Charlie Wall had survived another one.

Just then, a body slammed into me from behind.

Dinner at Our Lady started at four in the wide, low-ceilinged dining hall, set with eight-top tables topped by cream-colored cloths. At three, a skinny kid, on a break from college, rolled in the portable bar for happy hour. Two female residents, both former music teachers, took turns playing '30s and '40s hits on a battered, but in-tune upright. By six, most residents had finished drinks and the buffet dinner and were off to their apartments or to the nearby TV lounge for a VHS movie that ended by eight. Angie had never adapted to the early-bird lifestyle. She appeared in the dining room at 6, holding a cut crystal glass filled with chardonnay. Her unbuttoned cardigan revealed a pale blue smock, with tiny mother of pearl buttons sewn along the V of the neck.

Angie waved at a few widows who were lingering, their walkers lined-up by the front door like so many choppers outside a biker bar. By 6:30, most of the diners had rolled off on their "Hardly Davidsons."

Angie finished her chardonnay and walked to the buffet, bypassing the tin trays of roast pork, yellow rice, black beans and plantains. She picked up a plate at the salad section. She kept her figure by avoiding all that Ybor City food.

The skinny kid had left her a glass of Rioja on the portable bar. Angie poured it into her crystal goblet and settled at an empty table. She liked the quiet of the dining room at this hour. Two young waiters moved about, clearing the empty plates and glasses. Once the dishes were collected and the buffet table wiped down, they turned off the fluorescents. It was almost sunset, and a wall of windows poured honey-colored light over the tables and the bare walls. It was the time of day when Angie liked to think. A week after the shootout at Charlie's Wall's, she had a lot to think about.

Sammy, Our Lady's security guard, had been fired. Two of the younger widows had complained about a drunken guy in a uniform knocking on their doors after midnight, telling them he had to come in for the monthly check of the alarm system. Our Lady did not have an alarm system.

Larry applied for the job and two days after the shootout, he was strolling the halls in a crisp khaki uniform, with "Larry Pardo Security" embroidered above his shirt pocket. Larry wasn't a private eye, but he was also no longer a mousy van driver. Angie, a lifelong insomniac, joined him at midnight to watch black and white videos in which tough guy detectives in trench coats outshot the villains, set up the *femme fatale* for the fall, and trade sexy banter with their loveable, but ditzy secretaries.

The whole Buster thing had Angie reconsidering her sex life. Maybe she was putting too much effort into these relationships. Men were unreliable. They kept dying or disappearing. She loved all the sweating and panting, but hadn't she reached the age when she should just live off the memories? The real thing was great, but the heartache and complications were just too much trouble. Chasing an old hitman around Ybor City and witnessing the crazy shootout at Charlie's had been the last straw.

She held her wine glass under her nose, inhaling the aroma of plums and blackberries. A glass of wine, a late-night movie with Larry, some shopping trips to the new mall out near the football stadium, and regular manicures and pedicures should be enough, she told herself.

The double doors of the dining room swung open. Rubber soles squeaked across the terrazzo floor. And just like that, those thoughts fled. She felt the familiar icy hot tingle deep in what her mother used to call "her tweens." Angie flipped open her compact. The tiny mirror didn't reveal any wrinkles, just the coral on her lips and the touch of pink on her cheeks. Clicking the compact closed, she smiled up at the man slowly lumbering her way.

Angie patted the empty seat beside her. Buster, wearing his dark suit and Nikes, pulled the chair back and sat down, moaning quietly as he always did. She smiled, as his paw of a hand, scarred and hairy at the knuckles, settled atop her knee.

* * *

Outside it was full-on Florida summer, but inside Trip's tiny bedroom, the slatted venetian blinds kept things dark, and the chugging window unit kept things icy. Sleeping under a cotton sheet, Trip dreamed he was spelunking though a vast underground cathedral. He was lost, and freezing cold, and didn't know how to find his way back to the cave mouth. Awakened by a rattling surge from the air conditioner, he sat up and pulled a blanket around his shoulders. He tried to remember when he'd stopped writing the night before. It was late. Or early, depending on your feelings about 3 am.

He had stayed at the typewriter working on the pivotal chapter of the Charlie book—the shootout. The authors' bible, *The Elements of Style*, sat open by the typewriter along with the four-word note Katrina had left in the gift bag: "Keep writing. Love, Kat."

Despite all that had happened, he continued to follow her advice. Since embarking on the project almost a year earlier, he'd told Charlie's story as accurately as he could, checking dates and some of Charlie's taller tales against the newspaper articles on microfilm at the downtown library. But he'd always believed that Charlie's story, like Charlie himself, was larger than life. That's why he had taken some liberties with the chapter about the shootout. So what if Charlie didn't really shoot the hitman and live to tell about it. It was how the old man would have wanted his story to end.

Trip set about his morning rituals—brushing, bathing, making a strong cup of café con leche. Despite the caffeine, he felt another wave of exhaustion breaking over him. It had been a week since the shootout, but except for his time at the typewriter, which energized him, he was always tired.

The loss of Katrina and Charlie on the same day was a lot to process. He ached for the woman who was his first real love. He missed Charlie the way someone might miss a lost limb. He awoke every morning thinking the old man was asleep on the other side of the house. He caught himself making extra coffee or leaving a second mug on the counter. But he hadn't cried. What he felt wasn't grief. Just a void. He moved through his repetitive days listless, irritable, and easily distracted.

With his coffee in hand, he dragged Charlie's rocking chair out onto the front porch and settled into it, staring out at the Cadillac, the spiked fence, the live oaks, their sagging branches wearing mossy beards.

The porch was warm, the motion of the chair like a mantra. Like a Florida driver sliding across a patch of ice, Trip tried to steer his thoughts in another direction, but it didn't work. He was back to the crazy day that had started with a dose of mushroom tea and ended in the harsh light of a hospital emergency room.

The memory played out the same way every time. Trip watched from above, like he was a bird on a wire. He saw the Cadillac rattle to a stop, the chrome bumpers going silvery as the security spot flashed on. He saw himself emerge from the driver's side; saw the odd figure dancing across the fence near the oak tree, calling "Woo Hoo!" in that eerie, falsetto voice, saw a figure in a trench coat running across the yard, saw Charlie pull himself from the car; and finally, saw the black-suited hit man step from the shadows, cradling a shotgun.

Always at this point, the scene shifted into close-up. Trip rushed toward the strange man in the street, but he stopped at the fence and turned. He saw the gunman walk from the shadows and realized his boss had been right— he was a terrible bodyguard. He ran toward Charlie, tackling him just as the guy in the trench coat guy took down the hitman. He heard the boom of the shotgun, the sharp crack of Charlie's Colt, smelled the sour stench of the gunpowder.

Then, as it always did, the spotlight switched off, and the world went black.

Trip had taken his boss to the ground with a spinning tackle, that left Charlie on top of him. Charlie was lean and frail, but he was surprisingly heavy on Trip's chest. Trip eased Charlie off his chest and got to his feet, which triggered the motion sensor, and the night turned back into day. A truckload of hieroglyphs spilled across his eyes.

When his vision cleared, he saw the trench-coat guy on top of the burly hit man. The shotgun and Charlie's revolver lay a few feet apart on the grass. The strange dancing guy was gone, but an older woman, in a long cardigan sweater, was striding down the sidewalk.

Trip knelt beside his boss. Charlie's beaked face was drawn, his skin going gray, his mouth sagging open. He leaned close to Charlie's mouth, listening, but no air moved. Trip slid his hands over the seersucker suit but found no blood.

A moan made him look up. The hitman pushed the trench coat guy off his chest. The tall woman was on her knees, leaning over the hitman, who moaned again. Trench coat guy stood over them.

"Buster. Buster! Look at me. Are you hit anywhere?"

Trip realized he was looking at the man and woman he'd seen kissing in the van that night. It didn't make sense. What were they doing here?

Trip tried to concentrate. What would a real bodyguard do? He would secure the weapons, Trip decided. He picked up the guns and set them on the front seat of the Cadillac.

Trench coat guy retraced his steps and picked up a black fedora. It was two sizes too large and fell just above his eyes. Trip almost laughed. The trench coat, the suit, the fedora, the paunch; the guy looked like a chubby kid impersonating a film noir detective.

The hitman was laid out on the ground, like a giant slug. The film-noir detective and the tall woman bent over him.

"I think he's okay." The fake detective's voice was high and whiny. "Looks like they both missed."

Trip was sure the gunshots would draw out the neighbors, but when he looked around, the sidewalk was empty. In this bottom rung neighborhood, gunshots in the night no longer brought people out of their houses.

Charlie was not breathing. Trip ran inside, down Charlie's long hall, to the old rotary phone.

"My boss is on the ground," he told the 911 operator. "I'm not sure what's wrong, but it looks bad."

Trip rushed back and dropped to his knees beside Charlie. He pulled open his jacket and pushed on his chest. A single blast of air burst from Charlie's open mouth. Trip pumped again but got no response.

Looking up, he saw that the gunman was on his feet, though he looked lost and feeble. The woman led him down the sidewalk, her arm around his waist. The fake detective followed behind. At the gate, the hitman looked back, like a boy who had lost a toy.

Trip pushed again on Charlie's chest. The fake detective returned to stand above them. He cleared his throat.

"Do you mind if I grab that shotgun?"

Trip looked up, confused. "You want the shotgun?"

The guy nodded. "I'm not going to use it, or anything. It's, you know, special. An antique."

The guy looked harmless. Trip was sure the gunplay was over. He nodded toward the car and went back to work on Charlie's chest.

"Come on, Charlie. Breathe! Breathe!"

A sired wailed.

The ambulance crew eased Trip away. One guy took over the chest compressions. The other secured an oxygen mask to Charlie's sallow face. The EMTs were Trip's age, one Trip's height, the other shorter. Both had the broad chests and muscled arms you can only grow in weight rooms. After a few minutes, they stood, the tall one shaking his head and looking at his watch.

"What happened to him?" He asked Trip.

"He collapsed after getting out of the car." Trip didn't mention the hit man, the trench coat guy, or the old woman. He certainly didn't mention guns or gunshots. That's how Charlie would have handled it.

Trip rode in the back of the ambulance. One of the EMTs pumped Charlie's chest and checked the oxygen mask.

A stretcher was waiting at Tampa General, but no one seemed to be in a hurry. Charlie had not responded. The EMTs didn't say anything, but Trip knew his boss would not be walking out of this hospital.

He went into an emergency room lobby that smelled of sweat and antiseptic, sat on a seat of hard plastic that squeaked when he moved. He stood and paced the linoleum floor. At some point, a young resident pushed through the swinging doors. He was lanky, his skin the color of mahogany. Indian or Pakistani, Trip thought. The resident was visibly exhausted but polite.

"I'm sorry but Mr. Wall didn't make it. Are you his son?" He spoke a clipped, precise English.

Trip shook his head.

"I'm..." He struggled with the right description. "I live in his house. Drive him places. He doesn't really have any family. None that claim him anyway."

"We'll need someone, a family member or someone with legal standing to take care of the arrangements."

Trip thought of John Barnett. "He has an attorney. I'll call him. But can you at least tell me what killed him." Trip flashed on his takedown tackle. "Could it have happened when he fell?"

The doctor shook his head. "It looks like his heart gave out. I wouldn't be able to say with certainty without an autopsy. But this isn't a death that requires an autopsy. He had no visible wounds. He was old. A drinker, for sure, and a smoker. It was just his time, I think."

CHAPTER 48

"Stay there for now." Barnett's voice was gravelly but firm when he took Trip's 2 a.m. call from the hospital. "I'll take care of things. And I guess I should tell you; Charlie was very specific about what happened after he was gone. No service. A simple cremation. I'll come by soon with a bottle of champagne and we'll toast the old bastard. Until then, get some rest."

Resting was all Trip could manage. When he was awake, he felt like he was stoned or high. He had no energy. He entered rooms and couldn't remember why. Stumbling around the empty house, he found traces of Charlie everywhere, a pair of cuff links on his dresser, a half-smoked cigar in the bathroom, a coffee cup on the nightstand with a plug of curdled milk at the bottom.

Daniel Hebert, the *Tribune* reporter, wrote a front-page obituary. Trip had not answered the door when he knocked, but Hebert didn't need Trip for the story. His interview with Charlie was barely a month old, and the paper had packet after packet of clippings detailing the life of Charlie Wall.

He took the paper onto the front porch to read Hebert's story. He was struck by one sentence: "After four documented attempts on his life, Charlie Wall, 85, died of natural causes, according to John Dunn, a spokesman for Tampa General Hospital."

Easing back the rocker and lowering the paper, Trip felt his mind engage for the first time since Charlie's death. Of course, he thought, the only person who could kill Charlie Wall was Charlie himself. His laugh started small, just a chuckle, but it grew like a wildfire, until Trip was bent forward, coughing and laughing, struggling to catch his breath. Hot tears rolled down his cheeks.

Tears. Laughter. Grief. Regret. Trip let it all out.

* * *

After the breakdown Trip felt better. He returned to his writing with new energy. He was on the front porch two days later, sipping his second café con leche, when the ice blue Lincoln Continental pulled up out front.

He knew the car.

Ronald Armstrong Jr. had the same ruggedly handsome face and linebacker body as his son. He kept a weight room in the Palma Ceia house, and he maintained his 32-inch waistline and his bulky arms and shoulders with barbells, dumbbells and 200 sit-ups a day. His summer suits, and polished loafers were hand-made. His hair was graying around his ears but still hung over his forehead in a sandy-blond tousle, just like his son's.

Trip was in the cutoffs and T-shirt he'd pulled on an hour before. He thought about running inside to change but decided against it. He pushed his fingers through his uncombed hair and stood to meet his father.

Ron Jr. stopped on the broken sidewalk just below the porch steps.

"Dad." Trip said. "Good to see you."

His father scanned the old house, the ramshackle neighborhood, and his unkempt son.

"Someone told me you worked for him. Your mom showed me the obit."

"My stepmom."

"Yeah, Judy. She misses you. So do I. Son, I thought you told me you were planning to get on the right side of the law."

"And I did. I am. Except for one slip, I've been a straight arrow for almost a year."

"Working for the most notorious criminal in Tampa?"

"Working for an old man with a past. Charlie's been out of

the rackets since before I was born. I drove his car. Kept him company. All legal. Kind of a chance to figure some things out."

"From where I'm standing, I don't see a young man who has things figured out. Sorry, but that's what I'm seeing."

Trip's first instinct with his father was to argue, but he wasn't up to it today. And if the roles had been reversed, he might have said the same thing to his shaggy haired son, in torn shorts and a stained T-shirt, living in the house of a dead mobster.

"Let's say I'm a work in progress. But there is progress."

"Son, you're 30 years old. Your friends are married, starting careers. You haven't even been to college. Figuring it all out isn't really that hard. You just do it."

"I'm trying. It may not look like it, but I'm really trying."

His father climbed the porch steps. He stopped a foot from his son. He pulled a linen envelope from his pocket.

"There's some money in here. You're welcome to come home. I know lots of important people. I can help you. If you want it."

His father put the envelope in Trip's hand. Their faces, almost identical despite the age difference, were inches apart. There were fresh creases around his father's eyes. A slight sag below his chin. He had gotten older. Trip figured his father was seeing the same things in his son.

"Did Granddad ever take an envelope from Charlie?"

His father stared for a long beat before he answered.

"You'd have to ask him that, except that would be a real long-distance call. All I can say is this: Tampa was a different city then."

"How different? Who decides who's on the right side and who's on the wrong side? Is the bad guy the one with the envelope, or the guy who takes it? At least Charlie was honest about who he was."

Trip looked down at his father's envelope. Ron Jr. was right. Trip was a fuck-up. Charlie was dead. Katrina had fled, leaving no forwarding address. He had maybe $300 to his name. He had written a book but maybe it sucked. Even if it didn't what would he do with it? He had no agent. No publisher. No credentials.

Trip shook his head. He'd left his old life once before. He wasn't going back. He pulled open his father's sport coat and slid the envelope into the inside pocket.

"Dad, I appreciate the offer. I really do."

CHAPTER 49

It was late afternoon when John Barnett knocked. He had come directly from the golf course. His outfit was the same one Trip's dad wore on the Palma Ceia course—plaid slacks, a polo shirt with a tiny alligator on the chest, a Yankees ball cap. Barnett had switched from the tasseled golf shoes to a pair of brushed leather loafers. He still looked regal, his salt-and-pepper hair combed back, his manicured fingers curled around the handle of a leather briefcase.

Seeing the lawyer in the doorway triggered an image of Charlie on the gurney being wheeled into the hospital, his hawk's nose pointing skyward, his body suddenly small beneath the white sheet. Trip felt the room spinning. He took a hesitant step back. Barnett grabbed Trip's upper arm.

"I think you better sit down." He led Trip to the couch. "I've got some news."

* * *

I made a boatload of money. Heck, I probably could'a filled an oil tanker with all the dough I earned back in the day. But I never cared about money or the pleasures it might buy me. What I really liked was making it and using it to grow my business.

By the 1930s, my Bolita operation was the biggest in the country. The bars, the whores, the loansharking, the gaming tables, all produced. I handed out a lot of envelopes but those tithes to police chiefs and beat cops, to sheriffs and deputies, to mayors, county commissioners, governors and even a U.S. Senator were pocket change for me.

At the peak, my biggest money problems were counting it and stashing it. A passenger steamer ran daily from Tampa to Havana. I had a guy on that ship almost every other day with a suitcase or two stuffed with cash. Banks in Havana didn't report deposits to the American tax man.

I wasn't sure how much I had stashed in Cuba. It didn't matter, really, there was always more. I lost a lot when I handed over my Bolita and other operations to the Santo Sr., but once I converted the El Dorado into a burlesque house, the cash spigot flowed again.

When you don't really give a fig about it, money figures that out and finds ways to disappear. I spent plenty on exotic women and rare steaks. I enjoyed showing up every month or so at the Children's Home with a large, zippered bag stuffed with bills.

My years as a junkie didn't help. Money leaked away like water through a busted pipe. And even after I cleaned up, my brain was in low gear for a few years. In January of 1959, that asshole Fidel did what nobody thought he could do and overnight all my Cuban bank accounts were "nationalized." Which is another way of saying that bearded phony stole my money!

I got a decent payday when the government took the El Dorado by imminent domain. I used some of that money to buy a cabin just outside the Smoky Mountain National Park. I thought I'd like spending the dead of summer in the mountains, but the truth is, I was bored witless. I mean how do people live in a place like that? You spend all day careening around mountain roads trying to find a decent restaurant or a real bar, being reminded at every turn that "Jesus Saves!"

I missed my corrupt and crazy hometown, to heck with the humidity.

When I settled back into my house, my lawyer told me I needed to make some money. I shook the cobwebs from my head and looked around. It was the early '60s. The American economy was booming. The Dow Jones was setting records. I thought I'd try my hand at legal stealing.

* * *

"So, your boss was quite a guy." Barnett handed Trip a cup of coffee. He settled onto the couch with a crystal tumbler of Charlie's good bourbon. "He had a head for numbers. That's why he was such a good crook. He knew how to assess value and calculate risk. In 1960 he needed to start over."

"He never told me what he did after selling the El Dorado."

"That's because he thought it was the most boring part of his life."

"Boring?"

"Yeah, for a guy like Charlie, making money legally didn't come with enough excitement, but he did it. He had no broker. No expert advisor. The son-of-a-bitch just figured how to play the stock market. He also had an uncanny sense of timing. He cashed out ahead of the oil embargo and the late '70s recession. While others took a beating, Charlie took profits. He was good at it."

"When you say he was good at it..." Trip was fully awake now and leaning forward.

"He made a shitload of money."

"He didn't live like a guy who had any serious money," Trip said. "Look at his car. Look at his clothes. This creaky old house. He always said he'd stashed away just enough to get by."

Barnett sipped the bourbon, savoring it before he answered.

"That was Charlie. Money wasn't something he cared about. It was just a side effect of him putting his mind to something."

Barnett asked if Trip knew about the morning in April when Charlie came to his office in a Yellow Cab. Trip shook his head.

"He said you were off with some artist gal that day. Anyway, he had me draw up a new will. He made you the beneficiary, well, fifty percent anyway. The other half goes to Children's Home. He had a soft spot for orphans. I'm estimating here, but the estate is hovering somewhere around $17.5 million, just in liquid assets, tax-free municipal bonds mostly. He owned some real estate around town too. I'm still pulling that together. But this is your house now."

Trip stood up. The room was spinning again. He set the mug

on the coffee table.

"Do you mean…"

"He said a writer needed money to live on. He also said he didn't want you to have to go back to your family—how did he put it—with your tail between your legs.'"

Barnett said it would take a few months for the money to be available, and, so far, he'd checked just one of Charlie's ten safety deposit boxes. It held a fat roll of bills circled by a red rubber band. He opened his briefcase and pulled out a stuffed manila envelope.

"It's $30,000." Barnett handed the envelope to Trip. "Should tide you over."

Trip folded the envelope and stuffed it into the back pocket of his cut-off jeans.

"An envelope full of cash…" He smiled at the lawyer. "It's almost like Charlie's still here."

* * *

When Barnett left, Trip paced the house. The dizziness returned. It was barely 7 p.m. but he fell into bed. He was awakened the next morning by the roar of the lawn crew outside—Charlie had always spent money on a lawn service. He had a deep-water well and sprinklers that ran off a timer hanging on the back wall of the house. The old crook had the greenest grass in North Ybor.

Trip made his coffee while the crew finished up. He took the cup to the back porch, where he'd had one of his last conversations with his boss. He sat, legs dangling over the edge. The freshly cut grass smelled like celery and peat moss. Tumbleweed clouds rolled across a slate blue sky.

The old Trip would have celebrated his windfall with a joint or a cup of mushroom tea, but the new Trip just sat, letting the day unfold. His life now required no "artificial sweetening." He knew Katrina, the practical Midwestern poet, had a lot to do with that.

On the evening of the shootout, before they made the rounds to Charlie's old haunts, Trip had slipped the first draft of his book through the mail slot in Katrina's door. It didn't have an ending, but after all that had happened at Charlie's house that afternoon, he needed to let her know he had been writing. Seriously writing.

A few days after Barnett's visit, Trip found a pale blue envelope on the floor under the mail slot, partially buried under slick flyers for pool supplies and windows with a lifetime warranty. The envelope was heavy parchment, the kind you get with a set of fine stationery. It was addressed to Ronald Armstrong. On the ivory card inside were three sentences written in a precise cursive: "It's good, Trip. It's really good! Please stay sober and keep writing."

There were no other words. Katrina hadn't signed her name, though she had put a return address on the envelope. It was a street in Dayton, Ohio. Trip felt a burst of energy. He knew what he would do next.

As June gave way to July, Trip spent long days at the typewriter, adding the final chapters to the Charlie book, then he worked his way through two revisions and a polish. He'd found an antique car restorer in Drew Park, a squat, industrial neighborhood of auto mechanics and sex shops, on the bad side of Dale Mabry Highway, near Tampa Stadium. It took almost two months and $13,000, but Charlie's black Cadillac was freshly painted, the leather seats reupholstered, the engine rebuilt. The big V-8 hummed when Trip turned the key. It shut off without complaint. The mechanic assured him that the 1961 Cadillac, with fresh brakes, shocks and four brand new Goodyear white walls, was ready for a road trip.

"They don't make 'em like this anymore," he told Trip when he handed back the keys.

At the Ybor library, Trip made two copies of his finished manuscript, punched it into matching three-ring binders and added a cover page with the title: *Charlie—A Life*. Trip dropped the binders atop his clothes in Charlie's old suitcase. He put his electric typewriter in its case and gathered the road maps from the kitchen table. A young clerk at the AAA office had drawn out the best route from Tampa to Dayton. Trip would follow the blue ink line north to where it ended, at what he hoped was Katrina's home.

Night was falling, the sky over Ybor faded from rose to gray. Trip pushed himself up from the porch. He needed to put the house in order. He might not be back for a while. When that job was done, he'd walk to Rough Riders for a cheeseburger and some finger-sized French fries, then head home early.

He'd leave for Ohio at first light.

CHAPTER 50

I was dunked by Brother Abernathy, who promised me everlasting life, and for almost 80 years afterwards, I considered it a blessing. Now, I'm not so sure.

I had a lot of good years. I made the most of them but one day, you cross some invisible footbridge, you look around and you're someone else. Or maybe you're just a broken-down version of who you were. I can live with the achy bones, the demanding bladder, the brown splotches that appear on my arms and hands for no good reason, but what I can't live with is being obsolete, discarded, unseen.

That's where you end up. It doesn't matter how much money you've stashed away, or how big your brain is. You can't outspend or outthink obsolescence.

Now, I spend my time shifting through fading memories and trying to make sense of a handful of cliches.

I like the memories. Most of them, anyway. Memories of my mother. Of Ava. Of Dirty Joe and Tito. Of the decades when I was master of a wide swath of the world. Of those thrilling moments when guns were drawn, knives were wielded, and I teetered on a high wire between life and death.

The cliches bang together inside my head, like Bolita balls in a velvet bag. I spend hours staring out my bedroom window, while they jostle around. I used to think youth was wasted on the young and that I'd become older and wiser. But that's bull feathers. I mean, if youth is wasted on the young, then wisdom is wasted on the old. What can you do with wisdom, if no one is listening? If no one cares?

Maybe I should have died on my porch in 1955. Maybe that's what was supposed to happen. But here I am, 85 years old. Alive, but not so well. Maybe it would have been better to go out in a blaze of glory. But isn't that a cliché?

It's almost 6 p.m. The light outside my window is dimming. Time to put on the seersucker suit, grab my straw boater and rouse my young driver. At the Turf or Licata's, I'll eat a raw steak, drink too many old fashioneds, and tell the same old stories to the same old drunks. I'll fall into bed before midnight and wake up at noon the next day and do it all again.

After all that has happened, that tedious routine is all that's left of Charlie Wall's everlasting life.

On the sidewalk outside the department store, Seymour dutifully ran through each step the master had laid out. Become a warrior. Find the spot deep in your gut. Focus on it. He had learned the hard way that it was impossible to know for sure if the magic happened. You had to trust the process. Seconds later, he felt the world around him dissolving, his bowels constricting, his eyes bulging in their sockets, all the usual signs. He was optimistic.

The revolving glass doors spun him around, spitting him out onto the grey marble first floor of the downtown store. The air inside was chilled. Soft piano music played somewhere. Middle-aged woman, perched on silver stools, raised wrinkled faces to college girls in white smocks who bent forward as they applied creams and polishes.

For his final test, Seymour had chosen the original Maas Brothers department store. The company's suburban locations were sleek concrete boxes, rising atop asphalt arroyos, abutting six-lane highways, but the original four-story store squatted atop a full city block in Tampa's aging downtown. The place was wood-paneled, the ceilings low, the dark display cases scratched by the wedding rings of thousands of housewives, the marble floors scuffed by decades of spiked heels and hard leather soles. A red-suited, brass-buttoned attendant, a holdover from an earlier era, stood at attention inside the elevator, ready to pull back the collapsible, cross-hatched metal gates and turn the handle that would send the gilded box rising with a jolt—"Second floor, shoes, petites, ladies' lingerie, please watch your step."

Seymour's earlier appearances at this store had drawn the

beer-bellied security guard, who grabbed his upper arm and perp-walked him toward the spinning doors. But not today.

Seymour danced up the wide aisle, feeling like the scarecrow sashaying along the Yellow Brick Road. At the heart of his Emerald City was a bank of silver escalators, one going up, one coming down. He should have been giddy, but instead, he thought about his time with Buster.

Yes, Buster had lied about his intentions. People had been lying to him for years. There was Oppenheimer and the rest of the atomic bomb crowd, his Special Forces captain, the dean at the University of Tampa, and his running shoe partner—all those mouths dripping with mendacity.

Only the master had told the truth. On the starry night in the Mexican desert so many years ago, the little man in the ragged khaki shorts and a Snoopy T-shirt had revealed the secrets of the universe. "The impossible is always possible to the man who wants it badly enough."

"I want it badly"

At least that's what Seymour thought he had said. With all the peyote in his stomach, his words had emerged inside beach-ball sized bubbles that floated away.

The impossible was what he was attempting today at the department store. Four flights up, he stepped off the rolling staircase. For most of the 20th Century, eager couples had come to the Maas Brothers' houseware department to register for wedding gifts. The room was claustrophobically crowded, the tables and display cases buried under fine china, silver and stainless place settings, knife racks, Teflon frying pans, their long silver handles arching up like the swoosh on Seymour's tennis shoes.

Stout female clerks, their permed helmets dyed black or auburn, passed Seymour without looking up.

He found what he was looking for on a metal display rack thick with blenders, food processors, and silver and porcelain Mix Masters. He picked up a cherry red fondue pot, with a silver base, and a quiver of long, spiked forks, taped to the side.

Identical sets, sealed in boxes, were stacked on the shelf below. Seymour snagged a box and wrapped it in the long coat he had brought especially for the occasion.

He pictured the evening's feast at the shotgun shack. He had blocks of cheese and a dozen cans of Vienna sausages (all purloined that morning from a Kash 'n Karry, where he always skipped the Kash part of the transaction). He'd fire up the pot of oil, skewer the wieners and dip them into a simmering caldron of cheese. He had first created Austrian Fondue while working as executive chef in a Michelin Star restaurant in Salzburg. Of course, the snooty German chef had taken credit for Seymour's creation.

With the box tucked under his arm, Seymour hopped back on the escalator. Approaching the first floor, he spotted the security guard idling at the bottom, pretending to wipe off his glasses. The glasses bit was just a ruse so the guard could keep an eye on the customers coming off the silver stairs.

Seymour held his breath as he stepped onto the white marble floor. The beer-bellied guard seemed to stare right through him. Seymour strolled down the main aisle. At a perfume display, he stopped to spritz himself with the featured fragrance, an aromatic mix of mandarin orange, clove, plum, coriander and pepper—*Opium by Yves Saint Laurent*.

He reached the revolving doors and took one last look back at the busy store. Seymour smiled. It had taken years of practice and hours of intense concentration, but he had finally done it.

On this warm June afternoon in 1985, Seymour Grassley had become completely invisible.

THE END

The Everlasting Life of Charlie Wall is a work of fiction. The real Charlie Wall was murdered in his home on April 19, 1955. That murder was never solved.

Charlie showed up as I started writing a different book and quickly muscled in. While many of the events depicted in this fully researched book are true, I also took liberties with Charlie's life story. Trip Armstrong, Ava Corral, Buster Maniscalco, and most of the other main characters in this book, are products of my imagination. A few of the fictional characters, including Katrina Carey, first appeared in my short story collection, _Cigar City: Tales From a 1980s Creative Ghetto._

My great-grandparents were Sicilian immigrants who arrived in Ybor City at the beginning of the 20th Century. Francesco and Francesca Capitano started a dairy and tended cows for at least one Mafia boss. According to family lore, when World War II broke out a local Mafia boss called to say: "My son is now vice president of your dairy." Dairy farming was considered an "essential industry," and employees were not subject to the draft. The young VP never showed up to milk a cow.

The wild and corrupt city depicted on these pages did exist. Almost everybody took an envelope from Charlie and other mob figures. The bolita man was as familiar as a milkman and the butcher. In downtown Tampa and Ybor City, prostitutes openly plied their trade from second floor apartments and the upper floors of bars and gambling houses. Lots of mobsters, and some innocent civilians, were murdered. Most of those murders were never solved. It wasn't until the mid-70s that Tampa started seriously cleaning up its act and its reputation. For a more factual version of Tampa's mob history, I recommended

Cigar City Mafia, by my friend Scott Deitche.

Thanks to Scott, Gary Mormino, Terry and Dorothy Smiljanich, Arlene Hevia, Ed Miller, Karen Saint-John, and my editor, Sterling Watson, for help with this book. Thanks to Chris Calhoun for his support and advice. And to Amy Cianci and Joe Hamilton at St. Petersburg Press for their ongoing support of my work. And thanks to Eugenie Bondurant for always being in my corner.

ABOUT THE AUTHOR

Paul's new novel, The Everlasting Life of Charlie Wall, was released on April 15, 2026. His debut novel, Florida Hustle, earned a starred review from Kirkus and was named one of the "Best Indie Books of 2022" by Kirkus. The manuscript is currently under consideration at William Morris Endeavor, at their request. Paul's 2019 short story collection, Cigar City: Tales From a 1980s Creative Ghetto, won the fiction gold medal in the Florida Book Awards. A professional musician and award-winning journalist, Paul is currently executive director of the Palladium Theater at St. Petersburg College. He lives in St. Petersburg with his wife, the film and television actor, Eugenie Bondurant.